Augusta Campbell Watson

# Dorothy the Puritan

The Story of Strange Delusion

Augusta Campbell Watson

**Dorothy the Puritan**
*The Story of Strange Delusion*

ISBN/EAN: 9783744747646

Printed in Europe, USA, Canada, Australia, Japan

Cover: Foto ©Andreas Hilbeck / pixelio.de

More available books at **www.hansebooks.com**

DOROTHY THE PURITAN.

# DOROTHY THE PURITAN

## The Story of a Strange Delusion

BY

## AUGUSTA CAMPBELL WATSON

AUTHOR OF "THE OLD HARBOR TOWN"

NEW YORK

E. P. DUTTON AND COMPANY

31 WEST TWENTY-THIRD STREET

1893

Copyright,
E. P. DUTTON & Co.
1893.


Press of J. J Little & Co.
Astor Place, New York

# CONTENTS.

# DOROTHY THE PURITAN.

## CHAPTER I.

### DOROTHY.

WILD, gloomy forests through whose interlacing boughs the sunshine scarcely penetrated, and whose weird recesses seldom echoed to the footsteps of the white man, stretched for many miles beyond the little town, or rather hamlet, of Salem. This forest was admirable, as it displayed the grand proportions of uncultivated nature. To the homesick, pining emigrants, however, seeking an asylum in an unknown country, its mysterious, unexplored depths were tremendous obstacles to be overcome. These early pioneers, whose destiny it was to settle here, were indeed courageous souls.

It was an age of superstition. What more natural than that the Puritans should have peopled these unknown wilds with demons, witches, and strange beings, whose baleful influence, issuing from these dark retreats, spread destroying hands upon helpless humanity?

Of the Salem of those days few vestiges remain; two hundred years have obliterated many of the old landmarks. Our imagination must therefore come to our aid in picturing the little puritanical town and its sober citizens, with their superstitions and their straight-laced doctrines.

It is May-day in the year 1691; a brilliant flood of sunshine rests upon the grassy village street in long, warm, golden bars of light. A soft breeze, laden with the odor of salt, blows from the sea; the blossoms upon the fruit-trees are expanding into pink masses of color, and all the air is filled with the kindly warmth of spring.

Before a low wooden house, built on a narrow lane that leads from the principal thoroughfare, a young girl is swinging on a wooden gate. As she swings back and forth she sings in soft, cooing tones, the notes rising clear and true. The gate creaks on its hinges as she propels it violently backward and forward, sending forth a discordant protest against such ill-usage.

The unpainted, weather-beaten house, standing

back some distance from the road, was two stories in height, having four windows in both upper and lower stories; the door, however, instead of being between the windows on the lower floor, was for some unaccountable reason at the end of the house, and had above it a small, roughly constructed porch.

In the front yard bloomed in straggling disorder many vines and shrubs, which later in the season would blossom into flowering beans, southernwood, lad's-love and fennel, sweet-brier, ferns, and bay-berries. Back of the house lay the farm, its farthest fields terminating in a sandy beach on the shores of the harbor.

On the north side of the house grew a gigantic oak, its great branches resting upon the sloping roof, protecting the lowly, simple home from the scorching suns and beating storms: no doubt this king of the forest had been left standing when its companions fell by its side to build the farmhouse beneath it. On the south side a stately poplar reared its haughty head; straight, unbending, giving no shade, fit emblem of the austere character of the inhabitants of the little town.

This May-day was a glorious day; to be alive was happiness; the knowlege of having within one's

self the capacity of enjoying God's great gifts made
life indeed a blessing. The girl, swinging lazily
back and forth upon the gate, raised her voice higher,
and sent forth little trills of delight that soared
upward till the birds flying above her head paused
upon the wing, listened, and responded as to a loving mate.

Suddenly she stopped abruptly in her singing and
turned her head. Around the corner of the house
a woman came hurriedly. She was large and stout,
with a florid complexion, and her eyes were dark,
small, and bright. Her gray hair was drawn tightly
back from her forehea l. She wore a sober-colored
gown of coarse cotton; also a cap, whose frill flapped
about her face. Over the gown she wore a bodice
of dull-blue holland, and a white neckcloth was
pinned across her breast. Her sleeves were rolled
up, and her firm, well-rounded arms were covered
with some cooking ingredients.

As she approached the girl, she cried loudly and
angrily, " Dorothy Grey, thou lazy, shiftless hussy,
what doest thou, wasting thy time in song and riot ?
Out upon thee! I'll give thee a piece of my mind! "
Get thee to the well for the water." As she spoke
she surveyed the girl contemptuously, resting her

hands upon her hips and throwing her head back with an impatient motion.

"Aunt Martha, I'm truly sorry thou hadst to wait, yet thou knowest I sang but a little song; it was scarce louder than the robins sing. I caused no riot; none heard me save the little bird who did respond for very doubt but what his mate did call him."

Dorothy laughed; and when she laughed one became conscious of the wondrous beauty of her face. This beauty consisted partly in the freshness of extreme youth, her presence affecting one as does the early dawn of a morning in spring, or the pink bud of an unopened rose, the dew still upon its leaves, its sweet incense yet undiffused. Her eyes were of a translucent blue, innocent in expression, the pupils large and dark. Her hair was a light brown, gold when the sun touched it, bringing a shimmering luster to its waving confusion. Her complexion, bronzed by the sea air, was in strange contrast to the clear blue of her eyes, yet it but lent an added charm to the winsomeness of her face. Her figure, though slight and girlish, yet gave evidence of strength and endurance. She stepped down from the wooden gate, and stood irresolutely

swinging her foot to and fro upon the rough garden
path.

Aunt Martha glared angrily at the smiling girl,
and yet her manner was partly indulgent. " I want
to know if thou art going to bring that pail of water
from the well or no," she said. " Seventeen years
old, and no more use than a yearling colt! Thine
uncle and I berate thee from morning till night; it
is of no avail; thou dost not care; thou fliest in the
face of Providence." She paused an instant, then
continued more vehemently, " Dost not know thou
must give account of all thine idle moments? How
long will thine account be? Tell me that, Dorothy
Grey."

Dorothy kept her eyes downcast; her face was
covered with a cloud of discontent, her full red lips
were pouting. Then she glanced up shamefacedly,
yet impatiently, at her aunt. " I care naught about
the account," she muttered. " I add not up every
time I swing on the gate and sing."

" I shall argue no further with thee," interrupted
her aunt. " Get that water, and do not bespatter it;
bring it to the kitchen door, and hasten thy lazy
steps."

Aunt Martha finished her remarks as she walked

around the side of the house to the rear door, her
voice rising higher and shriller as she retreated.

Dorothy gazed a moment down the wide, straggling street, then went slowly over the grass-grown
path to the well, which lay at some little distance
from the house, under the shade of lilac bushes.
When she reached the well she threw her hat on
the grass, and commenced slowly raising the heavy
sweep, preparatory to dropping the pail into the
water.  She made a lovely picture as she raised her
strong arms to propel the sweep, the exercise bringing a bright glow to her brown cheeks, the quaint
costume of the Puritan maiden lending an added
grace to her pensive beauty.

Suddenly, before the pail was half filled, she
dropped the pole and looked down into the well.
She could see herself reflected in its clear depths,
her image looking back at her like a picture out of
a dark frame.  She leaned over the mossy curb,
and gazed long and earnestly, drawing her mouth
down solemnly, then smiling archly to catch the
different expressions.  Once she turned her pretty
head on one side, and shook her finger reproachfully
at the image in the water.  "Thou art an idler!"
she said.  Then she placed a little bunch of dande-

lions that grew in the grass near by in her hair, and
a spray of lilacs in her bodice, tossing her head as
she admired the effect.   Then she laughed softly a
little cooing laugh.

Aunt Martha and her errand were forgotten.
This pleasant occupation was certainly more at-
tractive than carrying heavy pails of water to the
kitchen.   Dorothy became so preoccupied in the
admiring contemplation of herself that she did not
hear steps approaching.

" Dorothy," cried a voice, " what art thou doing?
Art not afraid of slipping into the well, child? "

The girl raised her head quickly, and her eyes
rested on the stern face of her Uncle David.   She
tore the flowers from her hair and bodice and grasped
the well sweep vehemently.

David Holden was a stout, broad man, his figure
giving one the impression of great weight combined
with lightness of foot.   He had an honest face, a
pair of keen eyes, and an aquiline nose.   A head of
bushy gray hair, thick and rebellious, rose in rather
a formidable manner above a broad, intellectual
brow, while the lower part of his face was bearded
after the custom of those days.   His dress consisted
of knee-breeches, belted doublet, hose of leather, and

a high, stiff hat; across his arm rested a long mantle of dull-colored stuff that fell part way to the ground.

Dorothy turned toward him with an embarrassed smile. "I was but looking at mine image in the well. I must take a pail of water to the house, and must hasten; Aunt Martha is most urgent."

The old man's eyes had a twinkle in them, as he answered: "Hast never seen thine image before? Methinks thou hast. What does the good minister tell thee on the Lord's Day?" His voice took on a more solemn tone. "Thy time is not thine own: 'tis but loaned. We are in probation; waste not the fleeting moments."

. "He says many things that I do not always heed," she replied carelessly. "To speak the truth, I sleep more often than I listen." As she spoke she raised the sweep again; the pail fell into the well, emitting a gurgling sound as it filled with water.

"Dorothy," screamed her aunt, "I want to know if the well is empty, and thou goest a mile to the creek for water?"

"I am coming," called Dorothy, as she raised her eyes to see her aunt in the door of the kitchen, one foot raised, preparatory to descending the three stone steps that led to the ground.

Uncle David chuckled. "Thou hadst better make haste, Dorothy; she is wroth with thee."

Dorothy grasped the brimming pail, and stooping to one side, her arm stretched out to balance herself, she walked quickly toward the house.

Seven years after the landing on Plymouth Rock the colony of Salem was formed, and Salem village founded as its capital; the name typifying the peace which the brave and persecuted Puritans hoped to win in the New World.

The first permanent settlement of the place was made in 1628, John Endicott, the first governor, coming to the bleak, inhospitable shores with the immigrants.

In 1630 a body of colonists from England were introduced to the new settlement by the succeeding governor, John Winthrop.

Both Endicott and Winthrop held the welfare of the new province very near their hearts, and they laid many ambitious plans for its advancement. Their policy was excellent in inducing intelligent and worthy men to settle, bringing their energy and high purpose to bear upon the future of the town.

Naturally, the principal occupation in those early times was farming. By industry, patience, and thrift, the somber forests gradually gave place to rich and profitable farms. The wild beasts and the Indians were driven to seek remoter haunts, though the latter were a constant menace for many years to the early settlers, often entering the villages and committing many deeds of violence.

These self-contained, undemonstrative Puritans were possessed of a strong religious fervor, a fervor that permeated their every-day lives; their religion was their law. Neither friend nor foe was able to eradicate the clinging fibers of their creed, which, like the roots of a great tree, spread throughout their whole being. The Scriptures contained for them all the requirements needed for the saving of their souls. Their daily lives were to them examples of a faith which demonstrated fully that this short earthly span was but a probation in hardship for a happier existence. So cold, so austere, so unsmiling was the weary routine they practiced.

They had left their homes in England to seek in a new land both political and religious freedom, and there was no room in the new settlement for those who differed from themselves. Thus, unconsciously, they gave what they had received, intolerance for intolerance, narrowness for narrowness.

Some sixteen years before the opening of this story an emigrant ship sailed before a brisk wind toward the shores of Salem harbor. On the deck, eagerly scanning the fast approaching land, stood a woman, holding a baby in her arms. By her side stood a tall, muscular-looking man. These people were David Holden, Martha his sister, and their little niece Dorothy. Driven by persecution and injustice from the mother-country, they were seeking an asylum in the New World.

A year before their pretty, blue-eyed sister had died. Her husband, a rollicking trooper in the army of " Merry Charles," had been killed in battle, so Martha and David took their beautiful child to their hearts. They made the subject of her adoption a theme for lengthy and serious prayer, asking God that He would teach them how to do their duty by the little orphan, so that her feet might ever tread the narrow path—narrow, unfortunately, in more ways than one.

When Dorothy entered the kitchen her aunt was busy assisting a bond-servant to prepare the simple midday meal. She did not look up or address her niece. Dorothy placed the pail of water upon a low bench near the door, then, going to the window, commenced to drum upon the small diamond panes of the casement. She leaned lazily forward upon the deep window-ledge and gazed dreamily out into the sunshine. Just beyond the kitchen door, on the bough of a lilac bush a little, fat yellow-bird was singing sweetly, stopping now and then to peck at his feathers and glance cautiously around. Then he would throw back his glistening head, bursting into trills of exquisite melody, like some tiny, perfect organ endowed to chant the Creator's praise. Dorothy listened sympathetically, longing to join him in his chorus, envying him his freedom and lightness of heart.

Presently David Holden came in with slow and solemn gait. He washed his hands in the basin near the door, then seated himself not far from the table where Martha was working some pats of butter into various shapes.

Suddenly Dorothy turned toward them impetuously, deserting her view of the sunshine, her enjoyment of the song of the little bird. Her manner was nervous and excited. The rigid austerity of their countenances and demeanor, so at variance with her laughter-loving nature, oppressed her strangely. Perhaps there flowed in her quickly moving blood something more akin to her dare-devil father, the jolly trooper, than to her gentle

Puritan mother. Perhaps the beautiful May-day, with God's gift of flowers and sunshine, had made her feel with keener intensity the somberness and narrowness of her life.

"Aunt Martha"—there were tears in her voice as she turned excitedly toward the unsmiling couple, and she spoke rapidly, the sentences tumbling upon each other in a torrent of vehemence—"I would that I might go away from Salem; I am not happy here. Ah, that I might go to England to my father's people! Mistress Hobbs did tell me but yesterday that there they sing and dance and attend the plays; that great pageants are in the streets, and the great ladies wear embroidered bodices of scarlet and fine attire of linen and of satin." She paused; her breath came quickly, her cheeks were flushed, the light in her blue eyes glowed like stars. "I love the sunshine and the woods," she continued; "I love to sing and laugh. Why does the good Book forbid us to be happy?" she demanded impatiently. "Why should we be miserable when all else that are created are free to enjoy their lives?"

Martha had turned from the table and her work, and stood eying her niece in amazement and displeasure. Her uncle had closed his mouth grimly.

"Thou art an ungrateful wench," said her aunt sternly. "Have I not loved thee and toiled for thee? And now thou wouldst turn and sting me. Dorothy, Satan is tempting thee; beware of his foils; pray that thou mayest resist his wiles."

Dorothy flung out her hands wildly. "I must speak, I must tell thee both of my feelings; I can withstand this desire within me no longer; I *must* sing and dance; I like not to pray forever. Ah, that I might be free, free, just once to go forth into the great world—where, I care not, only to be free!" She choked hysterically; her listeners eyed her in amazement and dread. Before her scandalized aunt and uncle were aware of her intentions, she had frantically torn the little mob-cap from her curls, and taking hold of her skirts on either side, she lifted them slightly above her trim ankles, and, singing more sweetly than the yellow-bird that listened on the flowering bush without the door, she tripped lightly across the kitchen boards in a fantastic dance, keeping time to her steps with a sweet roulade heard from the gossiping Mistress Hobbs:

> "Ah, to be free, 'neath the greenwood tree,
> With my true-lover bold!
> There to sing, while cowslips bring
> Sweet dew in cups of gold."

Martha, her stern old face suffused with a blush, cried angrily, "Dorothy, cease, I say; cease, thou wicked girl! I will e'en tell Mr. Wentworth of thee; he will commission Mr. Parris to call thee out in meeting. Hast thou no self-respect? Thy dance is an abomination. Cease!" She started in pursuit of the laughing girl, who adroitly evaded her grasp. The rather unusual spectacle then took place of the staid middle-aged woman taking part in what appeared to be an impromptu dance. Round and round went Dorothy, laughing, singing, every motion filled with grace, her lovely face dimpled with mischief, as she dodged her panting, corpulent aunt, who followed in hot pursuit.

"Only one more round, Aunt Martha," she cried, "then I will ask thee to forgive me, and I know thou wilt; thou canst not help it."

She started again, and danced forward into a patch of sunlight that lay across the wooden floor; holding her skirts higher on one side and peeping over them, she gave a clear, rippling laugh, like that of a child caught in mischief. She looked back over her shoulder toward her uncle, who had turned his head discreetly aside, deeming the mere witnessing of this unhallowed scene a falling from grace; then with lowered eyelids, and making a deep, mocking curtsey, she rose abruptly, to behold the stern eyes of Mr. Wentworth, the foremost deacon of the Puritan Church, looking down reprovingly upon her from the open doorway.

Aunt Martha stepped forward and took the embarrassed girl by the shoulder, shaking her a little roughly. "She is a headstrong girl; thou must reprove her," she cried excitedly to the man who stood waiting expectantly upon the doorstep. "She has danced a most heathenish dance, here, in the Holden home; thou hast just witnessed those outlandish steps. My advice is not heeded; she is a degenerate sinner. I am indeed most fearful for the welfare of her soul."

Mr. Alden Wentworth, the new-comer, was the rising young advocate of Salem; in fact, he had already been called to the dignity of the bench. He was also a deacon in the church, and much esteemed by the Rev. Mr. Parris, the pastor of the Salem flock. He had held these two important positions but a year; in that short time, however, he had succeeded in gaining the love, respect, and confidence of the community at large, besides being held in high estimation by the governor. Mr. Wentworth was still a young man, being between thirty and thirty-five years of age; a scholar, honest, upright, conscientious, and the staunchest of Puritan adherents. Moreover, he was handsome, with dark, deep-set, penetrating eyes, and a firm mouth whose lines denoted gentleness combined with a strong will. He was tall and well formed, his muscular frame indicating health and great strength.

Dorothy looked frightened and embarrassed as Mr. Wentworth's reproving glance fell upon her. She hung her head; the rosy glow that had recently burnt in her cheeks spread to her brow and neck.

"A dance!" echoed the shocked deacon in dismay. "Dorothy, I scarce can credit these words; thou, a child of prayer!"

Dorothy looked up at him timidly through her long lashes, now wet with tears. "I am indeed a wicked girl, Mr. Wentworth," she glanced appealingly upward, "yet when the robins and the little yellow-birds sang I felt full envious of them. I must e'en join them in their melody, then the dance must needs come next; I could not still my feet, I had not power. Thou wilt forgive me if I transgress no more. Thou wilt not, oh, thou wilt not tell Mr. Parris? he surely will call me out in meeting."

Alden Wentworth did not reply immediately; he gazed earnestly at the pleading face upturned to his, as she stood in the patch of yellow sunlight, the clear radiance seeming part of her own vivacious personality. A strange, inscrutable expression shone in his eyes as he watched her. Then he stepped forward abruptly; the sunshine enveloping Dorothy became obscured by the tall shadow that fell across its brightness. With its fading a gloom spread itself upon the dull, smoked walls of the kitchen. The girl seemed snatched, as it were, from the sound of song and joy to the coldness, bleakness, and silence of night.

"Dorothy," he said in his quiet voice, its intonations solemn with a subdued, pious melancholy, "I shall not acquaint Mr. Parris of thy misdeed, though for the levity of a dance he surely would call thee out in meeting; but far be it from my policy to thus shame thee. Thou art as God made thee, filled with the life of youth and joy. That thou canst not help; 'tis thine inheritance." He paused, then continued more solemnly: "But be ever on thy safeguard that this inheritance draw not its net more closely around thy life and strangle thee. Satan hath many devices; he gives lightness to the foot

and sweetness to the song; beware lest he control
thy steps awry."

Martha and David listened respectfully to this
reproof, now and then shaking their heads in acquiescence, and glancing askance at Dorothy, as she
wiped the fast-falling tears with the corner of her
apron, her rosy, pouting lips trembling, as she endeavored to regain her self-control.

Presently she drew nearer to the reproving judge.
"Then thou art not wroth with me, Mr. Wentworth?"

"No, my child," he answered kindly.

She stepped close to him, and grasped his hand.
"I thank thee; thou art more kind than aunt.   I
will come to meeting always, and I will obey thee,
and never laugh in the Lord's house again when the
tithing-man strikes old Goodman Weldon with the
hard stick on his bald head for sleeping.   He cried
out loud last Sabbath.   Didst hear him, Mr. Wentworth?   It was such rare sport to see his grimace."

Mr. Wentworth smiled slightly, but did not
reply.

"Ah, that sermon," she continued mournfully,
"was full three hours long.   I saw the hour-glass
on the pulpit ledge turned so oft, and the sands fell

through so slowly. I cannot tell thee how weary I was. I wish that Mr. Parris would let some other minister preach. He drones and drones, till one grows weary with sleep."

"No, no, Dorothy, say not that; 'tis not respectful to thy pastor. Methinks the sermon last Lord's Day was filled with solace and godly sayings. Three hours is not long to hearken to the Word of God."

"'Tis long when the soul is far away," answered Dorothy dreamily. "Full oft I know not where I am till Mr. Parris calls loudly from the pulpit for attention."

Mr. Wentworth smiled indulgently. "Thou art but a child as yet; wisdom will come in time." He then turned abruptly to Martha and David. "I called to acquaint thee, Mistress Holden, with the fact that old Goody Trueman hath been seen again on the edge of the forest. They do say her cloak was of the color of fire; that a black demon stood by her side, and did hover over her as she plucked the poisonous ivy that grew upon the rocky hillside. When Jonathan Wells, who saw her approach, raised his stick to send her adrift she was no more seen; the stick did but cleave empty space; only a small red glow was visible against the clouds. It was as though she had risen with her imps in the air."

" I can well credit all I hear of Goody Trueman; she is of a certainty a witch, and hath signed the treaty with the Prince of Darkness," said David.

Martha made no comment. She looked distressed and troubled.

" Perchance thy words are true," answered the judge gravely, " yet we conjecture not aright always when we think we behold the agents of the devil. I do but speak to thee of these sayings that be abroad in Salem to warn thee to be circumspect, and if this creature do possess this dreaded power, to be on thy guard."

" Kindness is ever thy forte," replied David. " We thank thee for thy warning."

Mr. Wentworth replaced his steeple-crowned hat and stepped toward the door. As he changed his position, the shadow fell from Dorothy. She stood once more in the sunshine, his earnest glance resting upon her. " I bid thee good-day, Dorothy," he said. " I trust to see thee in thy place to-morrow at the meeting-house. Dry thy tears, and when thy feet are restless, walk to the Lord's house and commune with God in thy soul. 'Tis far better for thee than the riotous dance. When thou must sing, sing the psalms. Are they not filled with peace and all good promises?"

"Methinks I am not good as thou art, Mr. Wentworth. I have another self within me that does ever urge me in the wrong direction. Why has God willed us to be unhappy when He has given us so much to enjoy?" she concluded sadly.

"'Tis for discipline, the preparation for immortality," he replied earnestly; "pray constantly that thy probation be acceptable. We were not created for happiness, but that through our privations we might atone for our many sins, and through much misery be saved, and found at the last garnered into the Lord's house."

"I will e'en try, Mr. Wentworth, yet it is very hard." She smiled her pretty smile upon him; he bowed, and went his way under the drooping lilac bush, and the little bird upon its branch burst forth into merry song again.

Dorothy folded her hands demurely, and looking toward her aunt, she said contritely, "I am sorry I danced that awful dance, Aunt Martha. Shall I not help thee form the butter-pats?"

# CHAPTER II.



IT is well to state here the position in which the ministers of the Puritan days stood in relation to their people. None of the early colonists would have dared or, it is likely, wished to disparage their pastor's teachings, or in fact any of the ordinances of the church. No reproaches were tolerated, no criticisms condoned. Severe were the whippings and fines that befell any luckless delinquent who might express disapprobation of the length of the sermons or prayers of the pastor.

This unlimited control extended not only over the religious life, but also over the secular. The minister's word was law; even in regard to many trivial every-day concerns he was consulted, and his decision abided by.

The honor of being deacon was second only to that of being minister. The deacons had especially important duties to perform. During the absence of the pastor one of them conducted the service.

The deacons' pew occupied a position raised above the level of the ground, and there they sat in solemn state, leaning against their stiff, high-backed chairs, the objects of great respect, not to say reverential awe.

The Sabbath day was observed literally according to the command of the Bible, " Remember the Sabbath day to keep it holy ;" and many other strict laws were enforced, and in most part cheerfully consented to by the people.  To enhance the sacredness of the Lord's Day, it was filled from early morning till sundown with prayers, sermons, and singing of psalms.  All attended the meetings, some coming from a long distance and suffering much inconvenience in the heat of summer, or in the cold and storms of the long New England winters.

Little children came, tiny images of their solemn parents, while a tithing-man kept order with a long stick, prodding the unfortunate ones who fell asleep during the three-hour sermons.  The seats were hard, mere boards without backs; the men sat on one side of the edifice, the women on the other.

Unruly boys, " sons of Belial," as the deacons called them, had seats by themselves in the gallery, and the tithing-man hovered in their vicinity with

frowns and threatening gestures, his formidable bearing reducing the giggling, wriggling, weary little
Puritan boys to a condition of depressed submission.

The meeting-house was roughly constructed and
unpainted.  The rafters were exposed to view, and
spiders spun great gossamer webs from beam to
beam, airy, waving structures; an endless joy and
diversion to the poor little restless boys and girls
who nodded and twisted uneasily on the hard seats
below.

There were no shutters to the building, so that
the glare in summer must have been intolerable;
while in winter the aching feet and hands and be-
numbed frames of the pious church-members, seated
rigidly in the fireless building, surely showed of
what heroic material these old Puritans were made.

Between the services a lunch was partaken of in a
" Sabba-house," built on one side of the church for
that purpose.  It was a very solemn lunch; no hilarity being allowed, no jest or light word being permitted.  Then back they repaired to the meeting-
house to more psalm-singing, more lengthy sermons;
then home in the evening glow of the twilight to
the grim routine of the hard-working week to come.

This is certainly a drear, cold picture to contemplate, gazing backward through the centuries, from the luxury and ease of our modern days. It is not unnatural that the hardships they encountered in the mere struggle for existence, the fear of Indians and of wild beasts, their dread imaginings regarding the mysteries of nature, which lay yet hidden in the depths of the unexplored wilderness, should have imparted a gloom and a mysticism to their dispositions, and belief in the supernatural.

The settlement of Salem was somewhat scattered; its houses were simple but comfortable, built principally after a uniform pattern—large, dormer-windowed, and gambrel-roofed. The land was rocky and difficult to farm; the roads mere bridle paths cut through the gloomy wilderness.

Yet these Puritans gloried in their hardships. They had come to the New World for freedom of thought in their belief, and they had gained what they sought; they were content; they asked no more; their sufferings but increased the value of their freedom. As is the case, however, with all bigotry and prejudice, they drew the bands too tight; they snapped, and dire was the result.

From the frivolities and follies of the English court, from the lawlessness of the Cavaliers, they recoiled in horror. They preferred a life of weary hardship, with permission to worship God in their own way, to the daintiest home-nest in the mother-country. And so they came, a gloomy, solemn company, from over the seas, bringing with them in their characters the results of injustice and of intolerance.

The pleasant May had passed. June, glorious with the brilliancy of flowers and fleecy clouds, and the pleasant shade of full-leaved trees, had come to the little village. Dorothy wandered often by the edge of the forest, sometimes alone, sometimes with her girl friends.

She loved best to be alone; the straight-laced, sad little maids of the settlement were not much to her liking. She would gather the wild violet and the strange feathery ferns that bordered some little murmuring stream, and as she placed them in the bodice of her dress or in her hair, she would speak to them: " Thou art free, little violets and soft green fern; thou canst live thy life as thou wilt; none can hinder thee; thou canst sit in the shade and nod and dream right merrily till the summer grows hot and dry; then thou fallest asleep, till another year shall wake thee again."

The rippling stream would answer for the silence of the flower, responding to her queries in low, singing tones. It seemed to comprehend her loneliness and her seeking for the right to indulge in the natural gayety of youth. She returned one evening at dusk to the farm, after one of these wanderings prolonged beyond the usual hour. She had been alarmed by the appearance of old Goody Trueman, the acknowledged witch, whom she had seen standing on a distant hill and whom she held greatly in dread.

Dorothy hastened her footsteps, speeding lightly along over the grassy road that led through the narrow lane. The darkness was coming on rapidly; strange sounds issued from the rustling trees and from the summer foliage, growing thick and luxuriantly by the roadside. An owl hooted in a tall oak; a bat flapped his wings across her face. The air was filled with the soft, aromatic scents of shrubs and wild-flowers, their delicate perfumes intensified by the dew that rested on their leaves.

The realization that she had been in the actual presence of the witch, though distant from her, filled Dorothy with a nameless dread. When she reached the farm gate, she threw it open and walked quickly up the path to the little porch. Her heart was beating wildly and her breath came in short gasps. She seated herself on the rough bench in the porch, and removed her cap from her heated brow. ,

It was quite dark now; the night had come, a few pale stars hung twinkling in the sky; banks of somber clouds floated up from the north. Far off toward the east a circle of light glowed, the harbinger of the "Queen of Night." All was still about the farm.

Dorothy experienced a peculiar restlessness, a loneliness encompassed her; she felt as if she must speak to some one, at least feel a living presence, or from the sheer nervousness of fear scream aloud.

Suddenly the door opened, and Martha, closely followed by David, stepped to Dorothy's side.

"Dorothy," she said (there was a suppressed eagerness in her voice, an exultant sound, very different from her usual rasping, fault-finding intonations), "hast thou been here long? I did not hear thee come. Thy uncle and I have been waiting impatiently for thee; we have a subject of great importance to discuss with thee." She came close to the girl, laid her hand tenderly upon her shoulder, and leaned over to look into her face.

"I have been here but a short time. I have been

sorely affrighted, aunt. Goody Trueman was upon the hill, beyond the settlement; she did send a bat and owl to torment me. They flapped their wings upon me, but I did utter a prayer most fervently and hasten my steps, and they left me then in peace." She hesitated, then continued: "For the space of many moments I deemed she might cast her spell upon me; I covered my face with my mantle; when I dared look again she had disappeared. Dost think she mounted her broomstick? I looked most searchingly into the clouds but could see nothing." Dorothy asked this anxiously.

Martha tossed her head impatiently, but David shook his in acquiescence, and with decision. "No doubt she flew above thy head invisible. Ah, it is an awful thing to contemplate," he said. "A great danger surely confronted thee."

"'Tis arrant folly; broomsticks forsooth!" cried Martha scornfully. "I cannot understand such nonsense; the one who spreads such reports should have the broomstick laid across his back; yet, poor child, I have no doubt it alarmed thee." She paused, then continued more hurriedly: "Let that pass; words are but vain; we will not worry ourselves about this witch. I have great news for thee;

thou canst never conjecture. I will tell it thee right close by thine ear, my little Dorothy. Now hark ye: thy blue eyes and winsome face have won for thee the greatest honor thou canst imagine. Alden Wentworth hath asked thy uncle and me to give him our little niece in marriage." When Martha's voice pronounced the last words it echoed with a ring of genuine triumph and elation.

" Yes," said David, " our Dorothy hath made the greatest match in Salem village. Thou didst not scheme for it ; it came to thee, a great blessing and a great honor."

Dorothy did not speak ; she was bewildered, amazed ; she clasped her bunch of violets tighter in her hand, and arose from her low seat.

" Aunt, uncle," she gasped, " this honor surely cannot be for me. Mr. Wentworth hath scarce addressed me, save in reproof ; dost thou think thine ears heard aright ? "

" Surely we heard aright ; our ears did not deceive us. And let me tell thee, Dorothy, he loves thee deeply ; not in words do I judge of this, but his face shone with the great affection he held for thee. I read it there, and when he spoke he said, ' Tell her my heart is hers ; I pray that she may care for me.' "

" Oh, Aunt Martha, I never can, I never can!  My mind is filled with fear of him.   He is so far above me, so good, so different from me, when he draws nigh my life seems slipping from me.   I do honor and respect him, but can I love one who so sorely doth affright me?"

" Thou art but a fanciful child; thou knowest not whereof thou speakest; thou wilt learn to love him. Hast thou no ambition?   Why, thou wilt have the first place in the meeting-house, the first position in the colony.   Not one maiden in all Salem would hesitate.   As for his goodness, that is what thou needst. His age is also well; he can guide thee better."

The position enjoyed by the minister's wife and the wives of the deacons in those far-off days of Puritan New England was indeed a burdensome one, though probably filled with a triumph of its own.   No doubt this distinction was partly owing to the fact that there were few positions of importance to fill.

The wife who held so prominent a place amongst the women of the meeting-house paid in part her debt for that greatness by being continuously under the most critical supervision from the watchful eyes of the flock.   Her actions, her motives, her household management, and above all her observance of the Lord's Day, was freely, perhaps not always kindly, discussed. Still, the position was one of decided distinction; though the disadvantages were perhaps balanced by the benefits.

Poor little laughter-loving Dorothy recoiled in dread from filling this exalted place. She could not grasp its honors; she felt only that with it came an added shade of dullness and suppression. She looked out silently into the sweet-scented gloom of the summer night, past the tall shrubs that stood up ghost-like in the darkness, toward the distant line of sky that appeared to scintillate and throb with its thousands of twinkling stars.

A depression settled upon her spirits; her rosy-colored views of life changed to blackness. Her cage seemed to have become more heavily ironed, more cramped; she felt the fetters tugging at her heart, binding her tightly, strengthened by this destiny which fate had evidently ordained for her.

" No, no, Aunt Martha, I am not worthy to be the wife of Judge Wentworth. I would shame him by my levity. Why, even now I am a scorn to the good matrons in the meeting-house. Had he come to me, I would have answered him."

" Dorothy Grey," cried her aunt sternly, " I and thy uncle have promised thee; thou belongst to us to do with as we will.  We give thee to Alden Wentworth.  Come to thee, indeed, a willful child! He knew the respect due to us."

" Yet, aunt, without my will surely he would not take me;  he has overmuch pride for that."

" He comes again to-night for thy answer."  Her aunt spoke decidedly.  " Thou shalt tell him yes. Speak, David;  thou art her lawful guardian."

" Dorothy, I have promised for thee," said her uncle firmly.  " Thy happiness is my wish.  In this I see the hand of God; by that guidance I thus command thee.  Remember, thou art my ward; thou hast no voice of thine own."

Dorothy bowed her head, her whole frame trembled;  the nerveless hands that held the flowers clasped and unclasped, the petals fell withered to the floor of the porch.

" I must e'en say yes," she replied in a low voice; " my will is not strong enough to contend against thee.  And yet—yet—if Heaven," she spoke despairingly, " would but send a spark of love to aid me in this choice, it were not so hard."

" Thou art a good, obedient child; thou wilt be

happy.    I tell thee that all the girls in Salem will
envy thee.    That bold wench, Elizabeth Hubbard,
hath cast love-eyes for full six months at Mr. Wentworth, but he heeds her not, the silly thing, with
her wicked black eyes.    But thou hast won him
with thy sweet face, and I am proud of thee.    Why,
Dorothy, we will be among the first people in the
colony."

"Elizabeth is my dearest friend, Aunt Martha.
I would he had chosen her; she would make a
worthier wife than I."

"Out upon thee, say not such things!    Rather
thank an all-merciful Providence that hath given
thee this good place; thou art ungrateful.    We will
leave thee now to reflect; in a short space the judge
will be here.    See thou treat him kindly.    'Tis
'well the night is dark, else he would see thy pale
face."

Dorothy threw her arms with a desperate tenderness around her aunt's neck and laid her cheek
against hers.    "I would that he had frowned upon
me," she murmured; "I do so fear him.    Can I
ever be what he would desire?    No—no, Aunt
Martha, no—no."

" Hush, hush!  Compose thyself; all will be well.
'Tis but the suddenness of the offer."

She released the clinging arms and departed with
her brother, leaving Dorothy seated alone in the
porch.

It was not long before the girl heard the firm
steps of Alden Wentworth upon the garden path.
He joined her, and they conversed gravely for some
moments on indifferent subjects; then he drifted
gradually upon that deeper theme which filled his
heart.  An hour passed by; the moon rose high
among the clouds, her soft light resting upon Dorothy as she leaned listlessly against the back of the
old settle.  Alden Wentworth had risen and stood
looking down upon her as he conversed in his calm,
even tones, for the Puritans believed in moderation
in all things, considering it unnecessary to raise the
voice to impress the hearer.

" I am glad thou hast been sincere with me, Dorothy; I know now that thou dost not love me deeply
as yet, but thou wilt, thou wilt."  An undertone of
strong passion lent an intensity to his voice as he
spoke, though in all probability had he been conscious of this quality he would have crushed it then

and there. "My love will draw thee to me; I am patient, I am content to wait for what will surely come. Be thou always open and frank with me, as thou hast been to-night. Do not deceive me; be sincere with me. The future of my soul and thine requires that all should be as clear as noonday between us."

A shudder passed over Dorothy at these words, a coldness and a nameless fear. "I will never deceive thee," she said. "I will never deny to thee the right to read the truth between us. What could I withhold? I have led but a child's life under thine eyes in Salem."

"Thou art mine, then, forever."

"Ay, I am thine; be thou lenient to my youth and follies. Fate has given me to thee; I have not wished this honor. Be kind to my weaknesses."

"I will, Dorothy, I will."

"I am not calm like the people about me; thou hast heard of my father, and of the life he led at court as one of the favorite troopers of Charles. They say I have my mother's face and my father's temperament. It were a wrong to thee did I deceive thee in regard to my true feelings. Now never canst thou reproach me for a falsehood."

" Never," he replied. "All is fair between us. Some day thou wilt love me, and I will try very hard to make thee happy."

So Alden Wentworth went his way over the summer fields back to the town. Dorothy stood where he had left her, thinking. The brilliant moonlight enveloped her in its clear luster, her face was upraised to the heavens. On her cheeks rested tears. The soft wind blew across her face; it did not dry the tears. Ah no! they came too rapidly. A bat flapped his wings across her hair. "Again," she cried; " twice this day! 'Tis an evil omen; it comes from the forest witch. O Alden," she stretched forth her arms before her in despair, " no luck attends our betrothal. Would that I might recall my promise! I was so weak to yield, as though my life was not dull and lonely enough; but I must consent to still my song and stay my feet, and wed the foremost deacon in the church."

She sat very still for some time within the shelter of the porch, picturing vaguely the sad-colored path destiny was preparing for her as the wife of the Puritan judge. " This honor that has come to me is but void and dead," she murmured. " There is no love attending it to give it life. Had I the courage I would even now retract my promise. Should I do this, however, Aunt Martha and uncle would disown me; and I have no other home, no fortune. There is no doubt that I shall become the scandal of the town, for surely at times my spirits will gain the mastery." She smiled mischievously, and yet sadly, at this last reminder.

# CHAPTER III.



THE betrothal was made known, and great was the surprise and consternation that seized upon the good people of Salem. Many a wise head did wag in ominous presentiment of dire results. Many a sharp tongue did expostulate in the privacy of the home circle upon the grave judge being bewitched by the light in a fine blue eye, not seeking further for the heart beneath.

Be that as it may, Mr. Wentworth appeared content. It was with a tremulous eagerness he leaned from the deacon's pew the following Lord's Day, and gazed upon Dorothy, seated demure and pale among the stern-visaged matrons, the forced gravity of her face and manner being in marked contrast to her usual restless condition. Her hands were folded quietly in her lap, her gaze wandering dreamily at times through the bare, uncurtained windows to the low line of hills beyond.

It was to Wentworth as if all the inlets to his soul

were opened, and through them entered the sweetness, light, and love of a new world—a world that
held in its vague, intangible depths a vista stretching
over flowering vales to the possibilities of an existence made complete by Dorothy's little weak hand.
It appeared to him that the dull atmosphere that
lay thickly above the narrow path in which he had
trodden hitherto had risen and revealed a widened
road.  On that road there was room beside him for
one in whom all his dreams of unalloyed happiness
were centered.          .

Perhaps it was true, as the villagers said, that he
was deceived by a sudden fancy.  Be that as it may,
in this deception rested his hopes; he did not desire
the veil lifted.

Mr. Wentworth possessed to the fullest degree the
cramped, restricted, puritanical character; he shared
freely in the superstitions of his creed and age.  Yet
a wealth of silent sentiment lay buried under his
reserve, and deeper still the capabilities of a strong,
unswerving affection.

This element in his nature appalled him at times
by its intensity, when its object rose before his mental vision, effacing for the moment the customary
monotony of his life.  At such times he reproached

himself for permitting the earthly to overshadow the heavenly. "Still," he argued, "I am but a man, and I love her." Then relapsing into retrospection, he would question seriously: "Can it be wholly of God, this mighty love, or can it be that underneath it lie the temptations of the Evil One? Why should that fair face come between me and my Bible, and smile upon me from the leaves of my psalm-book, and cause me to wander in my prayers? If a Heaven-sent gift, why thus clog the wheels of duty?"

Dorothy, who had not yet felt within her the capacity for a great love, calmly acquiesced in the accepted order of things. And Wentworth, slow to express his feelings, did not cause any unrest within her mind by protestations of affection. The wooing went placidly on its calm way, like a smooth river, no warning ripples on its surface indicating the deep, dangerous channel beneath.

It was the custom at stated times of the year for the good matrons of the village to assemble in the great kitchen at the parsonage, each with her wheel, flax, and distaff, there to spin a goodly supply of firm linen to replenish the oaken chests where the minister's wife kept her household stuffs.

On a charming afternoon in midsummer quite a company of worthy dames were seated at their work, their tongues going almost as fast as the merry wheels over which they bent. The kitchen was long and low, its great beams overhead exposed to view. From them were suspended strings of dried Indian corn and sundry herbs; the latter distilled a faint spicy odor that permeated the atmosphere pleasantly. Very little furniture encumbered the room, with the exception of a heavy table and some high-backed chairs and settles.

Upon the mantel in tall candlesticks stood candles made of pale-green tallow, the compound of bayberries, gathered by the wayside, and " dipped " by the economical wife of the minister. The windows were open, letting in a cool, refreshing breeze laden with the sweet breath of cowslips, clover, and newly cut grass. The bees hummed noisily as they flew by, and occasionally the strange, wild note of a forest bird mingled with the call of the robin and the blackbird. The floor of the kitchen was of clay, damp and cool.

Mistress Parris sat among the women, plying her needle upon some homespun garment, now and then gazing delightedly upon the stout runs of linen thread that were gradually accumulating from the industrious energies of the spinners. This texture, she mentally pictured, would eventually take the shape of good sheets to fill her stout chests, and add materially to her wealth; for linen was held only second in value to silver.

There was no thought of idleness among these conscientious women; they were using the Lord's time, which was only loaned to them for a short space. So they diligently reeled, carded, and combed the flax.

At length a stern, dark-browed matron laid down her work for an instant, and looking up, addressed a woman seated near her, who had made a deprecating remark in reference to Mr. Wentworth's coming marriage.

" Perchance," said she in a cold voice, " it is not for me to question the motives of one who hath been set by Providence above me; if I err, I pray thee, pardon me, Mistress Parris."

" Speak on, thou hast a right; I question it not."

" They say," continued the speaker, " the judge doth not bring great credit upon the colony by his betrothal, or, for that matter, great credit upon himself. Why, good wives," she cried, her voice growing shriller as she proceeded, "what think ye of that vain, idle minx being placed above us in the meeting-house? Her levity, her laughter, and her antics are a scandal to the edifice. It is but a month or more come yesterday that she did tickle the neck of Goodman Wells with a mint-stick; he, poor man, having e'en lost himself in the seventhly of the sermon, was asleep. He did awake with a start, being confused, thinking a spider was on his neck, having spun from the beams aloft. He did fall forward, and strike his head with violence, so much so that a great bump did appear thereon the following day."

"Ay, that is so," echoed a chorus of voices.

"But," replied Mistress Parris, "that was before the announcement; since then most circumspect has been her demeanor."

"I wot it will not last," continued the dark-browed woman; "she knows what is for her good. Think ye she will lose this great honor by any vicious deeds at this late day? Not she. I have it on good authority that some time previous Mr. Wentworth contemplated advising Mr. Parris to call her out in meeting. She is sufficiently unruly to have a seat on the boys' bench and have the good stout stick laid across her shoulders. In faith she has bewitched him."

At the word "bewitched" Elizabeth Hubbard, whose head had been bent over her wheel, raised it and looked squarely into the speaker's face. There was a mesmeric influence in the girl's glance. Elizabeth was a dark-skinned, dark-eyed young woman, handsome in a wild, elfish way, with a heavy mass of hair of inky hue that waved about her temples in tangled confusion. There rested an expression of alert interest upon her face, the well-traced lines about her mouth denoting a fierceness of disposition and an untamed, headstrong will. Her presence affected the beholder with a weird, incomprehensible fascination.

"What dost thou mean by 'bewitched'?" she asked.

"Mean?" echoed Mistress Parris. "Why, that her blue eyes and pretty face hath cast a spell, as thy black eyes will do some day, Elizabeth."

Elizabeth turned impatiently to her wheel, and did not reply.

"Thou speakest of her antics at the meetings; what think ye all of her lonely wanderings in the forest? Oft hath she been seen on the edge of the great woods at evening, singing, and with her hands full of strange plants and flowers."

The dame who thus spoke had a low, intense voice. The rest of the circle gazed toward her where she sat in the farther end of the long room; her foot was upon the treadle, her head bent eagerly forward; she held aloft in her hand a hank of linen thread. The women drew closer together as though something in these words had alarmed them.

"What doeth she there?" continued the vibrating tones. "It were more to her credit did she bide at home, assisting with the farm work."

"Ay, thou speakest truly," said Mistress Parris. "Still, her family is of good repute; none better or stauncher church-members have we than David and Martha Holden. She is but a child, and seeks a child's pleasures. Why, it seems but yesterday that little Dorothy Grey ran heedless upon the village streets, the torment of her good aunt, and withal her happiness; for ye must confess she is full lovable."

These kindly words were met with silence, broken presently by the sharp voice of the woman in the distant corner.

"It is well known of the naughty baggage that she doth not do the will of her good guardians. Little cares she if they berate her; she is a wild thing, and, I fear me, the learned judge hath taken a firebrand into his heart. It is beyond my poor wits that a man of so great intelligence, and so filled with the strength won by prayer and a godly life, can so bemean himself as to choose this silly child for the sake of a fair exterior."

"Mercy on us, good friends," cried Mistress Hodgson, a sprightly matron who had not hitherto spoken, "ye are too hard; she is but young. Let her laugh while she can; let her gather the flowers. The years will come soon enough when perchance she cannot laugh, and when the flowers will fade. As for the meeting-house, I have smiled full oft myself at the hilarity in the boys' benches. And thou knowest that when old Goody Farnham called out 'The Lord have mercy on us' when the minister did start his sermon on the third hour—she being deaf, and having slept, thinking it time to respond in the psalm—it was hard to be calm and serious."

A slight ripple of suppressed humor ruffled the countenances of the stern matrons at this reminder.

It fell like a gleam of wintry sunshine upon a sad-colored landscape.

"Thou art right," said Mistress Parris, " the young should laugh betimes; tears will furrow their cheeks and make yet deeper wrinkles than do their smiles. And hark ye, charity is surely a godly virtue, and cloaks the follies of youth. Methinks ye should consider well the roistering, rollicking trooper, who did serve an ungodly master, and who has left to his daughter a light and verily a foolish nature."

"Thou art kindly disposed," said the cheerful Mistress Hodgson; "an inheritance like Dorothy's makes life a hard battle to conquer. They do say a more dancing, singing, light-minded trooper than William Grey never followed the service of that ' Imp of Satan,' the wicked Charles."

" I find not fault with her inheritance," said Dorothy's denunciator. " Yet hearken unto me." The woman arose from her wheel and came forward amongst them. She looked searchingly into the intent face of Elizabeth, raised expectantly toward her. " From the dormer-window of my garret chamber I have at the dusk of evening seen Dorothy emerging from the forest." She paused ; her listeners looked up eagerly from their work. " Not far distant, upon a rise of ground, the fading sunlight on her wicked face, stood Goody Trueman. Draw thine own inference. I say naught; I watch."

This announcement was received in a peculiar manner by the auditors. They did not speak, but drew their chairs closer together, looking tremblingly and affrighted over their shoulders toward the wide mouth of the great chimney.

" Did she vanish into air as thou watched?" asked Mistress Parris in an anxious tone.

" I know not; I dared look no further for dread of her horrid spell."

The women worked silently and steadily for some time after this. Suddenly the cadence of a low, humming sound resembling the sweet notes of the meadow-lark broke upon the quiet of the summer afternoon. The dames lifted their heads and listened, looking toward the open windows.

Elizabeth leaned forward over her wheel and raised her finger. " 'Tis Dorothy," she said; " I know her voice. She sings while we work."

The sound of a light step was heard without the kitchen door. The latch was lifted and Dorothy stood smiling upon the threshold. In the bodice of her gown a great bunch of purple clovers nestled and hung their honey-laden heads. She held her apron in one hand, and over its hem fell great masses of wild-wood ferns and columbine, and cool green sprays of vines and moss. The other hand held close to her ear the rim of a beautiful pink-tinted sea-shell.

"Dorothy," cried the minister's wife, looking up reprovingly, "where hast thou been? Methinks thy Aunt Martha believed thee at the spinning. Where is thy wheel, child?"

The girl threw back her head and laughed a clear, ringing laugh of girlish merriment. "My wheel, good Mistress Parris, my wheel, I judge, is rusting from want of use. In these summer days the flax doth stick and cling. I trow I like not spinning, but I will tell thee all where I have been. Surely a little diversion should be welcome after this laboring with the flax."

She paused and looked around mischievously upon the stern-browed group of women, who returned no answering smile. She heeded not their coldness, but appeared rather to enjoy their discomfort. Coming forward, she laid her hand upon the lathe of Elizabeth's wheel; it gave a loud whirring sound and stopped violently in the spinning. She laughed loudly as the flax broke with a snap, her pretty, teasing face glowing with merriment. "I am glad 'tis broke; now thou canst not work, and be a reproach to me in my idleness."

"I will tell thy aunt of thee," cried Mistress Parris, not relishing the loss of linen and time. "The years bring thee no sense or godliness, Dorothy."

"I fear not Aunt Martha overmuch; she forgives and forgets my misdeeds. Why not tell Mr. Wentworth? Yet, listen, scold me no more; I will tell thee whither I have been whilst thou hast worked."

The group looked up sternly into the laughing, roguish eyes, and listened, partly unwilling, yet partly won by her sweetness.

"I have wandered in the forest, where all was cool and quiet, and where the bird and butterfly did bear me joyous company. Thence over the fields and meadows have I walked, e'en down to the edge of the sea. I did rest upon the sand and watch the little waves come up unto my feet, back and forth, back and forth, tiny, blue, lapping waves, and they did sing a right merry song to me. Being warm and tired, I fell asleep beneath the shelter of a rock, and I did dream a bright dream." She paused; a dimness gathered in her eyes. "A dream of a home far away, beyond the seas, a home among my father's people. When I awoke I was still in this cold land, where they blame me when I laugh and sing. Ah, that I might have dreamed longer!"

" Hush, Dorothy, it is not grateful for thee to pine," interrupted Mistress Hodgson; " thou hast been snatched from the fire of wickedness in that benighted land. With thy temperament, thou wouldst most assuredly have fed the blaze which that degenerate people have built to their own undoing."

" Yet let me tell thee," cried Dorothy, unheeding this reproof, " something that will make thee all put thy wheels against the wall and go with me."

" What dost thou mean, Dorothy? What hast thou to tell?" asked Elizabeth quickly.

" Now hold thy patience, Elizabeth. When I did awake from my dream I did start and sit upright; mine eyes were dim at first, but presently far away against the sky, full as far as my vision could reach, I did behold a great ship. Its sails were unfurled like the wings of a spirit, and its bows were turned toward me."

The women all arose quickly, and gazed excitedly toward the speaking girl.

" And I did speak aloud, and say, ' 'Tis the good ship " Hope," so long expected. It is filled with new souls for the colony, and much merchandise.' I watched it growing larger and larger, and coming nearer and nearer; in my excitement I saw naught else: it seemed to fill the whole space between sky and sea."

" Sayst thou truly, Dorothy? " cried the excited women.

" Ay, truly, and I did place this sea-shell against mine ear, and it did speak to me of the sea and the ships. And it did whisper at first but faintly, then in a low and sadder voice, ' Dorothy, yonder ship brings some one to thee; some one looks thy way.' Think ye, Mistress Parris, it can be one of my father's people? For of a truth I did hear the shell say, ' Dorothy, Dorothy, I am coming to thee.' "

" Thou art a fanciful child; none can speak to thee that hath not life. 'Tis thine idleness, my child, that aileth thee; far better were it that no tidings of thy father's people ever reached thine ears. Come, let us hasten to the shore and bid a right welcome cheer to the emigrants. They have good winds to their favor, and soon, if Dorothy sayeth truly, will be beyond the bar. Waste no time; hasten to the harbor." She turned eagerly to the women, who had already commenced to place their wheels against the wall.

No news of such great and welcome import ever greeted the ears of the early settlers as that announcing the arrival of a ship from the fair, far-off land of England. It meant a wider interest; it meant news from absent ones; it meant gifts and added comforts; it meant an increase in the settlement, also a knowledge of the political situation of the mother-country. In short, it meant every joy desirable to the good people of two hundred years ago.

So the good wives gathered on the shore to bid the brave ship welcome. They did not hurrah and cheer, as we would of a later date; they stood sober and quiet, uttering little ejaculations of thankfulness to God for His great mercies. The good ship " Hope " came to anchor, the emigrants landed, and great was the sober rejoicing.

Alden Wentworth stood by Dorothy's side and gazed down upon her sparkling face, a look of tender yearning in his deep-set, solemn eyes. He constantly experienced, when with her, an unsatisfied longing, that, owing to his own conservativeness, gave little promise of gathering a plentiful harvest from that unawakened nature, yet hovering upon the narrow borderland between childhood and womanhood.

"Thou art glad, Dorothy," he said, "to see the landing?"

"Ay, truly," she answered; "I wot it brings me some one from England. I trust it brings some one of my father's kin."

He started at these words. "Thy father's kin!" he echoed. "And art thou not content, that thou shouldst seek the society of those unhallowed ones?"

She drew away from him; he frightened her, and she perceptibly shrank from him.

"They are of my father's people," she explained. "I know not that they are wicked because they differ from us."

As she thus spoke a gorgeous apparition stepped from the gang-plank to the shore. A murmur of disapprobation ran through the assembled throng. And, indeed, most appalling must it have been to the sober-minded, solemn Puritans to thus behold this splendidly attired personage, a full-fledged cavalier, their hatred and abomination.

The crimson velvet breeches, with ruffles of lace

hanging full below the knee; the russet-leather top-boots; the slashed satin coat, with soft puffings of mull between the slashes; the great hat with its nodding plumes held in place by a jeweled buckle; the embroidered gloves; and above all, the saucy, smiling, handsome face of a gay follower of a corrupt court and a licentious monarch. He looked upon the solemn assemblage with an amused smile; an expression of half-haughty condescension curved his short upper lip, which sported a blond curled mustache.

He was alone, and appeared to know no one. He passed through the crowd, which fell away from him as from one who was contaminated, and who might spread some deadly disease, moral, at least, if not physical.

Dorothy gazed openly upon him, her blue eyes wide and staring with unconcealed admiration for the glitter and glimmer of the stranger's magnificence.

He saw her, and started perceptibly, his step halting slightly, and looked boldly upon that sweet face, yet filled with but the glow of curious, innocent childhood. Curious she was, indeed, to see some one from the gay life of that land of which she dreamed and thought continually. Like a child whom the first glimpse of some unsuspected beauty has completely mastered, she gave a little gasp of delight, and bent eagerly forward. He passed on, leaving her blushing deeply at his bold glance and looking down.

Alden Wentworth turned to a neighbor standing near, and said, "Hast heard whom yonder bird of bright plumage may be? May the Lord preserve us from all such."

"They do say he is Sir Grenville Lawson. The account he gave of himself on shipboard is this. At least my cousin Timothy from Harrow, who is among the newly arrived, has so informed me. He was a cavalier at the court of Charles. Since the accession of William and Mary and the flight of James he hath been indiscreet, and for political reasons seeks an asylum in the New World till the storm blows past. Bestrew me, but he is a merry gallant, if one can read a countenance aright."

Alden Wentworth turned quickly toward Dorothy; she was looking after the departing stranger.

"Look not his way, Dorothy," he said. "Satan

hath many guises for his followers, and many tricks to catch the hearts of the unwary; this man belongs to the company of the lost, misguided ones."

Dorothy did not reply. She felt a coldness and depression coming over her as the bright presence of the stranger was withdrawn, even as a thick sea-mist shuts out the beauty of the land. When she spoke her voice was low and sad.

"The good ship 'Hope' hath brought no one to me. I did so earnestly believe it would. In faith, my father's people have forgotten me."

Alden turned almost fiercely upon her. It was as if the true nature of the man endeavored to out-step the bounds of austerity, which like bands of steel fettered his life of narrow conventionality. The aching and jealous longing of his heart at length found utterance.

"What dost thou desire, Dorothy, from another land than this? Thy desire should be here, in this thy home. Art thou not mine? Am I not thine?"

She drew away from him; he saw the motion with a cold sinking at his heart.

"Ay," she answered wearily, "thou hast my promise. I am thine—and yet—and yet——"

"Yet what?" he demanded quickly.

"I would I were more worthy of thee and that thou didst understand me better."

The people were now dispersing rapidly, and but few stragglers remained upon the shore. He leaned over her; when he spoke a depth of passion was in his words and tone.

"Thou art worthy, thou art! I am the culprit—God forgive me!" He made a frantic gesture with his hands as he spoke. "I seek to take from thee thy life, thy joyous youth; to steal the perfume from the flower ere yet its petals have unfolded; to crush thee into silence; to still thy song. And why? That I might make thee what I desire; to mold thee to a form that will rob thee of thy greatest charm. Forgive my selfishness. Thou art God's handiwork—forgive me!"

The intense feeling of the man appalled her. The mingling of this abandon of passion with his exterior coldness was beyond her comprehension. She released herself from his clinging clasp.

"I fear thee," she murmured, "I fear thee!"

"No, no," he said hoarsely, "say not those words. Thou canst not know, Dorothy, what thou art to me. I live in thee!" She drew closer to him again, and looked up into his face as a little child seeking forgiveness, yet hardly comprehending in what it has offended.

"I am grieved if I have pained thee," she said nervously. "I will endeavor to be to thee all that thou wouldst have me. Alden, thou wilt pardon me? I promise thee I will do better from this time on."

# CHAPTER IV.

## DOROTHY'S TEMPTATION.

A WEEK or more had elapsed since the landing
of the emigrant ship "Hope." Dorothy and Wentworth were seated side by side in the porch of the
farmhouse. It was evening, and the long shadows
were creeping stealthily over the lonely fields, noise-
less specters mourning for the death of day. These
forerunners of the darkness, with ghost-like tread,
spread themselves upon the land, clothing it in a
subdued, mysterious light. The heavily foliaged
trees stood out in one unbroken line of blackness
against the sky, from which the after-glow was
rapidly fading, leaving level streaks of palest red and
purple in its wake.

The sounds of night insects, mingling with the
croaking of frogs and the hoot of the owl, broke
upon the stillness with startling intensity. The
sweet scents of the shrubs, added to the spicy odor
of the ten-weeks stock that grew near the gate, rose
upon the air strong and penetrating.

The couple in the doorway had not spoken for some minutes. Wentworth was thinking deeply, and Dorothy's eyes were seeking to pierce the darkness; the solemnity of the hour depressed her somewhat, her sensitive organization being particularly susceptible to atmospheric influences. She gazed intently before her, toward the forest, as though loth to lose a glimmer of the fast decreasing twilight as it faded behind the great expanse of wooded country that towered in the west.

Presently Alden leaned toward his betrothed, and taking her hand, said in rather a strained, unnatural voice: "Thou knowest that the summer is rapidly passing by, that the days are shortening. When the autumn is here, Dorothy, I would that thou shouldst come to me. I have oft endeavored to speak of this, and have ever desisted for fear of alarming thee; now I can wait no longer—I must speak. What dost thou think, Dorothy?"

Dorothy arose hurriedly from her seat, and going to the front of the porch gazed silently over the garden to the road beyond. Then she turned and came toward Wentworth, and laid her hand upon his shoulder. He looked up expectantly, and even in the dimness he noticed that her face shone with a pale light.

"Alden," she said softly, and in her sweet voice was a cadence of deepest sadness, "I told thee once that I did not love thee as thou wouldst have me. I do respect thee and give thee all honor. I am proud that thou hast chosen me. Yet methinks that in my being is a font of affection that is not thine."

"Not mine!" he said hurriedly. "Dost thou then love another? Hast thou deceived me?"

"No, no, not so; I love none other. I wish to be upright and honest with thee, that is all. Art thou content, art thou fully satisfied to take me as I am? Perchance when I am older and wiser I shall learn to love thee as thou desirest, and my rebellious will and love of mirth time may yet subdue."

The child—for child she was as yet in years and experience—did not comprehend the nearness of the precipice upon which her feet were faltering. She simply felt that she owed Wentworth more than she could give. If he was satisfied, however, with part payment, her responsibility ceased; she had done all that was required of her, and the link that united her to him became strong enough for her conscience.

"Thou wilt learn to love me, my beloved; thou wilt," he said eagerly. "I am fully content with thee; I would not have thee other than thou art. Did I force thy true nature into another channel then I should indeed distort the real Dorothy, and in its stead find, no doubt, only a mirthless echo." He kissed her, and she submitted passively.

The wedding-day was set for early October. Wentworth would then leave the old manse, where he had previously resided with his superior, Mr. Parris, and go into a house of his own. A rather peculiar custom then prevailed, in direct contrast to the rule of our time at least. A man was allowed no independence whatever until after his marriage. He was obliged to submit in all particulars to the order of the court; he might not even live alone, but was forced to reside with some family, becoming a member of the household.

In fact, it is highly probable that these restrictions often forced the poor man into matrimony. The policy of the shrewd old Pilgrim Fathers was not so bad a thing after all; a householder certainly being a more influential personage in many particulars than a bachelor.

There was one man in the olden time who was not driven into marriage by the stern decree of the Puritan code. Wentworth, with the heavy odds against him of Dorothy's lukewarmness, worked, planned, and lived for the bright hopes of the future. He silenced the doubts that arose within him, crushing the slightest tendency to a possible disastrous termination of his desires, bidding the small voice be still that warned him of his unwise course.

The morning following the conversation in the farmhouse porch, Dorothy in her sober gown, brightened somewhat by a bodice of blue embroidered with silk thread, her dun-colored cape of " tiffany " across her shoulders, her little Puritan cap upon her head, took her way over the newly mown fields to the meeting-house. She held her psalm-book in her hand, and as she walked gazed demurely down at the ground, endeavoring to force her tripping steps into a mincing, sober gait, as became a Puritan maiden on her way to meeting.

She was thinking of many things; among others, that it would not be very long now before she would be Dorothy Wentworth. All would be so changed. She and Alden would walk side by side to meeting, and she would sit in one of the uppermost seats, the large square pew on the side of the pulpit, which faced the " foreseat," as it was called—the seat of greatest honor, kept sacred for the dignitaries of the colony.

This seat was raised some inches above the floor, and poor Dorothy knew that in this exalted position she should never dare smile during the sermon or the most lengthy prayer; it would scandalize the deacons, whose stern eyes she knew would follow her every motion.

Her mouth looked pensive and there was a listless droop in the willowy figure. She met many neighbors on her way, who greeted her with a staid inclination of the head. She walked behind her aunt and uncle, who stalked along silently in best attire, their faces drawn down into appropriate gravity for the service of the day.

On Sunday morning in New England in the long ago those whose homes were near the church edifice always walked reverently and slowly along the grass-grown streets to service. Those who lived at a distance rose early, sometimes with the sun; they saddled their horses, and with a pillion strapped on behind each saddle for wife or daughter they rode across the fields, or took the narrow bridle paths through the thick woods to church. No storms, no hardships ever interfered with this, their first duty.

Many curious eyes followed Dorothy's winsome, sober face as she entered the building and seated herself sedately by her aunt. Her uncle joined the men on the other side, that being the accepted custom.

Dorothy experienced a peculiar sensation of elation, surely pardonable, that after all she had carried off the prize without so much as preparing a single weapon of warfare. This thought lent a slight dignity to her youthful bearing.

Presently the minister and deacons entered. Dorothy flushed slightly as she encountered a grave, kind glance from Alden Wentworth. The service commenced after seating the meeting, which proceeding took much time. Though the Puritans disapproved of ceremonies and forms, yet, with praiseworthy inconsistency, each individual was assigned a place in the church according to his position of rank or importance, and a high seat in the synagogue was a boon earnestly desired.

One can see the picture distinctly, descending like a pale ghost through the mist of many generations, a sad-colored ghost indeed: the plain whitewashed walls of the meeting-house reflecting the glare of the sun from the staring, uncurtained windows; the rows of sober-faced, sedate men and women, upon whose countenances were plainly marked the traces of their mournful existences; the benches of unruly, riotous boys, belabored now and then by raps from the stick of the tithing-man, that fussy personage who flittered here and there as occasion required, no doubt delighted at the prospect of changing his position as often as possible; the monotonous droning of the psalms; the spiders spinning in the rough-hewn beams aloft; the nodding, weary little children, seated on their hard hassocks; without the church the sound of many birds and insects, and the distant swash of the waters on the shores of the harbor. There is nothing cheerful in this picture. We surely have the best of it in the nineteenth century.

The sun fell upon Dorothy's bright face as she sang in her sweet tones the quaint old hymns, the words of which ran into each other in a most puzzling manner, the meaning as abstruse as the tunes were grating. Still it was singing, and Dorothy greatly enjoyed it. In her absorption she was not conscious of a step that paused hesitatingly near her and then proceeded. Presently she became aware of a bright red glow upon the floor of the aisle—a glow that appeared to creep, like some living thing, along the floor. She turned quickly, almost dropping her psalm-book, and looked into the face of Sir Grenville Lawson, who stood but a few feet from her in the center of the aisle. The scarlet gleam upon the floor was caused by the sun reflecting the rich hue of his satin cloak. He gave her a glance keen and penetrating, then turned abruptly and took a seat nearly opposite her among the men.

Dorothy had seen Sir Grenville thrice since he came to Salem. Twice had she passed him on the village street, but had not then raised her eyes to gaze upon him. Had not Alden said he was a degenerate sinner? Once again near the forest, where, the path being narrow, he stepped into the brambles that grew on the side to give her room to pass. He had doffed his hat, and with bold glance and courtly bow had bid her proceed. She had smiled shyly into his handsome face, blushed, and passed by, conscious that he looked after her, and when she reached a safe distance she herself looked back and saw him standing watching her.

The psalm-book trembled in her hand, her voice ceased singing abruptly, and she watched him with covert admiration from under her long lashes. From admiration her thoughts drifted into interest. In

Dorothy's composition reverence certainly held a small part as yet. Any subject to occupy her thoughts during these wretched, weary hours was seized upon with avidity.

She fancied herself the center of some happy, impossible situation. Her mind soared far away from the monotonous voice of Mr. Parris, as he proceeded laboriously to expound his doctrines in sundry dreary, intricate passages, filled with doleful forebodings of everlasting damnation, to his grave, respectful flock. She did not see the little meeting-house, nor the hearers, nor the spiders spinning, nor the fussy tithing-man. Her imagination painted a much more alluring picture. She saw instead a beautiful home far away over the seas, in that pleasant land of England. She saw the king and queen, the splendors of the court, and she triumphant amidst it all; and by her side, not Alden, the staid Puritan judge, in his black attire and with his dreary views of living; instead, a gay and knightly form in satin, lace, and jewels. She laughed, sang, and danced, and acted out her nature. Poor little simple Dorothy dreamed and sang mechanically, absorbed in the airy fabrics of her brain.

The long, tedious service at last drew to a close;

the pious members rose, much elated that Mr. Parris had been able to preach two hours and twenty minutes on the ever-popular subject of the terrible punishment of sin by fire and brimstone.

Dorothy came out into the aisle, and Sir Grenville came from his place opposite, fate pointing with mocking finger at the pair as side by side they walked forth into the sunshine of that perfect Sabbath morning.

Mr. Parris and Wentworth, with the rest of the deacons, stood in the church door to greet the parishioners as they came forth, shaking hands, and asking sundry questions of interest, principally regarding domestic matters.

As Dorothy advanced, the glow of Sir Grenville's scarlet cloak seemed enveloping her sober-tinted gown in ruddy light. It touched her hair, her face, and thence wandered down upon her garments. Thus Alden saw her as she came out into the daylight, and a jealous rage arose within him, a spark of anger crept into his eyes. This nearness of his chosen one to this abomination of wickedness appeared to him like desecration.

Sir Grenville bowed and passed back of her, hesitating a moment as if intending to speak. He received no encouragement, however, from the black-browed clergyman or the grave deacons, who stood cold and erect. He smiled and hastened by, going alone up the village street.

The summer days passed rapidly, and beautiful September beamed with kindly smiles that held within their radiance some of the warmth of the departed season. The time of the cutting of wheat, the harvesting of apples, the gathering of nuts had come, with its added burden of work to the little town.

Martha was very industriously planning and spinning for the bride. Great preparations were making in the farmhouse. Dorothy grew quiet and morose, and expressed little interest in the proceedings, taking no part in the weaving. She went seldom to the new house now building on the outskirts of the village, the erection of which Wentworth watched with pride and interest.

Dorothy's aunt did not chide her, though inwardly she was much disturbed. If Alden was satisfied, she argued, why should she complain? It was for him to speak, not her.

It was now the 20th of September, but three weeks before the wedding-day. Dorothy was nervous and restless. The chain which she had at first been willing to assume now proved unbearably irksome. Each day, as it brought her nearer to that new position, brought with it dread. She betook herself one afternoon to her favorite nook in the forest, seeking a moss-covered tree-trunk that grew near a rippling stream, too remote from the confines of the woods for danger of interruption. It was a densely shaded spot, cool, damp, and still. Nature's sweet companionship soothed her into rest. Here she reposed and watched the dancing brook, addressing it in tones of tender endearment as it hurried on its way. The forest gloom was deep around her; a few stray gleams of sunshine fell through the heavy foliage, though scarce illuminating the somber surroundings, and causing the darkness to seem more dark where they did not descend.

As she leaned back against the tree an indefinable sensation crept over her, the consciousness of another's presence. Terrified at the thought of the possible proximity of some supernatural agency, she started from her seat, intending to turn her steps homeward.

As she did so, a man stepped out from the gloom of the overhanging shrubs and vines. He stood quietly an instant, the straggling sunbeams falling upon the jewel in his hat, thence down upon his rich apparel. She took a few steps forward, blushing deeply, her breath coming quickly. Like a timid woodland fawn uncertain of the good intentions of its hunter, she hesitated, and receded a few steps. Her timidity was exquisite in its naturalness.

"Do not be afraid," said the cavalier, advancing. "I have watched for you this many a day." He did not use the quaint *thee* and *thou* of the Puritans. "I have with patience discovered where you make your haunts. In yonder vile town, where they dread lest I breed a pestilence by my presence, I have sought and gained information. I know much of your history."

She came nearer to him, watching him eagerly. "Know much of my history!" she echoed.

"Ay, indeed," he said.

"Then tell me; I long to hear," she said earnestly.

"Your father, Trooper Grey, was known to me from stories heard at court. He was a well-known *protégé* of Charles." Here the cavalier paused, as if amused at some recollection which the uttering of this name aroused. He then continued more earnestly: "I feel some sympathy for his daughter, compelled to a living death among this stiffnecked people. "Your father angered the king when he married your mother, the Puritan, and indeed his marriage was a mystery, for a better mimic of these worthy saints never pleased a merrier monarch. Ah well, Cupid takes his revenge at times." He advanced nearer and took her hand, which she held out tremblingly before her. "Be not afraid; I would not harm a hair of that lovely head."

"Thou"—she gasped—"thou art Sir Grenville Lawson, the courtier. What seekst thou of me, the Puritan? Sayest thou truly thou hast heard of my father? It is no jest, no prank that thou wouldst play?"

"Truth is in my words," he answered. Her blue eyes shone with excitement. "I seek to offer comfort," he continued. "I can read a riddle: I know the story of the coming wedding in Salem. It behooves me to say the bride is not happy; she is even now distraught with perplexities and doubts—doubts of her right to wed the saintly Mr. Wentworth, with but coldness for him in her heart."

"What right hast thou, a stranger, to address me thus?" she replied quickly.

"The right I take in saving so much grace and

beauty from a fate so dire in this benighted spot of the New World. You are as yet innocent of what the world contains. I trow I could tell a story that would make a smile as bright as heaven come over the sweetest face the sun ever shone upon." As he spoke he leaned toward her and looked boldly and laughingly into her downcast countenance.

She gave him a shy glance, and said, "Tell me the story, Sir Grenville, I would fain hear it. Is it of fair England?"

He laughed softly. "It is of England. Ah, that I could with the power of words depict the joys of that gay city of London! It is pitiful that one born to grace so high a state should feel but half the pulse of living. Of a certainty it is death when one lays aside all that makes life bearable. One can renounce no more when he lies down in the cold earth forever."

Then followed a long account of the feasts and revels, of the court pageants, the gorgeous dresses of the knights and the fair ladies. Dorothy listened entranced, clasping her small hands and looking earnestly into his face. She became absorbed, carried beyond a thought of the impropriety of thus conversing in these lonely woods with a stranger, and one, too, so steeped in the wiles of Satan.

" And thou hast seen all this?" she asked. "Ah, that I might have just one little glimpse! But no, I never shall."

"Why not?" he said. " Surely you have a right in the disposal of your future; your life is your own."

She shook her head sadly but decidedly. "No, no, I have no right; I am a ward and under age. But let me tell thee why I was so sad when thou didst draw near to comfort me—for thou *hast* comforted me with thy beauteous story." She hesitated, awed by the unusual desire that assailed her to thus confide in a stranger. But Sir Grenville urged her to proceed, drawing nearer to her, and watching delightedly the varying expressions of her innocent face.

" I will tell thee, then," she said. " It was but this morn that I did search in the old chest in the garret for things wherewith to add to my wedding outfit. I did find there a gorgeous robe of blue tiffany and a red whittle embroidered in gold, and a coiffure with long silk lappets, and sundry other parts of a gala dress. They were fine!" she cried excitedly. "Furthermore, I did find a long chain of gold beads." She paused. "Oh, such bright

gold beads !   I donned this brave attire and did
descend to the kitchen to Aunt Martha."   The tears
gathered in her eyes ; she hesitated.

"Well, what then?" urged Sir Grenville.   "I wot
the old dame was wroth," he laughed.

"She was greatly angered with me.   She said
they were my mother's robes, given her by my godless father, and she did keep them hidden.   I must
e'en take them off and put them away.   She would
not let me have the golden beads, though I begged
with tears."

Sir Grenville threw back his head and laughed
loudly.   He had removed his large hat and thrown
it on the grass beside him ; his blonde hair shone
brightly in the light.

"That is of a certainty a grievous trouble," he
replied soothingly, becoming grave at her expression
of solemn surprise at his mirth ; "but fret not.   Come
here this time to-morrow, and I will give you a far
more costly chain of gold than that Aunt Martha
has refused to give.   Your trouble is one that will
quickly heal."

"Ah, no, no," she said, shaking her head.   "Aunt
Martha would not let me keep it."

He watched her curiously an instant, then said,

"Why tell her? Keep the secret. What she does not know will not trouble her; take this little gift from me. Come to-morrow and I will bring the chain. Be not alarmed; I will not bind you with the bauble."

She still shook her head. "I fear me it is not right, yet methinks I desire much to possess the beads. Yet if I may not speak of them they do not benefit me; as well might they remain in the old chest in the garret."

"Those treasures in the chest are not in your possession; there will be a great difference, as you will find when you own the gold chain. Our neighbor's good things, be they never so costly, equal not our own little jewel of perchance but meager price."

She still reiterated her denial. "I dare not," she said.

"Are they not worth this little walk and talk?" urged Sir Grenville coaxingly. "And they would so well become you."

"Perchance I shall come, then, to the woods again, if thou art sure I do no harm. Yet I will not take the beads; I will but look and admire them."

"Harm!" he cried. "As much harm as the dove

does, or the gentle lamb. I shall look to-morrow
at this hour for your sweet presence, and shall bring
the jewel for your inspection."

He took her hand, and bowing low over it, kissed
it. She blushed and drew it quickly away.

"I fear me thou art over bold," she said.

"It is the custom at the court," he explained.
"And be not angry if I bring the bauble; if you
are still hard-hearted I shall take it back. I cannot
force it upon you. Methinks," he laughed softly,
"when once seen it will prove a powerful argu-
ment." As he spoke these last words he cast a
piercing glance upon her.

She shivered under it. "I will come," she said
simply, and left him, not looking back, but going
quietly over the meadows toward the farm.

That night a new strength came to the girl, and
she resolved to go no more to the woods; yet with
this resolve mingled the desire for further converse
with the fascinating cavalier. When the morning
dawned her will had weakened; as the sun dries up
the dew upon the grass, so the light chased away
her good resolutions.

The soft glow of the afternoon sun, shimmering
through thick-leaved boughs, fell upon Dorothy

seated once more by the side of Sir Grenville. He had drawn the glittering coil of gold from the bosom of his lace-frilled shirt, and was holding it up to her admiring gaze.

"Ah!" she exclaimed, entranced. "It is most beautiful! I would it were not wrong to take it from thee; I fear Satan controls my will and forces me to wish for its possession. But let me hold it in my hand once—that will be no harm; I will give it back to thee."

He held it out to her, and she took it in her hand; the glittering chain seemed to coil around her slender fingers like some living thing. She leaned over it, examining its workmanship; then, holding it toward him, she spoke:

"Perchance I might take it from thee, were it not for a troublous dream I had yesternight. In my dream I saw my mother bending above me; she held her arms out toward me, as though to draw me to her, and she did say, 'Dorothy, my child, my child, may God protect thee!' I tried to go to her; I could not; something of great force held me back, and when I looked to see whence came this great strength, it was a chain of gold that did bind me. Then I did awake, and in the moonlight on the floor I thought I saw my mother kneeling. I heard low sounds of weeping, though of a certainty that must have been the wind; and I was cold and much affrighted, and did repeat, to reassure myself, one of the psalms."

For an instant Sir Grenville's hand that held the trinket trembled. He made a gesture as if to replace it in the bosom of his shirt; a troubled look came upon his face; then he threw up his head defiantly and laughed.

"Truly your dream was of a troubled nature. A dream is naught; forget it. The moonlight must have fallen across your face and addled your brain. Let me clasp this chain about your throat, then look you in yonder clear brook and see how well it becomes you."

"I will not promise to take it from thee," she pouted; "I will but place it upon my throat and then return it."

Sir Grenville smiled. "When it shines upon your white neck I wot you must possess it, else you were not a woman."

She allowed him to clasp the jeweled trinket about her slim throat, her blushes coming and going, and her eyes shining. Then, stooping over the clear pool, where the little brook had widened and made a natural mirror framed in a delicate fringe of softest green moss, she gazed intently at the reflection of herself.   She turned her head to catch the glitter of the beads as the sun shone upon them.   Sir Grenville looked over her shoulder, his handsome face close to hers, his breath warm on her cheek.   No warning came to the smiling girl that far off in the west a cloud was rising, a cloud scarce larger than a bubble, and scarce more tangible, but from whose infinitesimal beginning might ere long gather a mighty tempest.

Dorothy smiled at the two reflections in the stream, and said, " Methinks I will keep the trinket, it becomes me well; and I will follow thy advice and say naught of it."

Dorothy came again many times to the seclusion of her woodland haunt, and never did she sit alone upon the gnarled seat of oak.   Sir Grenville understood perfectly the nature he was dealing with, and was most wary and cautious in his advances.   He had been trained in the school of duplicity, and made an excellent instructor for so pliable and innocent a scholar as Dorothy.

Alden Wentworth was forgotten; his stern, quiet

image faded from her mind; in its place stood the gay, smiling face of the courtier. The domestic future that would have been hers in the new home now building gave place to a glittering life beyond the seas—a life so radiant with all this world can offer that her imagination soared upward in a tumult of exaltation and triumph.

The wedding-day drew near. October, cool, crisp, and beautiful, came with soft winds and a blue haze upon the hills. Among the woods the trees gleamed in gold and scarlet; the fields and late fall flowers glowed with a tropical splendor; in the woods and reedy marshes hundreds of fall birds came flocking to become a prey to the hunter. The little village basked pleasantly in the grateful warmth, which was the more welcome in anticipation of the rigors of coming winter.

Dorothy, her cheeks bright with color, her face radiant, flittered with an unusual restlessness in and out of the farmhouse. She kept aloof as much as possible from Wentworth, startling him at times with unaccountable fits of childish petulance. He watched her with a hungry wistfulness that was most pathetic to behold. He scarcely understood her varied moods, yet he trusted her perfectly, and loved her with a passion that had complete possession of him.

The strict discipline of his age and creed might have made him suspicious of the motives of others, but the innate goodness of his mind and heart counteracted this possible effect. He looked upon Dorothy through the lens of his affection—an affection not unmixed with awe, for he felt that she had qualities beyond his comprehension. She was to him as a beautiful wild bird, whose strange songs and fluttering wings would become quiet when her true resting-place was found.

The stolen meetings in the dim recesses of the woods continued. At length came a memorable day, when Dorothy, her hand held closely by Sir Grenville, upon her finger a jeweled circlet which was to be removed and concealed later, promised to leave Salem secretly, go with him to Boston, there marry him, then cross the seas to England as Lady Grenville Lawson.

# CHAPTER V.

## THE FLIGHT.

THE early morning sunshine cast pale, cold rays upon the wooden floor of the kitchen at the Holden farm. The breakfast-table was set for the plain, substantial breakfast, while Martha bustled about the stove, rattling pots and pans. David was seated near the window, looking out over the fields, where the wheat rose in stacks and the corn stood tied in hillocks, the yellow pumpkins showing between the rows.

The brother and sister had not spoken for some minutes; then David, turning from his dreamy survey of the fields, looked anxiously toward Martha; she, as if compelled by his glance, turned quickly.

"Martha," he said, a heavy frown upon his stern face, "I have suffered much this past night in my mind about Dorothy. The child's manner is unnatural, and yestereven, when Wentworth came nigh her, she shuddered and drew away from him;

I saw the motion with dismay. Alas! I fear some hideous outcome from this strange demeanor. Anxious thoughts of her robbed me of my hours of sleep."

"Out upon thy prating, man!" said Martha sturdily, brandishing an iron pot in her hand. "The girl is, as all girls are, silly and full of whims. I tell thee Alden Wentworth will tame her. He is patient now for blind love of her; when he is the master I wot he will clip her wings."

"I know not, I know not. Dost think we did wrong to urge the child? Perchance, had she her way, she would not have married him."

"I tell thee, David, thou art a weak fool. Why not bid a riotous colt go its way through the streets? Dost thou not bridle it till it is subdued and tamed? Dorothy is but a child; I take no doubt to my conscience but we did the right in compelling her."

"It may be; and yet for reasons that do assail me at times I am anxious. I have judged, 'tis true, but by her looks and fearsome manner."

"'Tis all right, take my word for that. Though at times I well-nigh lose all patience, I subdue my desire to punish her. So bide, David; let her go her way. Alden is a saint-like man, yet he is masterful. The results of his training will tell a different story a year hence, so fear not." She paused and took some steaming porridge from the fire, and placed it upon the table. Having accomplished this, she stood a moment in the center of the room, irresolute, then continued, "The child is late this morn; she has overslept. I will call her."

Martha walked across the kitchen to the inner room, whence her voice came loud and shrill, calling Dorothy to breakfast. No voice responded from the upper chamber. David leaned forward, his head bowed within his hands. "Yes, she is late," he said.

Presently Martha reëntered the kitchen; her face wore a strange expression. She walked slowly, and in her hand she held a crumpled sheet of paper. "David—David," she gasped, coming forward, "she —she has left us!"

The woman laid her hand upon the side of the kitchen table, as if to steady herself, and stared straight before her. David snatched the letter from his sister's hand. He did not speak, but the heavy frown deepened between his brows. Then he read the note aloud in a low, firm voice, his manner giving the impression that he had expected this, and was prepared to meet it.

"'AUNT MARTHA AND UNCLE DAVID: I am unhappy in Salem. I go to my father's people. I give Alden back his troth, and I beseech thee, if thou hast loved me, to forgive

"'DOROTHY.'

"That is all," said David; "she has forgotten all these years of love and care; there is no word of gratitude. Yet 'tis unlike Dorothy; she was ever grateful. Methinks some evil spirit hath entered into her, and she doeth this thing against her will."

"Against her will!" shrieked Martha, the rage that burned within her leaping all bounds. "She hath for her heritage the godless spirit of her father; she hath no heart or soul for good; she is an ungrateful, deceitful, lying wench. I cast her from me; no part within me holds she from henceforth; no home of mine shall she enter more."

David laid his hand upon the shoulder of the trembling, excited woman. "Martha, remember she is our little sister's child; remember the promise thou hast made to her dead mother."

Martha tore herself from his touch and burst into a torrent of sobs, leaning her head down upon the table, her shoulders shaking with a paroxysm of grief. David stood over her, looking down sadly upon her bowed head.

"Martha," he said, "God hath afflicted us." His voice had a solemn ring, like the voice of a minister when he reads the last rites over the dead. "He has permitted this grief to come upon us; all that He doeth is right."

The couple did not hear a step upon the narrow walk that led around the side of the house, nor did they move until a voice said:

"Good-morning, Mistress Holden. I am an early caller; the freshest bunch of Michaelmas daisies in all Salem I must perforce bring Dorothy, the dew yet wet upon their leaves. Has she not risen?"

Martha lifted her head; her swollen, tear-stained face was filled with terror and dismay. She held out her shaking hands toward Wentworth, who, sorely puzzled, stood upon the threshold holding the bunch of fall flowers in his hand.

"Alden—Alden, God give me strength to tell thee! She—hath left thee—hath given thee back thy troth; she has renounced thee, and we shall see her no more."

Alden Wentworth did not move; he had not grasped her meaning. He stood irresolute a moment, then advanced a step. "Given me back my troth? I know not what thou canst mean," he said slowly.

"Read this—read this! She was not in her room last night; she has gone; this is what is left us." Martha held the note out toward him.

Wentworth took the note, and the flowers dropped from his nerveless fingers upon the floor, and lay there, mute reproaches for their useless mission. He read the few words and handed the note back. A pallor spread itself over his dark face, a dullness settled in his eyes.

"Hath she left naught for me?" he said. "Surely, surely she cannot have forgotten that I would suffer most."

"She hath left naught," answered Martha.

The morning breeze blew gently through the open door, carrying with it the sweet, cool odors of the autumn; it rustled the leaves of the bunch of daisies that lay upon the floor.

"Naught?" he cried. "Then, O my God, I am indeed left desolate. Dorothy, Dorothy, thou hast broken my heart!"

He swayed slightly, but steadied himself, and passed his hand across his brow. Then he stooped and picked up the flowers, and handed them with a sad smile to Martha. "I have brought them for her burial, it seemeth. She is dead." He paused, then continued in a low voice, as if communing with himself: "Perchance such love as mine shall but slumber in hope, and in a better world will re-awaken, where Dorothy and I shall have eternity together. I might have seen this result, had I not forced myself into blindness. I have been a weak fool; she never loved me, and I knew it."

Martha was frightened. His quiet, self-contained nature had never, to their knowledge, overstepped the bounds of a gentle passiveness. In fact, there had been times when they had deemed him almost lacking in an interest in human joys. Now, like a mighty torrent, the suppressed, unsatisfied longings of his heart burst forth, and the brother and sister were dismayed at the very humanity of the man.

The depth of feeling and despair manifested in his words and actions compelled Martha to silence her own grief; and, rising from her seat, she laid her hand on Wentworth's arm. "Forget her," she said. "She was never worthy thy affection. Thou wast not guided aright in thy choice. Heaven forgive me for thus urging it. It was my pride and ambition—I did ever force the child."

"Forget her!" he said sadly. "Can the world forget the sun when it has hid its light and the darkness comes? Do the flowers forget the summer when the winter is here and they sleep in hopes of an awakening? Can I forget one who has been more to me than sun or many flowers—one who has been my life, whose image I have enthroned above my duty to my Creator?" He paused. "Let us speak no more of her. I have little strength left; I will go to my work."

He stepped through the doorway a little unsteadily, then passed out of sight, the weeping woman looking wistfully after him.

When Dorothy in the gloom of night passed down the creaking staircase of the old farmhouse and thence through the kitchen, where the tins upon the wall reflected the tiny moonbeams that stole through the chinks of the wooden shutters, no apprehension assailed her. The thought of leaving those who had been kind to her from infancy, and who, in accordance with all laws of nature, she should have loved, did not trouble her for the moment. Her mind was filled with dreams of grandeur and freedom from restraint.

As she went across the moonlighted fields, and

down the country road, she did not hesitate or turn back but once, and that was when the low hoot of an owl echoed mournfully from a tree by the way-side. She started at the cry and glanced nervously about her, a little wistfully, perhaps. She gazed backward an instant toward the slumbering village that lay so quiet and motionless beneath the stars, then her glance wandered toward the farmhouse, looking lonely amidst its wide fields.

"Aunt Martha will be grieved for me," she murmured. "But Sir Grenville has promised that some day I shall return in splendor"—she threw up her graceful head proudly—"and then all Salem shall see what a grand dame little wild Dorothy can make."

Sir Grenville had planned the elopement with all secrecy, and Dorothy had acquiesced, never demurring at any of the details of their contemplated journey. He, knowing, or at least fearing, that his disappearance simultaneously with hers might excite the suspicions of the villagers, had left Salem some days previous. He was then to return on an appointed night, when he would wait for Dorothy on the borders of the forest. With a good fresh horse and a pillion behind the saddle they would take the bridle path to Boston, a distance of some sixteen miles—not long in these days of smooth roads, but quite a hazardous undertaking over a rough, stony path, through a gloomy forest, and in the darkness of the night.

When Dorothy reached the trysting-place, Sir Grenville stepped hastily forward from the thickets, and, grasping her hand, drew her quickly toward him. "Ah, at last!" he murmured. "You are late."

"I have hastened," she replied; "yet methinks it reached the hour of ten before the house became quiet and I might with safety venture forth."

"We must delay no longer; all is ready. I will mount you upon the pillion, and we will hasten on our journey; I wish to profit by the light of the moon as long as may be."

She obeyed him, and they started, riding slowly and cautiously through the gloom. The horse picked his way carefully, now and then stopping to shy at some fantastic form that fell across the road occasioned by the gentle swaying of a branch.

Dorothy did not speak; her mind was too engrossed in the contemplation of the wondrous picture held before her delighted gaze, so cunningly colored by her admirer's hand that the true outline of the figure was hid in a blaze of deceptive splendor.

Suddenly an unaccountable depression settled like a heavy weight of iron upon her spirits. She remained passive in her seat behind Sir Grenville, speaking when he addressed her, but only in monosyllables. This depression (the first faint stirring of conscience) was no doubt increased by her surroundings. The murmurings in the trees resembled the sighing of human voices; the tinkling noise made by little wayside brooks sounded loud and ominous; while horrible forms and faces were conjured up by her vivid imagination from the restless swaying of the branches.

Sir Grenville was apparently occupied in guiding his horse, and indeed it was most necessary that he should do so, for now and then the steed would stumble and almost fall upon its knees. Once this mishap actually occurred. Dorothy started and trembled as Sir Grenville uttered an oath and reined the animal up so viciously that they were almost dismounted. It was the first time she had heard his voice in other tones save courtesy and affection. A shudder passed over her.

"Thou art cruel to the poor beast," she remonstrated. "He cannot see; he carries a double load."

"He must watch his steps, or he will become disabled. I like not the prospect of spending the remainder of the night hours in these woods, even with so fair a charmer."

She said no more, and in silence they traversed the remainder of the journey. When they reached the outskirts of Boston, Sir Grenville reined in the horse, and turning in the saddle said:

"I would have you dismount and rest a while before entering the town; I have made all arrangements for your reception in the place, yet methinks the ride has been long, and a change of position would be agreeable. Furthermore, I have something I wish to tell you before we proceed."

She detected a peculiar trembling in his voice that alarmed her; a muffled sound, and a halting inflection never heard before. She did, however, as he desired, and presently they were standing side by side, at no great distance from the horse, and near the trunk of a fallen tree. Through the interstices of the branches of some tall shrubs they could distinguish a few faint lights, indicating the direction of the seaport town. He had clasped her hand frantically, and was bending over her, seeking as he spoke to watch her face, which he could see but dimly, the lantern hanging on the pommel of the saddle emitting but a faint gleam.

"Dorothy, I know not why I tell you of this, unless it be a force from within compelling me, against which I cannot contend." He paused. She trembled visibly, but did not reply. "Perchance," he continued, "I am not the hardened wretch I deemed myself; or possibly from a superstitious terror of the warning evinced in your mother's dream, I perforce can deceive you no further." His breath came quickly, and he hesitated. "You have trusted me. What if I should tell you that in one thing I have deceived you; would you despise me?"

"How can I tell till thou shalt acquaint me with the secret?" She looked innocently and unsuspectingly toward him. "I am no witch, I cannot read thy mind."

"I have wronged you, Dorothy," he cried; "wronged you to win you; lied to you that you might become mine."

"Lied to me!" she murmured. "In what hast thou lied?"

"I cannot marry you," he said desperately. "At

the court of William and Mary e'en now there is a lady in waiting on Her Majesty who is my wife." He spoke as though the words were forced from him against his consent. " I did marry her some years previous. We were unhappy, and I left her; she hates me, and I do most heartily reciprocate. Yet the bond is still between us—the hated binding yoke; she is of the Church of Rome, that permits no divorce. The union was not of my choice, Dorothy, it was made for me."

Dorothy did not reply; she drew the embroidered whittle more closely about her shoulders, although the night was not cold, and stood motionless. Then she touched his arm and looked up into his face.

" I fear me I have not heard thee aright," she said. " If thou hast said truly, then why am I here ? "

" You are here," he cried passionately, " because I would not let that hated bond part us. I drew you into my heart—I could not cast you forth. You held me by your beauty, by your innocence. I could not lose you, could not release you. Yet since I heard from you that in a dream your mother came to pray for her child, to guard her from all harm, I could wrong you no further. The path is

now clear between us; all is told, and for the very
love I bear for you, whose depth has no measure, I
beseech you, forgive me—forgive me!"

He stepped from her side a few paces, and, fold-
ing his arms, looked down upon the ground.  As
he receded she followed him, and clasped his arm
fiercely.  Lowering her head, she looked into his
partly averted face.

"Then, Sir Grenville, I am naught to thee, nor
can I ever be; thou hast deceived me, else I would
not have fled with thee.  Yet in one deed thou hast
been kind; I thank thee that thou hast told me this.
Thou hast betrayed me, 'tis true, into a grave mistake.  Thou hast relented, and e'en now, if thou
wilt, thou canst restore me to my home ere yet the
morning cometh."

He turned vehemently upon her. · "How cool
and calm, Mistress Dorothy, is your voice!  Did I
go to this excess of trouble only to restore my prize?
Not I.  You mistake the man.  I have been a lucky
hunter—my bird is caught.  I have done wrong,
I own it, yet not I alone; I have left my wife for
you, you have tricked your rightful lover for me.
Are we not quits?  The stones you cast at me I can
e'en with justice return."

This insight into his selfish nature disgusted and

angered her. She the victim, he the strong conqueror! This chance upheaval of his nearly dormant conscience by a superstitious terror of consequences having been stilled by his confession, she was now to be dragged into the meshes of his net, to lose all semblance of goodness, to sink with him into the depths.

"Thou didst seek me," she cried angrily, "and cajole me. I know now full well it was not thee I cared for, else far different emotions would assail me now; but it was that exalted position thou didst promise me."

"Say you so, indeed, O worldly one? Well, that position is still yours."

"Thou knowest a falsehood is in thy words," she cried excitedly, stamping her foot upon the ground as she spoke.

"What may be pleased to be your wish, fair lady?" he said sarcastically. "We can talk in these woods no longer; the light of the morning will soon be upon us. Let me help to mount you once again into the pillion, and we will then ride into Boston town. On the way think deeply; I warn you it were better for you to bridle your words, and take the 'goods the gods provide.'"

"I will not go with thee!" she cried.

"I can compel you. Remember, I like not to use force, but as a last alternative I will bind a cord about you in the pillion."

"Thou dare not!" she exclaimed in a frenzy of terror.

"Listen," he said coaxingly: "no aid is near, no help can come; why not submit? You cannot return to Salem; your absence will have been noticed ere this. Those exalted pious people, the elect of God's earth, will turn the cold shoulder. Be discreet, be wise."

She looked down moodily upon the ground, and appeared to be thinking earnestly, then she spoke. "Well, then, mount thou first," she muttered sullenly, after some moments of apparent indecision. "The horse is restive. I want thee not to touch me. Mount, hold the steed's head firmly, and I will follow thee. Yet lay this to thy mind, Sir Grenville: I leave thee in Boston, and had I loved thee more I would be more aggrieved. I know now the ambition that was in my vain heart, and the wickedness of thine. Mine eyes are opened; I see clearly."

Sir Grenville hesitated a moment, then vaulted into the saddle and leaned over the pommel, holding out his hand to Dorothy. Like a flash she seized a stout stick from the ground, and grasping it in both hands she drew as near as was safe to the horse, and struck him a strong blow upon the hind legs, saying, as she did so, " Thou art a coward, Sir Grenville, thou hast lied to me!"

The horse, panic-stricken, darted forward, dashing headlong down the narrow stony road, out of sight, Sir Grenville cursing and straining at the reins as the frenzied animal swerved wildly from side to side. As the horse started, Dorothy observed two figures rise abruptly from the shelter of a thick clump of bushes and disappear in the shadows of the woods. She waited for no further developments, but turned and dashed precipitately from the bridle path into the thickness of the forest.

# CHAPTER VI.

## THE WINTER IN THE FOREST.

WHEN the terror-stricken and panting girl dashed
headlong from the bridle path, whither she knew
not, she was conscious of but one thing: that was of
being hotly pursued. The crackling of leaves and
twigs and the breaking of branches were plainly
audible. The echoing steps of Sir Grenville's rapidly
returning horse also greeted her ears, the loud thud
of the hoofs of the galloping steed sounding near and
menacing. She paused not to look behind her. On,
on she rushed, fear and desperation lending her courage and strength. She struck her head against low-
hanging boughs, lacerated her hands upon the briers
of the wild berry bushes and creepers, but still she
ran, all unaware of weariness.

Presently all grew strangely still about her. The
pursuing steps ceased, the sound of the horse's
labored galloping died away, and Dorothy, exhausted, trembling with fear, sank down at the foot

of a great tree. Her mind surged with a tumult of varying emotions, accompanied by the beating of her heart. It seemed to her that the fevered pulsations must be heard upon the stillness of the night. She touched her brow; it was wet. In the faint light that shone upon her from the now waning moon she saw that the wet stains upon her hands were blood.

"I am hurt," she said to herself; "yet methinks I felt nothing." She rested for a short time, leaning her head back and closing her eyes, yet listening sharply for any suspicious sound that might warn her of pursuit. At times she opened her eyes, and gazed upward at the great expanse of foliage above her head. Awful phantoms appeared to leer upon her from the oscillating boughs. To her highly strung fancy, some pointed the finger of scorn and derision, others opened their strangely distorted mouths and laughed at her discomfort, though no sound came from them, nothing save the hoarse murmur of the wind, whose tones seemed filled with mockery and glee over her hapless condition. The moon's light was growing paler, the sky was filled with myriads of bright stars, that twinkled tremulously in the cool air of the October night.

A terrible dread settled upon the tired girl. Perhaps she was not safe even here; she must hasten onward. She arose laboriously, her stiffened limbs refusing to act immediately, and looked fearfully about her, then fled like an affrighted deer, onward, onward, to some possible safe retreat whither her enemies could not follow. She hoped that when the morning dawned she would find herself near some settlement or clearing in the wilderness. She walked for perhaps a mile or more farther, dragging her wearied feet, her shoes torn and dilapidated, her head hanging forward, her mind scarce cognizant of her actions. Her one clear idea was that she must keep moving.

Presently she came upon a small clearing, apparently in the very heart of the forest. A small, weather-beaten house stood in the center of the clearing. It was built of rough-hewn logs, and was of one story in height, with an L at the back. A general air of neglect was apparent in the surroundings of the place, visible even in the dim light. There was no sign of life about the house, and no light in the window.

Dorothy crept cautiously forward, noticing, as she did so, that the clearing was surrounded by a wooden paling that inclosed a garden. The pungent odor of some fall flowers and herbs assailed her nostrils.

"Some one lives here," she murmured. "Perchance they will pity me and give me shelter, e'en though the hour is so late."

She entered the garden gate, and approached the house. The door stood open. Peeping cautiously within, Dorothy beheld a few flickering flames from a fire upon the open hearth flash upon the wooden floor. She hesitated, and stopped abruptly in the path. That fear of the supernatural, implanted in her very being and fostered by her training, rushed upon her with an irresistible force. There was something uncanny in the open door, in the dancing firelight at this late hour, when all honest folks were asleep. The picturesque solitude of the place seemed to warn her that this was the abode of no simple, honest woodcutter.

A numbness crept over her; her limbs shook beneath her as she clung for support to the broken palings of the little porch; great beads of perspiration gathered on her forehead and rolled down her face. She stood irresolute for an instant; then, as if impelled onward by a will outside herself, she crossed the threshold of the door.

"Is any one here who will give me shelter?" she said softly, with trembling tones.

No voice responded. The dying fire, fanned by the motion made by her entrance, flamed up, then died out to a tiny red spark. She stepped farther into the room, the dim light from the flames serving to make visible the furniture of the abode, which consisted of a bed, a few chairs, and a large oaken chest. The bed stood near the fire.

Dorothy sank down upon the floor near it, her head resting against its side. A few dried twigs were lying on the hearth, and she laid some of these upon the blaze. It started up again, casting distorted shadows upon the ceiling and walls.

Some occupants of the room, that had been dozing in a corner, now came forward and stretched themselves before the fire, gazing up into Dorothy's face with large, yellow, solemn eyes. These unexpected visitors were three black cats—black, without a single white hair. Their movements and the increased light aroused yet other sleeping denizens. Soon there was a flutter of wings, and a large white arctic owl perched upon the bed-post and blinked uneasily. Other birds in cages awoke and fluttered their wings, the cats purred, and the room seemed alive with all these gentle noises.

Dorothy did not speak or move; she was utterly exhausted. She sat staring with strained eyes into the fire. Presently an ominous sound greeted her ears; she started: the sound of heavy steps, accompanied by the click of a crutch. The steps came nearer—halting, uncertain, dragging steps, that seemed to scarcely advance, so slow was their approach.

Dorothy became as one without feeling. The steps and the click of the crutch sounded louder and more distinct, first upon the garden path, then upon the wooden floor. They had passed the doorstep and were coming forward into the circle of light.

The girl did not move; she clenched her hands, and her breath came in short, quick gasps. What was this thing, that walked as no human creature walked, that wandered abroad at midnight, that kept for company the owl and bat, and whose home was in the solitude of the forest, away from the abode of man? Dorothy dared not conjecture. The steps ceased suddenly.

"I hear human breathing," said a voice. "Ha!

ha! None can deceive old Goody. Come forward, whoever my visitor may be."

Like a flash the horrible reality burst upon Dorothy. This was the hut of Goody Trueman, the witch of the wilderness: the one who had signed the compact with the King of Darkness; the one who rode at midnight upon the back of a vampire, followed by thousands of serving imps; the one whose name stood foremost in the Black Book, and who was in league with the powers of the Evil One. The girl shrank into a heap upon the floor, her hands held out helplessly before her as if to shield herself from some horrible fate, her head falling forward on her breast.

" Why dost thou not speak ? " said the voice. " I saw thee, from the edge of the woods, enter my house. I have sharp eyes. Speak up, speak up! I know thou art here."

The voice had an odd, uncertain cackling in its tones. Dorothy leaned forward from her position upon the floor, trembling in every limb; she raised her eyes fearfully and kept them, as if fascinated, upon the withered, wrinkled face bending above her.

Goody Trueman was certainly in appearance the veritable type of a witch: small, shrunken, hunchbacked, her head resting low between her shoulders, her eyes catlike and deep-set, her skin like brown parchment, her nose and chin almost meeting, and her bony, restless hands crooked like the claws of an eagle. On her head she wore a steeple-crowned hat, and over her quilted petticoat a brilliant scarlet cloak, which, when the firelight struck it, glowed a flame color. Her shadow spread in gigantic proportions upon the wall, covering even across the low ceiling.

She appeared to Dorothy to be standing in the midst of fire, like the lost, hideous soul she was deemed to be. She was indeed the realization of that terrible creature so often pictured to the little Salem girl. The supposed witch advanced a step nearer, and held out her crooked hands to the blaze. One of the cats leaped forward and nestled upon her shoulder, purring as he placed his black, furry face close beside that of his mistress.

Dorothy gazed an instant at this fearful picture, then from her white lips came a piercing shriek, so startling to the feathered inhabitants of the hut that they fluttered in affright.

"Satan hath won me! 'Tis the witch, 'tis the witch!" she called loudly. "I am lost, I am lost! 'Tis for my many sins!" and throwing up her arms

wildly, she fell back unconscious upon the floor.
When animation returned, Dorothy saw that morning had come.  Through the small-paned windows
the somber, cold light of the early dawn was entering, bringing into clear and matter-of-fact relief those
objects which by the weird firelight enhanced the
terrors of the night.  A pillow had been placed beneath her head, a coverlet thrown over her feet.

Old Goody was standing before the fire.  She was
stirring some savory mixture in a saucepan, mutter-
ing to herself as she did so.  Perhaps the beams of
morning, perhaps the slight rest which unconscious-
ness had brought her, dispelled Dorothy's great dread
and fear.  She raised herself slightly and watched
the old woman at her work.

Presently Goody turned her head, bending her
withered countenance upon the girl.  By daylight
she did not resemble so decidedly Dorothy's idea of
a servant of the devil.  Her very human occupation
of cooking was certainly at variance with the popular
notion that witches did not eat, save at those terrible
orgies held with their imps at midnight in the forest.

"Thou art awake," said Goody.  "I have a good
and soothing draught brewed for thee;  see, it is hot;
thou must take it."  As she spoke she hobbled

across the room, and coming to the side of the girl where she lay upon the floor, leaned over her.

"No, no," said Dorothy, warding her off with her outstretched arm; "thou wouldst have me drink to my soul's damnation.  I can take no draught from thine hand."

"Out upon thee, child!  Hast thou no sense?  I am no witch, only a harmless old woman who seeks thy good."

"Ay, so thou sayest.  Dost thou not at midnight ride upon thy charger through the air, and fly above the houses in Salem?  Oft have the good people heard thee, like a mighty wind rushing by, thy imps with thee.  Dost thou not gather the deadly nightshade and brew a draught that weakens men's souls, so that they cannot say thee nay, but consent to sign their names in the Black Book thou hast always under thy arm?"

"No, no, child; those are silly stories; heed them not."

"Yet I am sorely afraid of thee.  I dare not take thy brew.  I have been ever taught that thou art an enemy to all that is good, and dost seek to harm all mankind."

"No, no, that is untrue.  I had a grievous trouble

once, long ago, beyond the seas in my old home. I grew afraid to trust all human love, so I did seek solitude in these forests. Much brooding hath made me what I am, distraught perhaps at times, but never seeking harm to aught. Thou must not fear, me, child. Thou must not turn thy pretty, winsome face from me. I seek to help thee."

"Then thou wilt not make me sign my name in the Black Book?"

"No, no; I know of no book."

"Wilt thou promise?" persisted Dorothy.

"I wish no communion with the witches. I scorn and fear their practices." The old woman laughed her discordant, cackling laugh. "I promise thee. If old Goody is all thou wilt ever have to fear in this world, thou needst fear naught."

"Then I will take the brew."

Soon Dorothy fell into a deep, tranquil sleep. When she awoke the cheerful sunlight was flooding the apartment, but she felt weak and her head was strange and dizzy. These were the premonitory symptoms of a long attack of fever which kept her a prisoner in the little house through the pleasant fall and bleak winter and even into the early spring.

The memory of those weary, miserable days never

passed from Dorothy's mind through all her future life. The utter loneliness of her existence; the terrible winter storms sweeping through the desolate woods, bending the monstrous trees; then the fierce snows and the bitter cold; the solitude, the apparent death of all things beautiful in nature, taking their rest, wrapped in their white ice-draped shrouds —all these things combined to make for her a memory of horrors.

Old Goody was kind and patient, and soon won Dorothy's heart. Her dread melted away before the true gentleness of the old woman's disposition. But the apathy that had fastened itself like an incubus upon the girl increased as the days passed. She could find in her heart no hope, nor even a wish to form plans for herself. The thought of returning to Salem was abhorrent to her. Tricked, deceived, humiliated, what story could she invent that would be believed or condoned? Ashamed to speak of her disastrous flight with Sir Grenville, afraid to tell of her habitation in the hut of the dreaded witch, she was indeed in a most perplexing situation.

One day, seated, pale, listless, and dispirited, on the old settle near the fire, her hands hanging before her, a hopeless, despairing look in her blue eyes, that appeared large and hollow for the dark circles surrounding them, her thoughts wandered through the wide field of retrospection.

Suddenly there burst upon her a torrent of self-reproach and remorse. Unable to quell the tumult raging within her, she broke out excitedly to old Goody, who had been sitting quietly in a farther corner of the room.

" Goody, Goody, speak a word of comfort to me!" Dorothy held out her thin, shaking hands. " If perchance this misery that I now endure had been the work of others, I might gain strength to bear it; but it was my own wretched ambition, my deceit, my discontent. All is over for me—no hope, no home, no future!" The despairing echo of the sad voice rang through the room in a cadence of deepest regret.

Old Goody arose from her seat, and coming to the side of the unhappy girl, looked down upon her bowed head.

" Methought," she said, " in time thy heart would unburden itself. It is good for thee; yet tell me only what thou wilt; be cautious, lest thou shouldst regret it later."

Dorothy did not reply at once, then she started from her seat and said impetuously :

"I will tell all, Goody, save the names; those I will withhold. Then give me thy advice and truly from thy heart tell me what I shall do, for of a certainty I am friendless and desolate."

"I will counsel thee," said Goody, watching the girl intently from under her overhanging brows.

"I have been ever thoughtless," Dorothy began, "hating all useful occupations, and filled with discontent. I was unhappy in my home. I longed for change, for a wider field. Then I was betrothed to one so noble, so good, so true." Dorothy paused; her lips trembled. "I broke plight with him, and for this wretched bauble thou seest on my neck, this chain of golden beads, which did seem to me to lighten up a way to riches and honors. I fled with one who deceived me, lied to me, and from whom I escaped to thee, Goody, that night I came through the forest to thy hut."

"Is that all?" said Goody. "Hast thou kept naught back?"

"I have told thee all, save one thing." As she spoke she tore the beads from her neck and threw them angrily from her. They fell, and lay like a glittering coiled serpent upon the floor. "I do despise and hate where once I thought I loved, and where I willingly followed. The one I wronged hath gained a great revenge: he hath come to me in other guise. In the darkness of the night, when all is still save the wind, I hear his voice; he steps from out the shadows that surround me; I see his face and gentle smile; then I awake and I am alone. Never more will he come to me save in dreams. With my own hand have I opened the gate that guarded my happiness and sent it forth. I stand without, where no hope is, and weep."

"Canst thou not seek his forgiveness?"

"No, no; there can be no forgiveness for me. The truth would but separate us further. I deem my misdeed hath in his eyes all the enormity of a great sin. The hand of God hath pointed no way, yet retribution hath come heavily upon me. In the bitterness of a broken spirit, Goody, I have learned to love the one I wronged."

"Then go to him; tell him all. It were better than the agony that now assails thee. My advice is, return to thy home, unburden thy secret, and perchance a kindly Providence will cause the light of peace to fall once more upon thee."

"I fear me never can thy prophecy be fulfilled. Thou knowest not, Goody, how weak are my spirit and will. I dread lest I destroy forever all hope by telling of my misdeed. They would despise and hate me. How can I account for my long absence?"

"The truth, my child, the truth," cried Goody; "it is thy only safeguard."

"I have no faith in myself; I dare not return. If, perchance, I could not bring to myself the effort of will needed to speak the truth, my soul were indeed lost; and if I speak the truth, they will disown me and cast me forth. I shall be excommunicated from the meeting-house."

"It is e'en now drawing near the spring," said Goody earnestly; "there is no time for thee to waste. Pray constantly for strength. Return, return; be brave. Tell this one whom thou lovest the truth, and all will yet be well with thee. God will be thy friend, if thou wilt but do what is right."

"Ah, that I could take thy advice!" Dorothy knelt by the old woman, and clasping her withered hand, kissed it. "Goody, Goody, I am grateful to thee for thy kindness. I wronged thee; thou art no witch. Yet in thy words is little comfort for either way—a truth or an untruth—I have killed my happiness."

Dorothy, full of deepest concern over Goody's advice, fell that night into deep musings. The days were lengthening; the first faint cries of the birds were again heard in the early morning; the winds blew less fiercely; the snowdrops peeped forth in sheltered places, and the sun's rays in their lengthened sojourn gave out an added degree of warmth. The words, " There is no time for thee to waste," echoed like a funeral knell upon the jaded nerves of the perplexed girl. No time, and she had already wasted four months; it was even now the month of March.

The strong desire within her at last compelled her to form a settled resolution. She would return to Salem; then, if she could summon strength, she would tell the truth and abide the consequences. The roads were not yet passable, but soon would be relieved of their obstructions of ice and snow. As soon as was practicable, the journey would be undertaken.

# CHAPTER VII.

## ELIZABETH HUBBARD.

THE circumstances of Dorothy's flight were necessarily entirely a matter of conjecture among the worthy people of Salem. There were no means of any accurate knowledge of her whereabouts being gained, even by the most astute of village gossips. The absence of Grenville was not commented upon. He had left the place some time previous to the girl's flight and had never been seen in her company, nor had he made a confidant of any one, having, in fact, rather shunned all companionship than otherwise. The women had discussed the unusual affair in all its bearings, and much sympathy had been expended upon David and Martha in their affliction.

The silent dignity maintained by Alden Wentworth forbade all curious prying into the sacredness of the trouble that had come upon him. If he grew thinner and paler, if his face became fixed in a settled look of melancholy, and if his dark, somber eyes appeared at times to rest upon some vision unseen by others, those others dared not question him.   In his gentle way he repelled all sympathetic interference.

"I tell ye, neighbors," said a brawny dame to her friends in the market-place one morning, "if the wench had had a different bringing up I wot this would not have happened.  The rod was ever spared because she was an orphan child; and look ye, what good hath it done?  My policy ever was, strike hard and long when the subject is a wayward one.  The rod is wholesome discipline; the young require its usage."

"People say," said another, "that she hath been taken by the Indians.  Ye all know she was ever wandering alone in the forests; she had no fear of the dark woods."

"I believe it not," said the harsh, deep voice of Elizabeth Hubbard.  "I was Dorothy's friend; I knew her better than others.  I do not think she hath been taken by the Indians.  She has been—in my poor knowledge I say this—bewitched by the black man, and is perchance e'en now concocting evil schemes against us.  She ever loved to be alone; he has taken her unawares."

The women looked askance at each other as these

words were spoken, and instinctively lowered their voices, drawing closer together.

"What have ye seen or heard, Elizabeth?" they said.

"I have seen naught and heard naught; I speak but on conjecture." Then more hurriedly she continued: "Why did Dorothy ever seek the woods alone? She was never God-fearing, so it was not for prayer and meditation. She hath been taken unawares, I repeat, and been forced to sign her soul away. Satan hath claimed her for his own."

As Elizabeth ceased a murmur of disapprobation rose clamorously upon the air, stilled abruptly, however, by the sharp, loud voice of a woman who had joined the chattering group.

"And thou art her friend and speakest thus? Truly a firm support in time of trouble, a good friend!" said the new-comer sarcastically at Elizabeth's elbow.

The girl turned upon the speaker a glance of deepest hatred and malevolence, her dark Spanish face growing white with passion.

"Speak of what thou knowest, Neighbor Holden. Dorothy was perchance of such credit to thee that thou art proud to speak for her; a bond, forsooth, of love and obedience was ever between thee and her."

"Thou false girl!" cried Martha angrily. "Thou dost malign her memory for a purpose. I have eyes and ears to see and hear. Thou dost throw thyself boldly at Alden Wentworth. Save thy pains: he will never turn from Dorothy to thee; thou hast too poor weapons at thy command. And let me tell thee, Elizabeth, traduce not the memory of the woman he has loved, and who was also thy friend. Build not thy future upon so false a foundation."

"I scorn thee," cried the angry girl, "and thy words! I shall remember them, nevertheless, never fear. Think what ye will. As for Mr. Wentworth, I wot he is glad to be rid of the silly thing, who possessed naught but a fair face. Such wounds as his do quickly heal." Elizabeth laughed, and when she laughed the company started, so hollow and un-natural was the sound.

"Go thy way, go thy way," said Martha. "I trust Dorothy is in a better world than this, where she is safe from all harm, poor little motherless girl! Yet thy words are a reproach to me. I was not always gentle with the child. Now that she has gone from me I know I was too harsh; but no one in my presence shall malign her memory." She left the women when she finished speaking, and walked swiftly through the market-place.

Elizabeth looked after her, an unfathomable gleam in her angry eyes. Some of the party smiled and glanced mischievously toward the scowling girl.

"Thou hast received a right just reproof from Mistress Holden," said one of the women. "Methinks God hath afflicted her sorely; it is not for us to make the burden heavier. And there is truth in her words. Twice, and even thrice, hast thou been seen on the village streets and in the lanes, and not alone, but by thy side Alden Wentworth. Say I not truly?" turning, as she spoke, to the listening women.

"Ay, ay," cried one, "thou sayest truly. Dorothy is forgotten. Perchance Elizabeth doth catch the prize on the rebound."

They all laughed loudly. Elizabeth blushed deeply, the color spreading into a flame over her swarthy face.

"I care not *that* for all thy envious speech." She snapped her fingers as she spoke, and tossed her head defiantly. "Let me alone; I ask not thy advice. Tend to thy own business. I would scorn to be called one with the gossips of the market-place."

The women laughed louder and more derisively than ever, their hands upon their hips, their buxom forms shaking with merriment. During the general outcry Elizabeth escaped, not once looking backward as they shouted sarcastic jeers after her.

Elizabeth Hubbard was the niece of Mrs. Griggs, wife of the physician of the village; she was also a member of his household. She had from childhood been possessed of a peculiar, erratic temperament, which, added to her tropical style of beauty, made her ever prominent in all gatherings of any importance that took place in Salem.

She was steeped to the utmost in the beliefs of the age. Witchcraft, that dread calamity that had swept over the seas from the shores of Europe, like a hungry vulture was hovering with claws extended above the little restful hamlet in the New World. To this whimsical creature all that was incomprehensible, all that lay below the surface, all that needed the gentle touch of faith to make tangible and perfect, savored to her of the supernatural. This morbid disposition throve upon the not unpalatable food prepared for it.

The belief in witchcraft was sanctioned by many of the most learned men of those times, and, under the protection of the clergy, flourished into a plant of prodigious growth.

Elizabeth was emotional, perhaps what in this day we call hysterical, and she magnified all naturally explained causes into spectral results. Her distorted imagination pictured strange, weird sights, and her ears heard the sound of spirit voices from the other world. These voices spoke to her from the trees and plants; they whispered in the air; they floated down to her from the clouds. By indulging these fancies they became realities to her, and she spake wondrous things, " as one having the voice of prophecy."

She had within her nature the power of a great passion, also the strength of an iron will that nothing could bend or sway, but hastened on, unheeding all obstacles to the desired end. Her affection for Dorothy had been firm until that fatal day when Alden Wentworth placed his preference upon the latter and asked her to be his wife. Then Elizabeth's rage, disappointment, and despair turned the stream of love into a new channel. Dorothy was hurled aside as an impediment to her own desires.

This great passion did not die when the young advocate's choice had been publicly proclaimed; far from it; it grew and grew, as a plant grows in a noisome soil. At times, when she sat with Dorothy in the old farmhouse kitchen and watched the preparations going forward for the wedding, murder was in her heart, if a wish could have killed.

When at last she realized that the field was once more clear, her joy leapt beyond all control. Her beauty increased, her black eyes shone resplendent. Woe be to the one that now stepped across her path!

The pleasant spring days were not far distant, though there still lingered in the air the parting chill of winter, and the wind still blew strong and fierce from the north. Snow yet lay in patches in shaded places where the sun's warmth did not reach. The trees had as yet put forth no foliage, and their bare gray boughs swayed against a cold sky.

Alden Wentworth was wandering slowly and listlessly across the fields one afternoon toward the latter part of March. He had been calling upon a sick friend, and on returning had taken a secluded by-way, seeking to be free from molestation. His mind was heavy. He envied that happy, waiting soul he had just left, so soon to be freed from earthly grief and care, so soon to enter into rest and peace. He was thinking of Dorothy. When did he not think of her, save in sleep, and then he dreamed of her. In these dreams, from which he dreaded the awakening, she was always near him.

This short span had passed, and in a new land, where all looked shadowy and unreal, she was by his side. It was as if their parting had never been; in the semblance of two blissful disembodied spirits, they rejoiced in the experience of a perfect unity.

His eyes were turned toward the ground, yet he saw not the wild-flowers that peeped cautiously forth from sheltered places and nodded as he passed. This pensive reverie was so absorbing, that, all unawares, he came upon the figure of a woman. Her head was bowed, her frame shaken with sobs; she was seated upon a wooden log placed against a gateway that led to the field. As he approached she raised her head.

"Elizabeth," he said kindly, "why art thou here? Art thou troubled? Can I help thee?"

He came close and stood looking down upon her. These ever-recurring meetings with the girl had not caused any suspicions to rise in his mind; his was not a suspicious nature.    He was always glad to see her; had she not been his beloved's chosen friend? Perchance, he reasoned with himself at times, when he could summon strength to speak of Dorothy whom better could he address than Elizabeth, her companion, who had loved her?

" I am in sore distress, Mr. Wentworth," said Elizabeth, glancing toward him.

He started, then stepped backward, for the first time conscious of the wondrous beauty of her face. " Thou knowest," she continued, " that many do accuse me and say I do dissemble when I speak what is within me.  This doubt of my sincerity pains me.  What object could I have in feigning this thing? "

" Heed them not," he interposed, " for surely the spirits of the air are amongst us, and it is necessary for us to be zealous."

" Can I help it if I have been chosen as a mouth-piece to denounce wickedness? "

" No, surely no," he said.

She continued: " It has come to me that I and others, perchance, do feel it our bounden duty, as the great call is within us, to accuse one who has been accurst this many a day ; whom all do fear, for the great calamities she hath power to bring upon us.  A witch indeed is in our midst."

"I deem I heard thee not aright," cried Wentworth excitedly.  "Thou surely wouldst not accuse one of witchcraft?"

"I?  Not I, Mr. Wentworth; I accuse no one. The voice that is within me controls my words, otherwise I should possess no power."

"Of whom dost thou speak?" he demanded sternly.

"Of one Goody Trueman, the forest woman. Thou knowest her well; all Salem knows of her, and fears her."

The young man drew a step nearer to the girl.  A shudder passed over him as he gazed like one fascinated upon this woman of prophecy.

"Yet surely," he said earnestly, "thou wouldst not desire the death of a fellow-being!  Well thou knowest the penalty of witchcraft.  Remember, Elizabeth, thou canst never return that which thou shalt take.  Accuse, but not openly, this wretched creature, if perchance she hath had counsel with those imps that do infest the forest.  Let her bide there; molest her not.  Beware lest thou fall into a grievous error."

"I tell thee, Mr. Wentworth," the girl rose excitedly, and held out her hands before her with a tragic gesture, "I will not rest night or day till the power that is within me shall have done its utmost to rid the world of these lost beings, who have sold their souls to the King of Darkness.  It is my mission; I shall fulfill it."

Again that shudder passed over Wentworth; his lips trembled and whitened.  "Beware, beware, lest in thy zeal thou shalt condemn an innocent woman.  A life, remember, is in thy hands."

They did not speak for some moments; then Elizabeth broke the silence.  On her face rested a cunning expression; she read well the man before her.  "I have not dared, ere this, to speak to thee of a subject near my heart and thine; yet methinks——"  She hesitated, then looked over the cold, somber-hued meadows and bleak landscape.  The wind blew her black hair about her face and shook her garments fiercely.  She clasped her cloak tightly with one hand, the other she laid timidly on the man's arm, glancing shyly up into his face.

He started.  "Thou wouldst speak of Dorothy," he said quickly.

"Ay," she replied.

"What of her?" he demanded expectantly. "Hast heard aught?"

"Naught. I wished only that I might speak to thee some words of comfort. She is as dead to us forever. Surely a chaplet of tears and kindly words we may lay upon her grave."

Alden Wentworth groaned aloud. "Say not those words," he cried. "There is ever a hope within me that she is living, and that some day I may see her again."

"And thou canst forgive her?" Her voice was filled with tremulous eagerness.

"She hath much to forgive also, Elizabeth. Thou dost not know all; I will tell thee. She was ever frank with me; she told me of her true feelings. No deceit could rest within her. She did not love me, and I, in my blind folly, did force her into my keeping. A wild dream of some time winning her heart controlled my wish to possess her. At the last, she left me to escape a life which she could not accept. I see it all," he continued dreamily, as though he thought himself alone. "My beloved, I have driven thee from thy home; thou art a wanderer on this earth. Hast thou found a resting-place? Art thou safe, my Dorothy?" He turned impetuously toward the girl, who watched him sharply. "Now, Elizabeth, thou knowest all my remorse and the vain regrets that I fear will ever be mine while I live."

Elizabeth did not reply; she tapped her foot impatiently upon the ground, and threw the rebellious locks of heavy hair back from her forehead. Rage at her own disappointment and scorn for what she considered his weakness were struggling for the mastery, but she quelled them by an effort of will.

"Dorothy," she said decidedly, "will never return. Perchance she is among her father's people in England, or with the Indians, or she may have been forced into compact with the spirits of the air, and may be now in their keeping." These last words she spoke slowly and cautiously.

"The latter is not so, that I swear," said Wentworth angrily. "No imps of darkness could live beside purity such as hers. No, no, Elizabeth. And beware lest thou speak thus to any save myself; spread not this calumny abroad. Yet truth may be in thy words, though thou know it not: be she with the spirits, as thou sayest, they are spirits of light in God's kingdom. Let us hasten," he concluded abruptly, "the night is coming; it is chill. I will see thee to thy home; then I must hasten to the manse to speak with Mr. Parris. I have many important matters to transact in regard to this same trouble with the witches, which doth engross much attention at present, having even reached the ears of the officials in Boston."

"Of a truth there is much to discuss," she replied eagerly, keeping step beside him as he strode across the meadow. "Hast heard of the yellow-bird that did appear to Farmer Morton and sit perched upon his mantel, and which when he strove to drive it off did ope its mouth, and from its tongue darted a flame of fire?"

Her companion trembled. "No, I heard not of it, nor do I believe it. This terrible thing is surely gaining great proportions. Mr. Parris is most strong in his belief. I think of a certainty that if it continues he will take a hand in punishing the witches. Heed thy words, fan not the blaze; it is an awful thing to take away human life."

"Yet thou believest?" she queried.

"In part," he replied, "not in all."

After Wentworth had bid her good-night at the door of her home, Elizabeth did not enter immediately. She waited until the echo of his footsteps had died away, then descended the steps of the porch and repaired to the garden. The night was cold and bleak; no moon or stars were visible; the wind moaned dismally among the trees. But she heeded not the darkness or the solitude, for the fire of passionate grief that burned within her. She clasped and unclasped her hands as she stood in the garden path, her rigid outline looming like some specter of the night above the shrubs that bordered the walk.

"I will not give him up," she muttered. "He has been restored to me from one who did not value him. She will never return—she is dead. Why should I fear? Though I make no plot, his heart must turn to me. Can a merciful Providence have placed this love within me, to requite me not? By the very power of my nature I will win him, if—if— she return no more."

# CHAPTER VIII.

### THE WANDERER'S RETURN.

OUR New England ancestors had undergone great persecutions in their homes beyond the seas, and had suffered many privations. These, added to the joyless existence that was their lot for many years after landing on the shores of the New World, caused them to become gloomy and taciturn, ever taking a depressing view of life. Their surroundings tended to increase this romantic, melancholy disposition—hence their credulity regarding supernatural agencies.

The country was too wild and unexplored for much travel, the hills and valleys being covered with dense forests, whose somber shades appeared to this superstitious people to be inhabited by witches, demons, black imps, and all horrible beings possessed of unnatural powers to work harm to God-fearing people. This condition of mind easily grew into fanaticism when fostered by the accounts that came across the seas from Europe, of the burning, hanging, and torturing of witches for their evil deeds.

On a certain evening Martha and David were seated together, as usual, in the kitchen. David leaned his head against the back of his high wooden chair, his stern countenance clouded by a shade of deep thoughtfulness. Martha sat near the window, watching the last lingering glow reflected from the distant clouds where the sun had descended in a blaze of glory. There were tears in her eyes, and her hands trembled as she brushed the drops away. Lying across her lap was a little child's garment.

" David," she said presently, " I am sad and conscience-stricken. When I look far across the fields, on such a night as this, to the west, I seem to see the opened gate of heaven; and then a great terror falls upon me, lest by my hand that gate has been closed to Dorothy. Ah, David, David! where is our sister's child? Did I do right by the little one? Did I do all my duty?" she concluded piteously.

" Torture not thyself, Martha; thou didst all thy duty. The child possessed her father's headstrong will; it proved too great for thee; thou couldst not gainsay it. I have forgiven the child. I pray she be safe with God. Yet I reproach not myself. I did what I thought was best."

"No, no," she wailed, "I did not all my duty. I did ever thwart her in all gayety and display. I did her a wrong; she was but young. Then worse, far worse than all, I did force the betrothal to Alden Wentworth."

"It is past," said David solemnly, "we can do no more. We must submit in all humility. Methinks this terrible thing that hath come upon Salem doth drive at times all thoughts of Dorothy from my mind. Thou hast heard of the three women that have been accused of witchcraft, and are to be tried in the meeting-house this day two weeks?"

"Ay, I have heard," replied Martha scornfully. "I heed not such folly. Such trials do but disgrace the meeting-house."

The kitchen was quite dark now, save for the pale light that fell from the crescent of the new moon hanging above the hills, its reflection resting in a curved line of silver upon the floor. "David, look!" As she spoke she held out before her the child's dress that had been lying across her lap. "The little robe that Dorothy wore on that long voyage from England—the last thing her mother made. I found it to-day in the garret chest. The child hath been in my mind all this day. Methinks I see her now, a babe, a little maid, and then a beauteous woman; for, David, thou knowest none could compare with our niece in all the village of Salem."

" Ay, thou sayest truly, Martha."

" I shall never cease in this world to sorely reproach myself for her misdeeds. I was too hard with her. Perhaps in time, had I been more lenient, this willfulness would have lived out its day, then left her. Yet as I bent over the old chest this morn, I did say, ' I will be kinder, more motherly, and I will forgive all, if a merciful God shall ever restore her to us.' "

" Thou mayst have much to forgive," he said gloomily.

" I lay no account on that. She was never wicked; naught but foolish and thoughtless. I did expect that William Grey's daughter could be a pattern of excellence; my years should have taught me more wisdom than that."

" He was a riotous, rollicking good-for-naught," said David impatiently, " ever ready with his unseemly song and his mug of spiced wine; truly one of Satan's most zealous followers. Yet let him bide. I care not to talk of him; he has gone to his account.

The thoughts that stir within me are of such dread and fear, they drive all else from me."

"What dost thou mean?" cried Martha. She dropped the little dress upon the floor, and drawing nearer to her brother peered down into his face. David rose quickly from his seat.

"I mean that the dread scourge of wickedness is amongst us; that the Evil One hath sent his messengers before him in the persons of these hags that do infest the forest and have signed their names in his Black Book—lost souls, doing the will of their master."

He walked excitedly to the window, looked forth an instant, then retraced his steps and stopped in the center of the room, where the faint light of the moon fell. "Light the candles; I like not this gloom. They may e'en now have sent their imps to molest us. These agents like well the darkness. Didst not hear a noise of wings without the door, or in yonder chimney? Thou knowest they hold their orgies when the moon is in the first quarter."

Martha silently lighted the candles upon the mantel-shelf, then turned abruptly to her brother, her hands upon her hips, her sturdy frame held erect.

"I am ashamed of thee, David Holden! Thou

foolish, credulous creature! And thou talkst of gossiping women, who, ye say, have not sense to question and find the truth of a story. I tell thee, give me a man for a fool when a silly yarn is afloat."

David looked darkly upon her, the candle-light flickering over his determined features. "Martha, it were better for thee if thou didst hold thy peace upon this subject. As there is a heaven above us, the authorities will punish these hags, who do follow the devil's teachings."

"If they punish those poor old babbling creatures, whose minds have gone astray, I give not an atom for their opinion, or for their knowledge of the ways of justice."

"Thou wast ever a rebellious, stubborn woman, Martha. Bridle thy tongue, I warn thee!" He went to the door while speaking, and stood some moments looking out into the darkness. Martha watched him earnestly a moment, then folded the little robe and ascended the garret stairs to replace it in the chest. Many tear-stains rested on the fine embroidery of the dainty garment as she laid it reverently away with her rolls of best linen.

"My poor little Dorothy!" she sighed. Then she locked the chest, and seating herself amidst the lumber in the garret she wept softly for the absent one.

While this conversation was taking place in the farmhouse, a girl, footsore and pale, with tattered garments and torn shoes from which her feet protruded, was making her way cautiously along the edge of the woods that skirted the settlement. Dorothy had walked all day since early dawn. Now, as the night drew nigh, she was creeping stealthily through the underbrush toward her old home. The thoughts in her mind were sorrowful in the extreme. Look which way she would, she always returned to the inevitable question, "Shall I tell the truth, or shall I withhold it?" Around this she fluttered with indecision and doubt. She knew what was right, yet feared that result which her experience led her to expect from the opinion of her townspeople. The reply that always came with the hollow note of despair to her sad communings, "If you tell the truth they will spurn you and cast you forth," caused her to tremble.

Her thoughts hovered as the pendulum of a clock, back and forth, back and forth, with no resting-place. The great love that had arisen within her from the ashes of so dire an experience would not sleep or rest.

She could not summon the moral strength to cast it forth and bid it die. "No, no," she murmured, as she slowly wandered over the rough fields, "I cannot tell them—I cannot tell him. He is nothing to me now. Yet his thoughts of me may be tender. If I speak the truth, that I did fly with one who deceived me, I could not look upon his face and live."

When she neared the outskirts of the farm, she paused to rest upon a bank that rose on one side of a newly plowed meadow. It was a glorious night: the stars twinkled and flashed in a nearly cloudless sky; the crescent had crept lower, until now it hung just above the distant line of sea; the feeble piping of a few early spring birds sounded from the neighboring trees.

The little hamlet lay almost in darkness, save where here and there a stray glimmer shone from some cottage window. Dorothy glanced wistfully up into the heavens. Wondrous stories came to her memory—stories she had heard in childhood, of happy homes far away in each bright star. If some angel spirit would but descend and bid her follow, how gladly she would obey! Suddenly a cloud came blowing up from the north, and a soft wind fanned the girl's face.

Dorothy felt herself seized with an unaccountable desire for a sign from above that might point her the right course to pursue in her present great dilemma. She rested her back against the soft, damp earth that composed the bank, and clasping her hands upon her breast, raised her head and gazed intently into the radiant sky.

"If that little cloud that comes blowing from the north," she said aloud, "doth cross the moon and dim its light, I deem it a sign that should I tell the truth, all the light in my life would depart; then I will not speak. If it passes by the moon, then I will tell the truth, and take it for an omen that the light shall still shine for me again." With the relief of having the decision made by an agency outside her own will—a voice from heaven, as she had chosen to interpret it—she rose from her low position, and stood watching the oncoming of the cloud.

There was a weird fascination in thus having nature indicate what fate still held in store for her. On came the cloud, driven swiftly before the wind. At first it appeared to avoid the moon, and shifted in an uncertain manner; then it broke slightly. Suddenly the wind rose to greater volume, and with a sound like the beating of the surf upon a rocky shore, it whispered hoarsely among the trees in the not far distant woods.

The scattered drifts of clouds formed into somber masses; in an instant the light of the moon became obscured, and the beauty of the night was dimmed. Dorothy, her hands clasped before her face, her form shaking from the reaction which came to her, burst into a passionate flood of tears and leaned her head down upon the dewy bank of earth. The moon went down enveloped in clouds and mist.

The hours of the night passed slowly by. Dorothy arose and continued her way over the few remaining fields that lay between her and the farm-house. She walked with a buoyant tread. Had not fate decided for her? Was she not free? A sign had come from heaven: by that sign she would guide her fate. Once more her life was clear and open; the reproachful memories of her past follies were dead, buried, and forgotten. No one need ever know. She would be silent; her ingenuity would help her to invent some plausible tale that would be accepted, and no witness could disprove her statement.

Presently she noticed a dark object coming toward her over the meadows. The object approached slowly and cautiously, keeping its head toward the ground and growling ominously. "Old Rollo! Old Rollo!" called Dorothy in a low voice. "Come here, good fellow, come here."

The farm dog, hearing her voice, hastened his pace, and was soon careering about her with dumb expressions of delight and welcome. She threw her arms about his shaggy neck, and laid her face close against his. "I need not lie to thee, good fellow," she said tearfully. "I could tell thee all, and thou wouldst think no less of me." The dog looked up into her face and whined. "It is because thou hast no mind to judge that thou lovest me. I would that others were as kind as thou art, poor dumb beast! Never, never wilt thou turn reproachful eyes on thy old friend Dorothy."

The dog thus appealed to drew closer to her, and with low murmurs of delight and affection licked her hands, and laid his paw in her lap as he nestled to her side. "Come," she continued, "protect me. They will not drive thee, a dog, away. They may then have pity upon me, a poor human penitent."

The two united friends walked over the little distance remaining of the Holden property. All was very still around the house; no lights were seen, for the hour was late, and all were asleep. Disheartened and frightened, Dorothy seated herself on the settle in the porch, and with the dog close by her side she decided to wait until morning. In a short space of time she had fallen asleep. It was a deep, dreamless sleep, produced by extreme exhaustion and excitement.

Aunt Martha rose early the following morning, as was her usual custom, and thinking she heard a noise in the porch, went to the window that overlooked the front door. Her eyes fell upon Dorothy, still fast asleep, her listless attitude resembling the deep repose of death. The dog looked up and whined when the window above his head opened, but he did not desert his charge. In another moment two excited old people came hurriedly down the creaking staircase. "Come to the back door," whispered Martha. "Do not frighten her; let her awaken naturally."

When Dorothy opened her blue eyes they rested upon the happy faces of her aunt and uncle. "Aunt Martha!" Dorothy's voice was soft with wistful pleading. "Forgive, forgive!" She could say no more, but held out her wasted arms.

"My little girl," said Aunt Martha, "thou art

welcome home!" and kissed her. Supported between the two, the wanderer entered the farmhouse.

And so the prodigal was received with joy, and the fatted calf was killed for the penitent. Yet she was only half a penitent, for with remorse came not confession.

Her aunt and uncle fully believed her story. She had left her home, she said, for very weariness and hatred of her existence; also on account of the forced bond of her betrothal. She had wandered in the forest, endeavoring to reach Boston, but had strayed from the bridle path and lost her way. At length she had been taken in by a kindly woman, a wood-cutter's widow, living in the heart of the woods, who had nursed her through a long attack of fever. Then she had for a time feared to return, but at last, hoping for forgiveness, had summoned the courage.

The old life was now resumed, save that the still small voice was never silent in the ears of the mistaken girl. For some days she refused to leave the farmhouse, making her aunt and uncle promise that they would not yet tell in Salem of her return.

"Not even Alden Wentworth?" asked Martha. "Methinks it is but his due."

"No, no," said Dorothy with a shudder, "not him; I must have strength to meet him. I am still but weak."

Martha was puzzled at this repugnance to meet one to whom she had been so indifferent. "Why, Dorothy, child, thou wert ever careless of his opinion. He cannot harm thee, and surely he will not reproach thee, save in his capacity of deacon to one of the erring flock. He is a proud man; he will never seek to force himself upon thee again. Fear not."

"Is he, then, so indifferent to me?" asked Dorothy humbly. "Have I offended him past all forgiveness?"

Her aunt gave her a sharp, curious glance. "Of that I cannot say. He doth not speak of thee. There is one whom gossips say he hath been seen much with. I set no store, however, on the idle talk of the women."

"Who is it?" asked Dorothy, "that seeks so soon to fill my place?" There was a touch of bitterness in her voice.

"Elizabeth Hubbard," replied her aunt.

"Surely Elizabeth can be no friend of mine!" She spoke angrily.

"Keep thy temper, Dorothy, keep thy temper. When thou throwest precious goods away, some there will ever be to pick them up. But I have said I would not reproach thee, and I never will."

"Aunt Martha," replied she solemnly, "what we possess we often set no store by. What we lose, of a surety that we do prize, but we do hate the one who profits by what we recklessly have lost."

Aunt Martha drew near her niece, and with a tenderness unusual in one of her self-contained disposition, kissed her gently upon her brow. "Dorothy, I fear thou hast lost the greatest blessing of thy life. Heaven help thee if the love which it was once thy right to feel has come to thee too late! I fear thou hast killed it in that other one with thine own hand."

Dorothy threw herself upon her knees, laid her head against the old kitchen settle, and sobbed. "He might have remembered me a little while," she said brokenly. "Forgotten in a few short months, and he said he truly loved me!"

"Hush, child. I know not that he has forgotten; 'tis perchance but idle gossip." As Martha spoke she stroked the bright brown hair. "Surely," she said, "thy misdeed has brought its punishment."

# CHAPTER IX.

## THE WITCHES.

THE strange and terrible delusion of witchcraft had fallen upon Salem with great virulence. Horrible tidings had found their way from distant lands, of the wholesale destruction of victims accused of this crime. In England, France, and Germany was this superstition prevalent. Witches were burned by hundreds and thousands. This belief did not confine itself to the poor or illiterate; many of the highest in all lands shared in the error of the day.

In England one Matthew Hopkins assumed the title of Witch-finder, and invented horrible tests whereby to vindicate his claims to such an exalted position. One of his most cruel proofs was this: after capturing the supposed witch, to tie the thumb of the right hand to the great toe of the left foot, then proceed to drag the poor wretch through a pond. If the frightened creature floated, there could be no doubt whatever that she was a witch—and she always floated! Through the instrumentality of Hopkins it is said that nearly sixty persons lost their lives by fire and hanging.

Our ancestors believed that a witch had willingly given her soul and body into the keeping of the devil: she had signed her name in his great Black Book. This ceremony accomplished, she was his forever. He, in return for her allegiance to him and her work in his behalf, endowed her with wondrous and supernatural powers, whereby she might do harm to all she wished, and to all who opposed her will.

These supposed witches had most marvelous gifts conferred upon them by their master: they could raise a storm at sea; they were given unusual physical strength; they could cause a tornado, fire churches, pinch, throttle, cause disease, destroy reason, and even take human life. Their actual presence was not considered necessary for the consummation of these terrible evils; an apparition or shape, sent in the form of some animal—a dog, cat, toad, spider, or the ever-popular yellow-bird—was sufficient for the success of their undertakings. These witches were supposed to go through weird, uncanny dances with their imps and ungodly followers, under the forest trees.

Another favorite pastime consisted of swift flights

through the midnight air, generally astride a broom-stick, their attendants from the lower world following them with fiendish cries and hideous laughs.

When the good people in those old days of New England heard strange, unaccountable noises on blowy nights, in the chimney or around their houses, they did not rise and with candle in hand investigate the cause; instead, they shuddered and lay still, whispering with bated breath, "The witches are abroad to-night; they are riding above the house-tops!" The mother clasped her little one closer, and murmured, "God keep thee, my child!"

During two preceding winters, those of 1691 and 1692, a society, or rather a circle, as it was called, consisting mostly of young girls, had been formed in Salem. This circle appears to have had for its first object amusement, the young people of those days sadly lacking any diverting pastimes. Gradually, however, these evening meetings, which took place principally in the house of the Rev. Mr. Parris, as-sumed a more serious aspect, and instruction in the black art became one of the main features of the en-tertainment. Mr. Parris had in his employ two ser-vants, or rather slaves, a man and his wife, named John Indian and Tituba.

These slaves Mr. Parris had brought with him from the Spanish Indies. They were steeped in witchcraft, and understood many of the horrible practices of the ignorant tribe from which they came. They instructed the circle, and kept it well supplied with material calculated to inflame the imaginations of the already intensely excited young people. The result of all this conjuring was that a species of hysteria seized upon the girls, and their antics soon began to give evidence—according to the popular idea—that they were bewitched.

Elizabeth Hubbard's erratic temperament had made her from the start a prominent actor in this magic circle. She now became possessed of the marvelous power of interpreting the spell of the witches; at least she claimed this honor.

The good people of Salem, at first surprised, soon became alarmed at the curious performances of the members of the society. They finally consulted the village doctor.

He was nonplused, read some learned documents, shook his head gravely, declared the disease unknown to science, and considered the girls certainly under the dreaded spell of witchcraft. They went through some of their antics for his benefit, creeping under chairs, uttering piercing cries, falling into convulsions, laughing and crying, until the poor, bewildered old man fled in dismay.

The afflicted children, as they were called, went triumphantly on their course, and were looked upon with sympathy and tenderness by the community at large. At last, intoxicated by the exalted position they now sustained in the village, they grew bolder, and openly accused three poor old helpless women of having bewitched them. From this small and apparently innocent source sprang the terrible torrent that swept so many blameless lives into eternity.

When Dorothy returned to Salem it was to find her old home given over to the wildest confusion. The daily work was neglected, the fields were not sown, while the people gathered, with bated breath and grave countenances, upon the streets, to discuss this appalling condition that had come amongst them. Three old women lay terrified in prison, awaiting their trials, on the testimony of the accusing girls.

Alden Wentworth had kept aloof as much as possible from the general alarm and confusion: not that he was an unbeliever in witchcraft—that would have been an impossibility in such an age, with such surroundings and teachings, to say nothing of natural temperament. He did not believe, however, in the power of human agency to discover a witch; and he predicted that many grievous mistakes would follow a trial by law of such an anomalous crime. He had faith in the efficacy of prayer and good deeds to avert, and in time to overcome, this fearful affliction; but he advised no violent measures.

The allusion that Elizabeth had made to Dorothy's being in the keeping of these lost creatures had alarmed and disturbed him; not that he seriously considered her words, but for the possible effect they might have on others, should Elizabeth speak of her suspicions abroad.

In March two distinguished magistrates, John Hathorne and Jonathan Corwin, came to Salem to try the accused witches. Alden was present in the meeting-house during these trials, though he took no part in the proceedings beyond that of interested listener, having peremptorily refused from the beginning of the witchcraft trouble to sit in judgment upon the accused parties so long as spectral testimony was taken in evidence. The trial was attended with considerable pomp and ceremony. Great crowds watched the proceedings with awe and respectful attention, drinking in with credulous eagerness the absurd testimony tendered by the girls.

It was the last day of the trial. Old Goody Trueman, who had been taken into custody shortly after Dorothy's departure from her home, lay very ill in the jail. It was impossible to bring her from Ipswich, where the prisoners were confined. The crowd was in a fever of expectancy, awaiting the verdict. All were silent; the unusual event had made a deep impression upon the populace. Now and then one of the "afflicted children" would disturb the solemnity of the scene by screaming out that one of the witches was torturing her; then she would fall upon the floor in a fit or a faint.

Wentworth, wearied, sick at heart of this horrid spectacle, left the church and repaired to the quiet resting-place of the dead, whose narrow confines bordered upon the meeting-house grounds. He looked down upon a newly covered grave: a few new shoots of tender grass grew upon the damp earth; the early spring sunshine fell warm about him. He removed his hat reverently, and gazed upon the peaceful scene. He did not hear a step on the soft ground near him, when, turning suddenly, he encountered the keen eyes of Martha

Holden watching him intently. She now came quickly forward, lifting her skirts as she stepped over twigs and brambles that lay upon some of the neglected mounds. He did not speak; something in her face drove the words from his lips. She had reached him now and stood close beside him. "Alden," she said, then hesitated, "I have something to tell thee."

"Yes," he said quickly, drawing near to her.

"It is of Dorothy. Methought I would seek thee here and speak, while those gaping idiots are trying the poor old dotards, placing their keen wits against their befogged brains!" She glanced angrily toward the meeting-house as she spoke. "I knew thou couldst not stay in *there* for long!" She pointed contemptuously over her shoulder as she finished speaking.

"Yes, yes," he interrupted impatiently; "but what of Dorothy?"

She gave him a searching glance, then said abruptly, "She has come home."

He paled a moment; then a light like the glow of the sun when it is highest in the heavens overspread his countenance. "Home!" he gasped— "home!"

" Yes, she has been home some days; she wished it not told abroad."

" Where has she been?   What says she of—of—me?"

" She has spoken but once of thee, and then in tones of deepest contrition.   She left thee for the wrong she thought she would do thee, did she marry thee without loving thee.   She hath been ill in the house of a kind woman who pitied her when, after wandering in the forest, she lost her way.   She was seeking to reach the seacoast, to embark for England."

" God bless that kindly woman, whoever she may be," said Wentworth reverently.

Martha continued: " Speak not much to her of her wanderings when thou dost see her; she is yet over weak, and allusions to her troubles do but harass her greatly."

" Will she see me?   I fear she may not desire it after all that I have brought upon her; for thou knowest, Martha, fear of me drove her from her home."

" Not so," said Martha.   " I do love the child, yet I can see her faults: she was ever unhappy, seeking advancement.   Be not too humble; women like not men that do bemean themselves. Show her that thou art master. If I were a married woman, I would not let thee into this secret." She laughed. "Too much leaven makes the bread hollow."

For very happiness he laughed too, then checked the mirth as a sound unbefitting the sacredness of the place where they stood.

"I will not let her know that I have seen thee," said Martha warily. "Come some time as though by chance. Remember, she has changed. She will not meet thee dancing that heathenish dance, as thou hast once seen her; her heart is not so light as then." She paused, and continued sadly: "No doubt this discipline is better for her, but she is little wild Dorothy no longer."

They were startled from further converse by shouting and screams and the tramping of many feet. They turned, to see crowds issuing from the doors of the meeting-house. The verdict had been rendered, the trial was over. The prisoners were being led, or rather dragged forth, by their jailers. Following closely came the "afflicted children," calling loudly after them:

"See where they go, their imps surrounding

them! They do pinch us, and prick us, and choke us."

"They do seek our souls!" shrieked the deep voice of Elizabeth Hubbard, as she strode, tall and menacing, in their wake, the picture of an avenging goddess loth to let her prey escape.

The two poor friendless old women, cowering and trembling before her cries and frenzied attitude, raised their hands imploringly. Their eyes were dim with age, and their forms bent by the infirmities of many years.

"Away with them!" she cried. "Their eyes do pierce our souls like coals of fire! Take them from our sight, else we suffer from the torments they do send upon us."

Then followed fits and swoons, and gestures of apparent terror and dismay.

"I am no witch!" called one of the prisoners angrily, in a high, cracked voice. "Ye do dissemble. I have no contact with the Evil One; ye have, for ye seek our lives."

"She tortures these poor children," said the magistrate, from his position on the upper steps of the church. "See ye not their sufferings? Put these accursed fiends into the cart, and hasten with them to the jail.  Pollute our presence no longer by these hags of wickedness."

Amidst great confusion on the part of the crowd, and groans from the two terrified old women, the latter were placed in the cart; and followed by jeering, hooting boys hurling sticks and stones, they proceeded down the country road in the direction of the prison.  Martha and Wentworth gazed upon this spectacle with varying emotions: Wentworth with deep pity, yet powerless to interfere, for were these prisoners not tried by law?  Martha with anger uncontrollable.  She turned impatiently to her companion.

" Why seek ye not to influence Elizabeth Hubbard?" she said.  " Methinks she would heed thee, the wicked baggage!  Out upon her, with her heart of stone!  She is the leader in all this wickedness."

Elizabeth had been standing for some minutes with her back to them, not seeing the two figures watching quietly among the graves; she was gazing gloomily after the retreating crowds.  She now turned quickly, hearing her name, and encountered the grave, reproachful glance of the young judge and the wrathful eyes of Martha.  But her gaze did not fall before theirs.  She came rapidly toward

them over the rough ground, not avoiding the resting-places of the dead, but stepping heavily upon
the raised hillocks as though there was no sacredness in the place. As she neared them, she turned
defiantly upon Martha and touched her arm.

"Why were ye not at the trial, Mistress Holden?
It was a rare scene."

"I detest such sights!" said Martha angrily,
twitching her arm from the girl's grasp. "When I
make war, I make it not on two poor imbecile old
women. Ye had better be about some other business, or methinks ye will do better work for Satan
than aught thy victims can do."

Wentworth laid his hand on the outstretched arm
of the excited woman. "Be discreet, be discreet,"
he said.

"I approve not of such deeds, and I am not
afraid to say so," she replied.

Elizabeth watched the angry woman with a hard,
determined expression. "Discretion were better
for thee," she said slowly. "Mr. Wentworth advises well. Yet let me tell thee the import of the
trial. In a few weeks they will be hung, Old
Goody Trueman with the rest, or as soon as her
health permits her to mount Gallows Hill."

"Surely, surely not!" cried Alden Wentworth in dismay.

"Ay, 'tis true and just; the magistrates have so decreed it."

"I say it is *not* just," interrupted Martha hotly. "Thou art a wicked girl; yet thou wilt receive thy reward. Methinks thou hast received already a portion of it. Fate can spin a web stronger than thou canst, Elizabeth. Whom dost thou think has returned to Salem?" As she spoke Martha smiled triumphantly upon her angry auditor, cocking her head on one side, and laughing softly. "Thou wilt not have it all thine own way now."

"Who?" inquired the girl. "I care not who comes and goes from Salem."

Alden Wentworth was not taking part in the angry discussion between the two women. He had retired a few steps from them and stood motionless, his head raised, a happy, dreamy light in his fine eyes. Elizabeth watched him intently an instant and read the answer to her question on his face.

"Dorothy," she said, "Dorothy has returned." Her voice sounded strained and unnatural.

"Yes, forsooth, Dorothy, thy old friend, whom I heard thee malign in the market-place. No doubt thou wilt be happy to welcome her again," she con- cluded sarcastically.

"Where has she been these four months?" demanded Elizabeth.

"What is that to thee? Thou canst have no interest in the matter. If thou canst not prove thyself a friend in need, in good times we want thee not. I wish thee to come no more to the farm."

"Yes, Elizabeth," said Wentworth, the sound of Dorothy's name recalling him from his reverie, "she has returned amongst us. The heavy remorse I have carried within me is no more. My prayers are answered. We should all bid her welcome, both for her own sake and for the sake of her good aunt and uncle."

"And ye advise me thus?" she said, stamping her foot passionately, and striking her hand violently against a headstone raised upon an adjacent grave. "Ye are blind, ye cannot see. I wish that I were dead, dead, lying here below where my feet tread. There is no hope, no happiness more for me."

Wentworth and Martha started in dismay at this exhibition of anger and despair, and drew back a few paces.

"Ye may well shrink from me," she cried. "Ye have ever said that I was wild and had no reason in me. Ye have doubted that I did see visions." She drew nearer to them and peered into their faces. "Look, I see one now; it rises from yonder grave." She pointed, as she spoke, to a sunken depression in a neighboring plot. "Ye cannot see it. It is well that ye cannot. It rises from the dead, to the dead it returns. And ye—ye—have made me see this vision." She clutched the young man's arm convulsively, and her voice died away in a low echo that resounded over the lonely field.

"Calm thyself, calm thyself," said Wentworth, much alarmed. "These witch trials do but make thee beside thyself; thy mind is dwarfed. To me thy words are riddles."

"Riddles!" she cried mockingly. "He calls them riddles. Perchance ye will have the wisdom given thee some day wherewith to read them." She laughed that eerie, haunting laugh of hers.

"Hush, Elizabeth, hush!" he reiterated.

"I will not," she said. "I will have my say, then I will depart. As I have entertained thee well, I will soon bid thee good-day. Be not disturbed, Mistress Holden, I will not call at the farm.

Yet wait; I have a message for Dorothy. Tell her from me, that when she marries and is from under thy influence I will bring her a wedding gift."

"She wants none of thy gifts, thou false girl!" said Martha.

"Nevertheless I will bring her one, and it shall be woven good and stout, and shall be of goodly length."

She left them abruptly. When she reached the gate of the little graveyard she paused and glanced back over her shoulder. Her face looked so dark and menacing, her eyes so black and baleful, peering forth from the masses of somber-hued hair, her whole expression so malignant, that Martha, shuddering, drew closer to Wentworth.

"What meaning lies in her words?" she gasped. "She must be crazed. Was ever girl so daft?"

"She means harm to Dorothy," said Wentworth slowly. "Yet surely I cannot understand why she should hate her, her old friend."

"Ye men are stupid," answered Martha impatiently. "I know well why she hates her. Thou canst not see through a clear glass—ye have no discernment."

Wentworth looked helplessly upon his companion,

but did not reply. They waited a few moments longer, communing with their own thoughts. The wind blew damp and chill about them; the sky was fast deepening into the gray tints of a somber sunset; the little graveyard grew bleak and dull-hued.

Suddenly he spoke: " Come, let us be going; 'tis cold among the graves."

" Yes," said Martha, " let us be going; at home, perhaps, we can drive the ill-omened words of this girl adrift. My heart is heavy; this hillside is an uncanny spot."

# CHAPTER X.

## THE RENEWAL OF LOVE.

THE air was growing warm with the sweet breath of spring. The wild violets, anemones, and the wind-blown grass flowers were gazing coyly forth from their winter resting-places. In the orchards the pink and white masses of buds upon the fruit-trees flung out their fragrance to the breeze. The little brooks sang merrily through the woods, joining with the joyous songs of birds. Upon the bare, bleak hills the foliage spread and covered the gray boughs, and the brown earth lay hidden beneath richest verdure.

The door of the farmhouse was open, but the soft air, the sunshine, the fragrance, and the songs of the merry birds were all unnoticed by the girl who sat within the threshold, her head bowed above her spinning-wheel. Her hands were busy, her foot was upon the treadle, but her thoughts were far distant in another spring, just one year ago. Poor, erring Dorothy!

" Just one year ago," she mused, " I did fling my happiness aside, and now, like a child who has no power to help itself, I weep for the ruin I have wrought."

She dropped the linen she had been weaving, and rising, went to the open door. She looked across the smooth fields to where the line of sea glittered, then upon the cattle grazing peacefully in the meadows, then to the blue sky above her head. " I seem to care for naught," she said aloud; " it is as though I had no feeling left in me. Yet once a day like this, and I could have danced and sung, as happy as yonder bird who hastens to his nest." She drew her hand across her eyes: they were filled with tears. " I had thought perhaps he would have come—and yet, why should I wish to be more miserable than I am? He cares not for me, he has forgotten."

She returned to her work. Round and round went the busy wheel, the lint from the linen flying through the atmosphere, the whirring sound echoing pleasantly, like the song of a good housewife happy at her task. Dorothy's passage through the fire of tribulation had purified much of the light dross which had been hers both by inheritance and temperament.

The merriment of her nature had toned to a gentle humor, which, though seldom seen, shone forth occasionally, like the rare glimpse of the sun on a winter's day.

Her beauty had increased and expanded. The childish contour of her face was replaced by firmer, sweeter lines, while a pathetic pensiveness had taken the place of her former mischievous archness. Her perverse, irritating moods had departed, and in their stead came a quiet acquiescence that amounted at times almost to indifference. This latter change in Dorothy was the cause of much disquietude to her aunt.

Alden Wentworth, true to his word, had not yet called upon his old love, and she, all unsuspecting Martha's interview with him, watched and waited, hoping, yet fearing his coming.

As Dorothy sat before her wheel this day, she made a pleasant picture. She wore a blue petticoat, a bodice with slashed sleeves, a lace neck cloth around her slender throat, and upon her pretty drooping head a silken hood rested, the brown curls falling in little rings upon her forehead. Her small feet were shod with high-heeled shoes with silver buckles, and the pretty apron that covered her dress in front was daintily embroidered.

The practice of the Puritans in regard to dress was in some respects at variance with their theories, many vanities of the toilet being allowed. This was probably in defiance of the severity of the attire of the Quakers, a sect whom they abhorred.

The shadow rested near the hour of four upon the dial in the garden path. Dinner had long been over; David had returned to the field; Martha was in the milk-room, busy with her churning. The house was very still; old Rollo lay curled up on the doorstep, fast asleep.

Dorothy took her foot from the treadle, bowed her head upon her arm, and leaned forward upon the wheel. The breeze stirred her soft hair and fanned her neck, but she was oblivious to all surroundings. Her thoughts were blended in a maze of regrets and remorse for the past year—the year of her grave mistake. She did not hear a step pause upon the walk, or the rustle of the shrubs near the door.

She did not move until a well-remembered voice said, "Dorothy!"

She then started quickly, and rose to her feet, a blush mounting over her pale face—a scorching, crimson blush.  She held out her small hands deprecatingly; her sensitive lips quivered like a frightened child's.

Wentworth took a step forward, watching her intently as he did so.  "Welcome home, Dorothy," he said, " welcome home."

By a great effort of will she quelled the hysterical desire to sob, and in a voice scarce audible replied, " Thou art kind to bid me welcome;  I merit not such words from thee."  She leaned tremblingly against the spinning-wheel, and gave him such a pleading, piteous glance that Wentworth was deeply moved.

" Be not afraid of me, Dorothy;  I would not harm thee.  No thought against thee has ever found place in my heart.  The wrong thou hast done me is balanced by the wrong I did thee."

They stood facing each other, the yellow sunlight from the open door falling over both.

At these words a tremor passed over Dorothy. " No, no," she said vehemently, " say not so.  I am all to blame.  I left thee—I left thee——"  She could not continue; her voice broke, and she turned away her head.

He came nearer to her, and clasped her hand firmly in his. " I know thou didst leave me, and I know wherefore. I will not reproach thee; thou hast ever been frank and true. Let it be between us henceforth as though this had never been. Let us turn our feet into a new path, leaving the landmarks on the old forgotten."

" No, no," she said, weeping, " it can never be the same again. How can it, when this my misdeed is ever between us? We cannot bury it, for, like a buried seed, it will grow and bear fruit. I fear myself, I fear myself!" She tried to draw her hand from his grasp, but he held it firmly, and forced her to look upon him.

" Thou art weak yet from the fever. Thy words are not the truth of thy heart. I will wait. Time is naught, if it bring me at length what I once thought was mine. Dost thou feel as cold toward me as formerly?"

She threw out her disengaged hand with a passionate gesture. " No, no, Alden, no, no. Yet— I am not fit to be to thee what thou wouldst have me—I am not fit."

" Not fit!" he said. " Thou art too good, too pure, too true for me."

As he spoke these words, she trembled so perceptibly that he thought she would have fallen; her face grew white and drawn. "Sit here near the door, on the settle," he said anxiously, putting his arm about her and guiding her steps. She leaned against him helplessly. "I have alarmed thee," he said. "Forgive me."

"Nay, it is not that. I am not good or true; I am neither; I have done that which can never be forgiven."

He, thinking that in her weak condition her overtaxed nerves caused this magnifying of her offense, soothed her, speaking gently to her, now and then placing his hand tenderly upon her hair. When he did this, she shrank as from a blow. Seeing this movement he drew his hand away, but not in displeasure, for he had read in Dorothy's manner and words something that caused his pulses to throb and his heart to beat joyously.

"My child," he said, "let us converse calmly. I will not pester thee with questions of thy feelings; tell me of thy wanderings. Did the dark forests not affright thee greatly? Who was this kindly woman who took thee in? I would I might requite her for her care of thee."

A gray pallor overswept her face, more alarming than had been her previous whiteness. She could not answer him; her lips became dry, her tongue dumb. Requite her! If he but knew of those beads of gold that Goody had taken for her recompense—those beads that bought her to follow a lying deceiver, that glittering chain that bound her to her own destruction—he would scorn and spurn her, she thought, looking up into the kind face observing her, a voice within her convincing her that that face could look cold and stern and pitiless.

"I cannot talk of that dreadful time," she said. "Ask me not; it frightens me to recall it. Tell me of thyself and Salem, and of this terrible sorcery that is in our midst."

He did as she required. "I can well believe that it pains thee to speak of so much sorrow. I fear, however, this witchcraft plague is not a more cheerful subject. It is growing to great dimensions. Many have been arrested and now lie in prison awaiting trial."

"I hear Elizabeth is one of the foremost of accusers."

"She is vehement in her charges; yet not she alone, for most of the people do affirm that there is

a diabolical agency in this strange demeanor of the
afflicted children."

"Aunt Martha bides at home and forbids me to
attend the trials, though indeed I desire not to see
the doings."

"It is no place for thee." He spoke decidedly.
"Hast heard that old Goody Trueman lies in Ipswich jail yet very ill? Thou wilt remember her.
Thou hast seen her on the edge of the forest at
sundown, a glow upon her form like fire. Many do
affirm, though I must confess I have seen it not,
that a black dog appears and disappears by her side
in the twinkling of an eye; and they do say further,
that at midnight, in the glen, she leads the dance of
the witches."

"I believe it not! It is false!" she cried excitedly. "I believe she is a good old woman."

He eyed her curiously a moment. "Thou art so
good, Dorothy, that thou canst see no harm in
others."

She winced at these words, and her hands worked
nervously as they lay in her lap.

He arose presently. "See," he said, "the evening has come; already the sun is sinking. I must
leave thee. I have pressing business at the manse.

A great meeting of the clergy will be held this night week in reference to witchcraft; as deacon of the Salem church, I must prepare a discourse for that occasion. Dorothy, good-night."

She rose from the settle and placed her hand in his. "Good-night," she said simply.

He hesitated an instant on the doorstep, then said slowly, "Thou hast naught to tell me why I should not come to see thee oft? Wilt thou welcome me?" he pleaded wistfully.

She tried to speak, but no sound came from her lips.

"Am I not welcome, then?"

"Thou art welcome," she said at last, scarcely recognizing her own voice, it was so strained and hoarse, "and—and—I have naught to tell thee."

"I shall come, then, again, and soon." He went from her presence down the garden path in the fast gathering twilight.

When he reached the gate she called him back. "Alden, Alden!" she said. He was by her side quickly. "I know not why I called thee back," she said brokenly; "perchance an impulse to tell thee something. It has gone from me again; I cannot remember; it was no doubt but a trifle." She spoke feverishly and grasped his arm. "Tell me, tell me, hast thou forgiven me? Give me some penance, that I may perform it—some hard deed that I may do to prove that I have indeed been pardoned, and for my soul's peace."

"I have forgiven thee, freely, fully; it is as though thy desertion had never been. Wilt thou not believe me? We have both erred and have both forgiven."

"Thou hast not erred, thou hast not," she said. "Couldst thou forgive everything for the love thou hast for me—all weakness, all wrong?" She dared not look into his face as she asked this question.

"No, Dorothy, not everything: not deceit, nor unfaithfulness; methinks that would kill all love in me. But why thus torture thyself? I deem that there still lurks the fever about thee."

"Ay," she replied, "but not fever of body. Good-night, good-night, Alden. Dream of me as thou knewest me a year ago, not as now. Dream of me." Her voice sounded sweet and gentle.

"I shall dream of thee now, as always, my beloved one, who holds my heart and faith and hopes." He clasped her passionately and kissed her. "Thou lovest me, thou lovest me," he murmured.

"Ay," she said, "I love thee; yet pity me, pity me, Alden. My will is weak. Oh, let me go, let me think!" She released herself from his arms. "I am so tired. I have battled against this love; thou hast won—wilt thou be merciful?"

"Dorothy, thy words are strange; I understand them not. Dearest, all is right between us once more. It is as though the sun of happiness had spread his rays upon us, to lighten the way in which our feet shall tread. Surely God has been good to us; He has tried our affection and found it strong." He went again down the path, looking back once when he reached the gate.

In the fast waning light she strained her eyes for the last glimpse of him as he passed from her sight. Then she leaned her head against the doorpost, her eyes wide and dry, and looked straight before her, seeing nothing: not the gorgeous coloring in the western sky, where shafts of crimson and of gold stretched across the heavens; not the white mist of the coming night, that lay like a shroud upon the trees and shrubs; not the long line of cattle crossing the meadows to the barnyard; not even old Rollo, looking affectionately up into her face. Ah no, her thoughts were turned inward, were communing in that secret place where none had been admitted.

She realized fully that the disclosure of her flight with Grenville would cost her the love of Wentworth. Furthermore, the knowledge of her long residence in Goody Trueman's hut would cause the suspicions of the excited populace to descend upon her, and these once aroused, there was no conjecturing what the end would be. This latter conclusion did not affect her with that shrinking dread and quaking at her heart as did the fear of losing one whom she now felt to be more than life to her.

Then the horrible doubt dawned upon her, that he would not believe the account of her residence with the witch and her escape from Grenville, and she had no witness to prove her words. Who would credit the evidence of a lost creature such as Goody? "I know not, I know not," she murmured, "which way to turn for counsel." Then in her ears sounded, with grave decision, old Goody's warning—"Tell the truth, tell the truth." "I dare not, I dare not; the price is too great." She clasped her hands and looked up into the sky, now dark with the coming night. "Oh, for a voice from that great throne above, not to tell me what is right

—that I know—but to give me strength to fling aside what I most desire." No voice came from the somber clouds; no sound was heard except the rustle of the wind across the fields and the evening songs of the little birds in their nests, joining with the whirring of insects. "Methinks God has forgotten me for that false step," she whispered sadly, "and as I once did err, has taken from me all strength to resist temptation."

While she thus thought bitterly, old David came across the path. He walked slowly, for he was wearied by a hard day's work. He took a seat beside his niece upon the doorstep.

"So Wentworth has been here," he said, glancing sharply at Dorothy from under his beetling brows; "I saw him leave the house."

"Yes, he has been here."

"Is he coming again?" he demanded quickly.

"He is coming again," she answered quietly.

"Then take heed, Dorothy, if it be thy wish that he comes to thee, that no more shall thy tempers, thy follies, and thy whims rise up between thee."

She did not reply.

"Dost thou hear me?" he demanded. "Now let me say further, then I shall speak no more upon

this subject: he has forgiven thee, freely and fully."
He paused, then continued gravely: "If I read the
man aright, he could be pitiless and cruel to one
whom he deemed had injured him. Be sure that
thou goest to him with all thy heart, no secrets hid
from him. I am an old man, Dorothy, and my interest is in thy welfare."

Instead of replying she left her seat hurriedly and
stepped into the path and took a few hasty steps to
and fro, then cried angrily:

"Why dost thou irritate me, uncle? What could
be kept secret between us? He knows all. Shall I
crawl upon my knees to him? Perchance that is
what thou wouldst have me do." She laughed hysterically. "I will go to the milk-room and help
Aunt Martha. She is ever kind to me since my return; she does not cast suspicious gibes at me."

Thus Dorothy thrust aside another opportunity,
and with each baffled effort the spinning of the web
grew stronger, and the little spider of deceit ran
gleefully up and down the strands, carrying ever
fresh materials for the structure. We deceive ourselves when we consider that the enormity of the
sin lies in the sin itself. If such were the case then
would there be but one victim to suffer for a

broken law, and that one might pay the penalty by atonement and restitution, and all be made perfect once more, unheeded by the thoughtless one, however the mighty consequences stretch out their clinging, penetrating fibers, drawing in all who come within the reach of their influence. It is indeed one of the most torturing symptoms of remorse that we cannot suffer alone, but that those we love and fain would shield must also be dragged down into the deep waters of tribulation with us.

Dorothy buried her secret for the present; it rested not in the grave she dug for it, but arose and stalked forth in the broad light of day. To her feverish imagination it seemed that a being resembling herself, yet different, and unseen by all eyes save her own, walked forever by her side. It stood close beside her in the market-place, in the house, in the church, in the fields, in her dreams. And that other self, the one being who knew the secret of her heart, mocked and jeered, pointing the finger of scorn and derision. "Thou deceivest others, but there is One thou canst not deceive, One who looks down upon thee from the heavens, One who knows all, One to whom the judgment of mankind is as nothing." It was as if a new life was hers and she but a part of that life, for another shared it with her—a hated presence, that sent its poison into her being, obliterating the spell of peace and draining the springs of her will.

Dorothy was fighting hopelessly against a tender conscience. It was doubtless true that the awakened power and passion of her affection kept her silent. Had she not dreaded losing her lover she would have unburdened her heart to her aunt and uncle and abided by their decision. The words trembled constantly upon her lips, " I have deceived, I have lied." But the thought always followed, " I cannot give him up; death were far better."

# CHAPTER XI.

## DOROTHY'S CONTRITION.

WENTWORTH, after leaving his love standing in the doorway of the farmhouse, went directly to the abode of Mr. Parris, where he remained for some time in close conversation with his pastor. The result of this interview was that some impatient, if not angry, words passed between the two men.

"I fain would counsel thee," said Mr. Parris in his harsh, decided manner, "not to overdo this matter. This witch, this Goody Trueman, of a surety is an accursed creature. Why does the soul which she has sold require the offices of the church? It would be but a hollow mockery."

"I differ from thee in this matter, Mr. Parris; not doubting the verdict of the magistrates who have condemned her to death, but for the sake of a humanity which she possesses with us all, I think it her right that some spiritual—yes, perhaps earthly —comfort should be meted out to her."

After a pause, during which Mr. Parris looked closely at the younger man, he said sarcastically: "What wilt thou do? go to Ipswich and hold prayers in the jail?"

"No, certainly not. I shall not usurp thy office. I shall simply see these condemned women, and perchance speak some holy words to them. This old Goody is aged, diseased, and helpless."

"I fear me, Wentworth, thou hast not considered well this step. Thou surely canst not be in sympathy with these lost creatures!" As Mr. Parris spoke, he looked suspiciously upon his parishioner, who returned the glance defiantly.

"My sympathy and my purpose are my own. I need no other man's guidance." Wentworth spoke decidedly, though respectfully. "I need not tell thee that I believe in witchcraft; I do certainly credit the power of the spirits of the air. Yet I do affirm that this kind are but exorcised by fasting and prayer. What good is accomplished if we take their miserable lives? We do but send them to their master. Were it not better to force that master to relinquish his hold upon them on this earth, while there is time for repentance?"

"Go thy way," cried Mr. Parris angrily; "go

thy way. I promise thee thy work will be useless; thou wilt sow thy seed on barren ground."

When Alden informed Dorothy the following day of his intention to visit the condemned witch, she turned as pale as the bunch of white blossoms she held in her hand.

"Is it required of thee?" she said slowly.

"Not ordered by my superiors, oh no," said Wentworth; "the clergy have no sympathy with the witches; yet I feel as though this undertaking were but part of the life-work I have chosen as deacon of the church, to visit those condemned to die. The layman has a duty as well as the pastor."

"When wilt thou go?" she inquired in a low voice. She appeared calm, but her heart was beating so rapidly it seemed he must hear its throbs.

"In a day or so," he replied. "To-morrow I attend a meeting at a town not far distant; perchance the following day I shall go to Ipswich."

The result of this conversation was that at an early hour of the following morning, as Alden journeyed to his meeting, Dorothy started in the opposite direction with a small basket in her hand and a roll of some material, prepared for bandages, under her arm.  She had risen early, in fact with the first gleam of dawn, explaining to her aunt her intention of spending the day with friends living on a distant farm.  Instead she turned her steps toward the jail in the adjoining town.  The broiling, blinding sun beat down upon her as she walked, the perspiration started upon her forehead; she shifted the basket from one hand to the other as though it contained some weighty substance.  The road was many inches deep in dust.  Little clouds of powdery earth rose in yellow mist about her feet.  It was a tedious walk, with little shade, the monotony of the way unrelieved save by the occasional passing of a farm wagon.  Once a good-natured farmer offered her a seat beside him, but she declined, shaking her head, and plodded sturdily along.  Back from the hot road were shaded glens, through which flowed cool, deep streams, running between fern-clothed banks.  She dared not pause and rest among them, for time was precious; she must return to Salem before night set in.  So she looked neither to the right nor the left, but walked rapidly on, breaking into a run when the road was clear of passers.

After about two hours or more of this energetic proceeding, she stood before the jail.  It was a stout wooden edifice, with iron doors and small, grated windows. After much parleying with the jailer, she was conducted to old Goody's cell. Dorothy had claimed relationship with the prisoner, saying she had come from a great distance beyond Salem to bring her a remedy for her disease, which she was lying ill of and near to death.

" It is contrary to rules to see the prisoners at this hour," said the keeper, " yet for thy long walk thou deservest some reward. Thou mayst talk to the witch for a few moments. But be cautious; go not nigh her, for she hath spells we know not of. If ye see a spider or a toad or rat in her cell, call the jailer."

Some moments later the keeper opened the heavy grated door and admitted Dorothy into the gloomy cell. Coming so suddenly from the outside glare, she blinked an instant in the darkness before being able to decipher objects before her.

Old Goody lay upon her back on a pile of straw in the corner of the cell. She had heavy irons upon her arms and ankles. The small shaft of light that came from the narrow window in the upper part of the wall shone across her withered features. She looked indeed hideous and haglike.

"Goody, Goody," said Dorothy softly, stepping across the stone floor to the center of the cell.

"Who calls me?" answered the cracked, cackling voice of the old woman. She did not open her eyes or move as she spoke.

"I, Goody, a friend." The girl stepped to the poor creature's side and bent over her. "See, I have brought thee a little basket of good things, a roll of linen, and some fine salve for thy sickness. Thou surely wilt remember me."

Goody opened her dim eyes; a spark of loving gratitude shone within them. "Ay," she said, "I know thee. Could I forget my little wild-flower of the forest? Ah, well indeed I remember the night thou camest to bloom for me in my poor home."

"Hush," said Dorothy, holding up a warning finger, "hush!" As she spoke the jailer passed the door of the cell, placing his eye to the grating as he did so. "Be cautious; speak lower, I beseech thee."

Goody gazed earnestly at the pretty, troubled face bending above her.

"I have brought these things for thee; see, here are some sweetmeats and other things of use," said Dorothy in a high voice, for the edification of the jailer.

"Are these all for me?" queried Goody. "Was it thy pretty face, then, that gained thee admittance to the jail? Thou art my only friend; no one has yet called to see the poor old witch. They deem me lost, yet I have done no harm; I am but a poor distraught creature whom man maligns."

"One will come to see thee perchance to-morrow," said Dorothy earnestly, "and I implore thee, speak not of me to him. I have called to-day with a double purpose—to see thee, to comfort thee, and to tell thee this."

"Why this secret, child?" said Goody, rising from her lowly bed, and looking sharply at the partly averted face opposite her.

"I cannot tell thee why, yet I do implore thee, speak not of me, of ever having known me. This is more than life to me. O Goody, Goody, if thou hast ever loved me, promise me this." Dorothy clasped her hands and looked beseechingly at the troubled face of the old woman.

"I surely will grant any wish of thine; I could not refuse it, my faithful little comforter."

"I thank thee, Goody, so much, and I fear sorely for thee; these cruel men have punished thee greatly. Would I could aid thee! When I was ill no one could be kinder than thou wert to me, and I am grateful. I had a little gold saved; I made it by my own spinning. Perchance it may buy thee some little comfort; thou canst bribe the jailer. It is in the basket underneath the box of salve." The tears were running down Dorothy's face as she spoke.

"Weep not," said the old woman; "it is but for a little while. I am very old and sick; my appointed time is near. Pray ye that God will call me to Himself soon."

"I will, I will; every day will I pray for thee. I love thee, Goody, thou hast been so kind to me. Would I were possessed of power to unbar thy prison doors!" She smoothed the wrinkled cheek, then kissed her gently. "To-morrow, when he comes, he will comfort thee; he is so good, so just; but remember thy promise—I am a stranger to thee."

"Yes, yes, I remember."

"And now, now the time is up; I hear the jailer coming. I will bid thee farewell."

"Farewell, little forest bloom. Perchance when we meet again it will be in a better world than this."

"Ay, Goody, God will it so some day."

"Mistress, time is up," called the stern voice of the jailer.

Goody lay back upon her straw bed, and Dorothy passed from the gloom and dampness of the prison out into the sunlight.

When she reached the narrow lane that led to the farm it was growing dark. She was exhausted from her great exertion and the nervous excitement of the day; her limbs trembled beneath her, her face was flushed, and dark rings encircled her eyes. She seated herself upon a rustic stile for a few moments to rest and gain composure before entering the house, and as she did so beheld Wentworth coming hastily across the great grass-meadow that lay near the shore and which sloped downward to the harbor. He came directly toward her, waving his hand in welcome as he approached. She arose to meet him, advancing a few steps. He smiled as he accosted her. "I wot this has been a weary day for thee," he said; "the Leavitt place is a good three miles from here. Didst walk all the way? Thy aunt has told me it was a sudden resolve on thy part to make this visit. Thou art a whimsical little one," he laughed.

"I walked all the way," she answered wearily.

"We will not go to the house," he said presently. "Come to the shore and rest; I have much to say to thee, and the time is short."

"No, no," she answered; "I must go home, I must see Aunt Martha, and I am very tired."

"I am more important than Aunt Martha, am I not?" He laughed again. "Come with me to the shore."

She took a step forward, then one backward, still hesitating. A strange mood was upon her. In shadowy outline she beheld that other self close beside her, holding up a warning finger, her lips framing the words, "Thy last chance." "Methinks it is damp by the sea," she said; "I like not to cross those marshy pools at evening." She spoke like a fretful child.

He laughed once more, then taking her by the hand led her across the salt marshes down to the shore. She did not object further, but followed as in a dream. Looking far over the water, her gaze upon the sails of a vessel in the distance, her hand within her lover's, won by his earnest solicitation she named the wedding-day. As she named it a cold horror took possession of her and made her shiver and tremble. Was it the forerunner of the breeze that stirred the ocean, as yet miles away, where it lay like a dark mantle upon the wide expanse of water? She knew not. She drew her cloak more closely about her and glanced fixedly as if fascinated at the profile of the strong face beside her.

"Wilt thou ever be harsh to me, Alden, if I offend thee?" she said wistfully, her pretty, sensitive lips quivering as she spoke.

"No, dearest, I never will be harsh to thee."

"If I did something that was very wrong?" she urged.

"Nothing that thou wilt do could be very wrong; so long as thou art true and sincere, and thy love is mine, I can ask no more of thee."

"And thou wouldst never believe evil of me?"

"Thou couldst do no evil; that word belongs not to thee," he said quickly.

It was quite dark now, and the outline of the distant vessel on the horizon that was sailing swiftly before the wind had faded from view; a flock of seagulls were flying toward the south, calling loudly and in discordant notes; the soft lap of the waves on the beach sounded faintly in their ears; in the sky hung the beautiful evening star. Dorothy arose from her low position, and standing before Wentworth spake words that sounded incomprehensible in his ears.

"Alden, Alden," her voice rang with a pathos and deep regret, "wilt thou blot out all that has gone from thy memory—all, all, and take me from this moment as I am, and with the help of One who is above us all? I will be to thee so true, so faithful, that no reproach shall ever fall from thy lips for my misdeeds. I come to thee, Alden, with no past; I am born anew in thy love."

"My dearest, my little Dorothy!" That was all he said. He could not understand her vehemence, her tone of entreaty, and her pale face startled him. "Thou art tired; this has been a hard day for thee."

She clasped her hands tightly in her lap and spoke no further. He did not understand her and she could not explain. They walked home, over the fields, in the sweet, mild night. The air from the sea blew in their faces; the solemnity of the evening hour cast its pensive spell upon them, compelling them to silence.

The wedding was to take place in June, but a

short time hence; yet why delay? The bridal outfit was ready, the new house was ready, and the
lover urgent.

That night, as Dorothy sat in her casement window brooding deeply upon her sad position, she fell
asleep, her head leaning upon the window-ledge,
the dews falling upon her hair, and the chill night
air blowing over her. In this sleep she was visited
by a dream, or rather by a vision—a vision clear
and startling in its significance. She appeared to be
wandering alone in a dreary valley; great cypress-
trees grew thick about her path, obscuring the light
of the sun. At her feet were pools and morasses,
slimy and green; horrid creeping things appeared
and disappeared from out their stagnant waters.
The scene was dismal in the extreme, and fraught
with great danger; to advance or to retreat seemed
equally hazardous. Suddenly a figure shining with
an unearthly luster came forth from beneath the
drooping boughs of the trees. This bright being
was clothed in flowing drapery, and upon its forehead was a star that shone as with the light of the
sun, its powerful rays spreading through all the
lands of the earth. Dorothy trembled and stood
motionless. "My child, my child," she heard a

voice of rarest sweetness say, "there is but one way for thee." As these words were uttered, the wondrous stranger pointed to a narrow path that led beyond the pools and morasses and noisome reptiles. "At the end of this path is the temple of truth; I am its guardian. Behold, I have opened the way." Dorothy held out her hand, but her radiant guide had disappeared as mysteriously as she came.

Dorothy stirred uneasily and awoke. Her hair and face were clammy from the falling dews, and the night air caused her to shiver; but she paid no heed to these discomforts. Going to her dressing-table she took from it paper and pens. Seating herself, she wrote a full confession of her flight with Grenville. After having finished this task, she held the letter in her hand an instant, looking sadly down upon the folded paper. "My death warrant," she murmured, "signed by mine own hand." Then she placed the document beneath her pillow and crept quietly into bed.

She did not sleep during the remaining hours of the night; her mind remained full of activity; she lived again through the scenes of her past life. As regarded her future she made no prophecies, reasoning thus with herself: "Without Alden there will be for me no future, only a blank lapse of time." That he would forgive her, she did not for one moment dream. Had she not been living a lie? His faith in her would be forever shaken, and without faith his affection would be incomplete. She must reap as she had sown; she must bow her head to the whirlwind; it was her righteous punishment. A falsehood could never win for her the kingdom on this earth that she desired; she must build her hopes on a firmer foundation.

When the morning dawned she arose weak and languid, scarce able to leave her room. She crushed back the tears, and forcing her countenance into a semblance of repose she descended to the kitchen.

"Alden has been here," said her aunt, looking up from her work; "he stopped to leave thee these blossoms. He was on horseback, on his way to Ipswich; he will be gone two days. He is a kindly man to thus interest himself in these unfortunate old women."

"I saw him pass from my casement," said Dorothy listlessly, taking the flowers from her aunt's hand as she spoke, her heart giving a joyful bound of relief at the news of this respite. She had de-

cided that no one should hand Wentworth the confession save herself, and now fate had doled out to
her forty-eight hours in which to reconsider her
decision.

A remarkable change took place in Dorothy's demeanor; it was as if a prisoner condemned to die
had received the tidings of a new trial.  She smiled,
chatted, then walked with a song upon her lips
down the flower-bordered paths of the old-fash-
ioned garden.  A certain self-congratulation assailed her.  Had she not the means at hand to
debase herself?  Had she not of her own free will
yielded up all she valued?  Why begrudge her
these few hours of peace?  As if in mockery to the
sincerity of her atonement, she eagerly grasped at
this slight temporary delay.

All her light-heartedness and buoyancy of spirits
returned to her.  She seated herself beneath a
flowering fruit-tree, close to the old dial.  In the
darkness and silence of night the mysterious message brought by the beautiful dream visitor had
impressed itself upon her emotional nature with all
the distinctness of a command from above.  In
the light of day, amidst the charms of nature, the
vision became as other dreams that pass away, leav-

ing in its place but a faint shadow of its unreal presence.

"I have not done so very wrong," she thought; "I will keep the confession, and not tell him yet. I will think further upon it. I was alarmed at the dream last night. Why should I thus throw away my happiness?" As she argued thus, she walked down the box-bordered path.

When she neared the confines of the garden, she noticed a tall figure coming down the country road. It was the figure of a woman walking swiftly. Dorothy saw that it was Elizabeth Hubbard. The latter did not glance toward the girl in the garden path until immediately opposite her; then she veered round excitedly, as if compelled to do so by an impulse beyond her control.

"Well, Mistress Dorothy, a good-morning to thee." She paused, then continued mockingly: "So, forsooth, we are to have a bride after all at the new house on the outskirts. Dost thou know thy mind this time, or wilt thou give Salem another surprise?" As she spoke she looked sharply at Dorothy, a curious expression in her black, staring eyes.

"Yes, Elizabeth," said Dorothy simply, "I am

to be married; the time is but a short way off now."

"I wish thee luck; still, I ween Mr. Wentworth had better be in attendance on these great events of the day; he is ever negligent of his duties. Dost thou know he did not attend the three last trials of the witches? He spends his time with thee to the scandal of the ministers and magistrates."

Dorothy flushed angrily. "His attention to me is his affair and mine," she replied.

Elizabeth smiled. "I will not quarrel with thee. Hast thy aunt told thee of the wedding gift I am weaving for thee?"

"No; is it fine?" asked Dorothy eagerly.

"Ay, fine and strong. When thou art married I will give it thee. If thou dost not marry Alden Wentworth, then it shall not be thine."

"Perchance it is a great roll of linen?" queried Dorothy.

"Ha, ha!" laughed Elizabeth. "No, not linen; thou shalt know in time." She glanced craftily at Dorothy's puzzled countenance. "It is but just begun, though I work swiftly, and I protest no other gift like mine shalt thou receive among all the offerings of the dames of the town." She then passed on with her stately step, turning back her head once to smile.

Dorothy, leaning over the gate, looked after her until she disappeared from view. "Elizabeth is jealous," she thought. "She hates me; she would be in my place if she could." This idea, so suddenly suggested, appalled Dorothy. Having made her bargain of self-sacrifice she had not taken into account the possibility of another's filling her place.

She had pictured Wentworth alone and wretched, even as she herself would be alone and wretched. That he would ever yield himself to the charms of another was poison to the life of the partly formed resolve of confession. "She shall not have him; he is mine," she said aloud.

All the good impulses that had risen within her became dulled, stupefied, by this unexpected turn of affairs. She could renounce him, but she could not give him into the keeping of another; that was simply beyond all power of will she possessed. She remained in the position in which Elizabeth had left her for some time, looking with strained eyes down the winding road.

At last she turned and hastened back to the farthermost part of the garden. Beneath the roots

of a spreading shrub that grew near a sheltered
ledge the written confession was buried. After
having smoothed the earth above it, she stood a
moment irresolute. "It is written," she thought,
"and at some future day I will take it from its
place and tell him, but not now, not now."

The feeling that she had accomplished at least
one step in the right direction served to impress her
with the sense of a possible entrance at some future
time into the confidence of one to whom she owed
much. To be sure, the paper was but an inanimate
object, but she had written it with the right intention; that was certainly a good beginning.

# CHAPTER XII.

## THE MARRIAGE.

SWEETLY bloomed the wild roses along the way-side on that bright June morning long ago when Dorothy and Wentworth were married in the little Salem meeting-house. The atmosphere was redolent with the sweet scents of the early summer, the lilacs were in bloom, the foliage upon the trees was fresh and green. The harbor was bathed in sunlight, and far distant, where its waters joined the sea, it sparkled with the glitter of brilliant gold. Bees and butterflies darted through the air; and the birds fluttering near the little church blended their clear notes with the strains of the marriage hymn, the scarlet-crested songster mingling his lark-like tones with the sad cadence of some forest wanderer.

All the people of the settlement turned out to do honor to the wedding of the handsome, distinguished, popular Judge Wentworth. Some were present from interest, many from curiosity. The wedding was a welcome break in the midst of the terrible depression that lay like a mantle of death upon the spirits of the multitude. But a few days previous one of the professed witches had been executed on Gallows Hill, in the presence of most of those now watching stolidly the simple ceremony of the Puritan marriage.

Dorothy moved like a white spirit from another sphere, so emotionless, so passive did she seem. Her lovely head drooped like a lily on its stalk; her face was pale in the midst of the pretty bridal finery; her eyes were downcast, and the hands that clasped the psalm-book trembled slightly. Her voice was scarcely audible in the responses.

When she passed out into the brilliant light of the bright day, she shuddered even in the warmth of the sun, and when her neighbors pressed about her, and addressed her by her new name, Dorothy Wentworth, she listened eagerly, yet did not seem to understand its significance. She stood an instant upon the upper steps of the church porch, and glanced languidly over the heads of the people. Her hand rested tremblingly upon her husband's arm.

Suddenly a spasm of fear crossed her features—a visible contraction of the muscles of her mouth, a nervous closing of her lips. In that curious watching throng she had recognized one countenance, the handsome mocking face of Sir Grenville Lawson, his gorgeous apparel and great cavalier's hat making him most noticeable among his more somberly attired neighbors. She gazed upon him as if fascinated, her glance riveted upon his bold eyes—those eyes that compelled her attention by that mesmeric force that once had won her from her true allegiance. In her thoughts she had dreaded this possible encounter at some future time, but had put it aside with all its accompanying danger, and in desperation had taken the great risk.

There was an inscrutable expression upon the face of Sir Grenville as he watched her intently. Though his features remained passive, yet to one knowing him as Dorothy did there were manifest tokens of his more than common interest in the scene before him.

Involuntarily she drew nearer to Wentworth and caught his hand convulsively. As she did this, she heard a whisper in her ear, and turning beheld the dark countenance of Elizabeth close beside her.

"I do present all well wishes for a happy life to the bride," she said, bowing low as she spoke, and inclining her head mockingly. "That well-woven gift I promised thee shall be thine in good time."

"I thank thee, Elizabeth," said Dorothy, her white lips forming the words mechanically, her ears scarce hearing them.

"Dearest," said Wentworth in a whisper, watching the deathlike countenance of his bride, "this has been too much for thee; we will hasten to the farmhouse for the feast, and there thou canst rest."

"Yes, yes," she answered, "let us get away, and quickly."

So the bride and groom walked across the flowering meadows, followed by the invited guests, to partake of the collation spread in the best room of the farmhouse. When Dorothy reached the door of the house she looked back. Upon the brow of the hill she beheld Sir Grenville standing motionless, his figure outlined against the sky, his face turned toward her.

Wentworth's eyes followed the direction of her gaze. "'Tis that godless fellow from England," he said. "This is thrice he has been to the settlement; twice since thou hast been away. I know not what brings him hither, save, perchance, a morbid interest in the witch-trials. His silly fopperies do bemean a man; I scorn such empty pates."

A low, gasping sound issued from Dorothy's lips. "Alden, I am wearied." She tried to smile. " It was the heat of the meeting-house; I am not quite as strong as I was a year ago; let us go within the house."

So the friends and neighbors took part in the sober festivities, and in the cool of the pleasant evening Dorothy went to her new home, the fine house on the outskirts.

After Sir Grenville's fruitless attempt to recover his escaping prey, as related in a previous chapter, he took up his abode near the borders of the woods, confidently expecting that hunger and fear would eventually drive Dorothy forth from her hiding-place. He dismissed the two men whom he had employed to assist him in case she should prove fractious after hearing the disclosures he intended to make in regard to his previous marriage.

" Now mind, you fellows," he had said, " I have paid you well, and I give you added gold to keep your mouths shut."

" A sorry trick she played you," said one of the men, smirking.

"Hold your insolence!" cried Sir Grenville angrily. "How dare you discuss the affairs of your betters?" Then he hesitated and appeared to be considering deeply. "If I need you further I shall acquaint you with my wishes."

"Very well; we are always ready to earn a little gold; any business, so long as it pays," said one of the men eagerly.

"I am aware of that," said Grenville, eying the evil face before him contemptuously. "That is all for the present; when I need you I will send a message."

Sir Grenville's little plot had been a failure; still he could not leave Salem, but returned twice to the town to wait and watch. Like the moth that flutters round the decoying candle, he haunted the vicinity of his thwarted plans. She could not be dead, that he would not believe; fate would certainly play into his hands in time; he would be patient and wait. So by chance he met her once again standing in her dainty bridal dress upon the steps of the church porch.

As he watched her an intense anger took possession of him, an uncontrollable rage. She had escaped him, and by a way in which he could not follow; she was beyond his reach forever. If it had been possible to have taken revenge upon her then and there, to have crushed her, humiliated her, ruined her, he would have done so. But what would that avail him, he reasoned, now that she was married? No, he would let her suffer the agony and fear of his daily presence; he would thus torture her, make her life a spell of constant dread.

Being a keen judge of human nature, he appreciated fully the manner of man Wentworth represented. Grenville felt confident he knew nothing of the elopement escapade. His rigid puritanical code would have forbidden a union with one upon whom the finger of scandal could place its scathing mark. What her story had been, Sir Grenville could not conjecture. He gave her credit, however, for a greater subtlety than he had believed she possessed, knowing that she must have succeeded well in deceiving all parties. So Sir Grenville took up his abode in the village.

He passed the new house daily, often glancing toward the partly opened casement, from which a form would quickly retreat at his approach. Then he would smile wickedly to himself. "She fears me. Well, I have her in my power. The little bride most surely lives a life of torture; full well I know she has a sensitive nature. My presence is not so welcome, I trow, as when she sat beside me in the forest."

Sir Grenville conjectured truly when he described Dorothy's existence as torture. She knew no rest, day or night. The appalling knowledge of his near presence, the constant dread of disclosure, the intuitive perception that he had undertaken some scheme of revenge, made every hour a wretched ordeal. She comprehended her husband thoroughly.

He was a man of great uprightness and unstained honor. Perhaps in these days he would be considered narrow and prejudiced; that, however, was not the fault of his mind, but caused rather by his creed and environments. He had a code of morality that allowed of no diverging; it was a straight line without softening curves. Yet he was unsuspicious, loving, and tender, capable of a great and enduring affection.

The horrors of the witchcraft delusion were increasing. A month had passed since Dorothy's marriage; it was now approaching the latter part of July.

On the 19th of July five condemned witches, after

a mere mockery of a trial, had been executed. These victims were Sarah Good, Sarah Wildes, Elizabeth How, Rebecca Nurse, and Susanna Martin. Their accusers were the afflicted girls, prominent amongst whom figured Elizabeth.

These trials were attended by most astonishing proceedings. The accused had no council to plead their cause; they simply were called upon to answer a number of absurd and conflicting questions. These trials were constantly interrupted by fearful performances executed by the five cold-blooded girls, who, we trust, were ignorant of the great evil they were doing, and in which they apparently gloried.

Susanna Martin stands out prominently against the dark background of this dread period. She was a widow living alone. Having, it is presumed, incurred the enmity of the magic circle, she was arrested on a charge of witchcraft and thrown into prison. When brought to her trial before the magistrates and many prominent personages, she stood her ground defiantly, and answered in a fearless manner. When she was brought before the judges for the final verdict, the witnesses immediately went into fits. One of them on recovering threw her glove at the undaunted woman; another declared that she was choking her; the rest were struck dumb, their tongues refusing to move.

"Of a certainty she is a witch," cried the learned judge.

Susanna laughed, saying such folly was beyond her.

"Is it folly to see these children hurt?"

"I never hurt man, woman, or child," she answered.

At this one of the girls shrieked, "She is hurting me now! I am in torment!" So the farce went on, and the courageous woman met her fate on Gallows Hill.

The girls now began to have all honors conferred upon them, being treated with the greatest respect and consideration. Their words were listened to as though they possessed the power of the oracles of old. They went from village to village, accompanied by an escort, ferreting out witches. Woe be to the one that incurred their displeasure by expressing doubt of the purity of their motives!

This acuteness displayed in detecting a witch was considered a peculiar gift, conferred by Providence upon these now all-powerful girls. They became the instruments, as it were, to cleanse the earth of this foul plague-spot. When they "cried out," as it was called, upon a suspected person, the unfortunate individual was summarily dispatched to the prison to await trial on their evidence.

It seems hardly possible, looking backward through the dim mists of years, that such an ignorant delusion should have gained the prominence it did in an enlightened and God-fearing community. Yet great and undoubtedly sincere men authorized the law to take its course, the legislature making provision for all necessary expenses incurred for the trials of the accused witches.

Dorothy took no part in the general consternation. She crouched upon her knees upon the floor when the cart containing the condemned passed the windows of her house, not daring to look forth.

" God pity them, God pity them!" she moaned. " O Goody, Goody!" And she placed her fingers to her ears to still the cries and execrations that arose upon the air from the jeering crowds that followed. She was in a condition bordering upon frenzy; she realized that she would succumb to a serious bodily ailment did her tortured mind not soon find relief. She was suffering acutely from this unnatural condition one morning while standing

in the diminutive garden that lay between tehh ouse
and the road.

Wentworth had just bade her farewell, as he expected to be absent for the day.  He was going to
the presiding judges, to endeavor to use his influence in preventing the contemplated arrest of a
lady, high in social position and of great goodness
and purity, one upon whom the avenging circle had
cast its evil eye.  He was in much distress of mind
when he took his departure, and did not look back,
as was his wont, but walked hurriedly in the direction of the abode of Mr. Parris.

Dorothy watched him out of sight, scarce seeing .
him for the mist of tears that gathered in her eyes.
"If he knew!  Oh, if he knew!  Yet could the
misery of that knowledge and his contempt be
greater than what I suffer now?"  She turned
wearily aside and stooped over some beds of simple
flowers, touching them tenderly and inhaling their
sweet fragrance.  She was not aware, in her absorption, of the approach of a stranger, till a shadow fell
across the flower-bed.  She turned quickly, to encounter Sir Grenville's mocking gaze.

"Sir Grenville," she gasped, placing her hand to
her side and stepping backward, "what dost thou

seek?  Hast thou not injured me enough?  Must thou remain to look upon thy work?"

"Dorothy," he said, and the old sweet seductiveness was audible in his voice, "think not so evil of me.  You have escaped me, but I am not wholly depraved.  I shall not seek revenge in the way that you seem to fear: I shall never tell your husband.  What would that profit me, save to incur your hatred?  No, no, I work from deeper motives."

"What wilt thou do, then?  What can I do that will send thee from this place, that I may see thee no more?  Tell me, tell me!"

Sir Grenville laughed softly.  "I shall stay here, my fair pupil; it is my present wish.  And another reason chains me to this spot: the fascination of your presence has not been dispelled as yet.  I have not forgotten you, Dorothy, and our little love idyl in yonder forest, while the good and learned judge in all innocence deemed you dreaming of him, perchance.  Dost think six months a lifetime and my memory defective?"

She flushed painfully at these words.  "I can acquaint my husband myself; then thou canst have no power over me."

"Yes, but you will not.  You have learned to

know the man as I read him when I first beheld
him by your side.   Rouse him not, Dorothy ; light
not the flames of a temperament such as his, or the
destiny that lies before you as his wife I dare not
picture."

She shuddered, and turned piteously upon him.
" For the affection thou once professed for me, when
I believed thy words," he winced at this speech,
" have pity on me, molest me no further!   Canst
thou not see the fear of thy presence is killing me?
Yes, killing me!   At times I wish that death might
come, that I might find rest in yonder churchyard,
if such a false heart as mine can find rest anywhere."
She passed her hand across her brow, pushing back
the heavy curls of hair.   He noticed how thin her
hand was, how clearly the blue veins showed beneath the skin.

" I shall not molest you—simply pass your house
occasionally.   That will not cause suspicion to rest
upon you.   I shall never seek to recognize you in
public.   Yet for the trick you played me. I must
seek a little quiet revenge, by remaining near the
shy bird that but for a silly, mawkish touch of feeling I had so nearly snared.   Bah," he continued
angrily, " what a fool I was, to let sentiment over-

rule me! But for that weakness you would be with me now beyond the seas, away from these soured old Puritans, who make life a curse with their narrow bigotry."

"Hast thou no heart?" she cried. "Canst thou look upon my wretchedness and thus mock me?"

"Once you made my happiness," he answered passionately. "Can I forget so soon? I was as capable of loving you as the stern, dark-browed man you have chosen; yes, and a millionfold more, for I loved you in spite of all. He loves you as the one perfect woman he has chosen, the flawless object he has built his hopes upon; I loved you with your faults."

"Hush, hush!" she said. "Thou shalt not speak to me thus; I must not hear thy words."

"You shall hear them," he answered fiercely. "Then, if you possess the courage, seek your husband and tell him all."

"Wilt thou not leave me," she pleaded, "ere I fall at thy feet? This trouble has made me weak. Have mercy!"

"I will go; yet remember, I leave not Salem. In the dark watches of the night, when no sleep comes, listen: you will hear my steps without your door.

I shall not leave you, Dorothy; there is a bond between us, a bond so strong that no power can break it, save the courage which shall unseal your lips."

"Or death," she said solemnly.

"I ween that e'en when death comes, no strength would cause you to tell your husband. Tell me," he continued curiously, "what causes this morbid fear of him?"

"Shall I tell thee, Sir Grenville?" She drew closer to him, speaking in a hoarse whisper. "It is because I fear to lose him; it is because I love him: in this lies both my happiness and my misery. Thou by thy deceit hast proved to me the cruelty of one man, and hast also opened mine eyes to the honor and goodness of another, and so I have turned to him forever." A little sigh escaped her at these words; she held out both hands beseechingly. "Thou saidst once thou didst have affection for me; for its sake leave me in peace; I ask no more of thee."

An incredulous expression passed over her companion's face; he turned abruptly from her. "Your words belie the substance of your speech," he said. "If it were love of him, you would not fear. Does not the Good Book say, 'Perfect love casteth out fear'?"  He spoke no further, but left her abruptly. As he reached the summit of the hill he met old Martha coming laboriously up the steep ascent to visit her niece.

Martha turned in the road and looked disapprovingly after the gayly attired worldling.  "Foolish bedizened follower of this earth and its vanities," she muttered, "what canst thou seek in this quiet spot?"

As if by some mysterious means he interpreted her thoughts, and turned in the narrow foot-path, removing his hat and bowing deferentially.  "Good-morning to you, worthy dame," he said.

Martha vouchsafed no reply; holding her head stiffly, she passed on, but heard his laugh following her as she did so, echoing until it died in the distance with a gay, rollicking sound.

# CHAPTER XIII.



WHEN Wentworth returned to his home at evening, grief and disappointment were apparent in his manner. "I have availed nothing," he said. "Mr. Parris is deeply impressed with the necessity of dealing summarily with this most appalling situation. Doubtless in much he is correct, yet I fear me in this case he makes a grave mistake."

Dorothy listened in silence. "Have they arrested this good woman?" finally she said.

"To-night they make the arrest. The afflicted children do affirm that she hath hurt them several times. They say she hath been in the forest at that terrible meeting which takes place at midnight between the imps of Satan and the witches, when they do dance together on the greensward."

Dorothy listened attentively, leaning forward in her chair.

"I argued and plead with the ministers and

magistrates that they investigate further into the matter, but all to no purpose."

Dorothy left her seat, and coming slowly toward her husband looked closely into his face, then placed her hand upon his shoulder.

He noticed, with misgivings at his heart, how weak and faltering were her steps, how her breath came in short gasps, and how thin and pale her sweet face was growing. "I am fearful for thee, dearest," he said tenderly, drawing her closely toward him; "each day thou growest more frail. Am I absent too much? Perchance thou art lonely all day alone. This most wretched business has absorbed my time. Truly, our people are bereft of all peace of mind; Satan is busy amongst us."

"Alden," she said solemnly, "I think not on my bodily condition; it is my mind that is diseased, and through that ailment my body suffers." She glanced wistfully into his clouded face.

"My own," he said, "what troubles thee? Tell me; perchance I can help thee. Am I not thy husband and thy best friend? Is it thine household cares that are too great for thee?"

She clung to him convulsively, dry sobs shaking her slender form as the wind shakes the reeds in the meadows. She essayed to speak, but no sound came from her parched lips.

"Tell me not," he said soothingly, "if it is so hard for thee. I can conjecture it is of thy health. I shall send for Dr. Griggs to see thee to-day. Fret not, it is not serious. This witchcraft trouble has shaken thy nerves."

"No, no," she said excitedly, drawing away from his clasp, "I will see no doctor; they can do nothing for me." Then, lowering her voice, she continued, as if speaking to herself, "Perhaps God will take me to Himself. He knows all, and He has promised forgiveness."

"Tell me, Dorothy, what is it that troubles thee?" She had placed her hands before her face; he drew them down and held them forcibly in his strong clasp. "It is my right. What is this secret? Surely thou canst trust me."

A convulsive tremor passed over her; her head drooped. "Thou art right," she said finally, "it is —it is—my health; I fear—I fear to leave thee," she faltered. Another strand in the web was tightened; the poor victim's struggles became weaker.

"It is, then, as I conjectured; the doctor will give thee some soothing draught. All will be right again; if not, we will go to Boston for change.  I will endeavor to procure time."

"No, no," she said vehemently.  "I care not to go to Boston."

He was puzzled at her incomprehensible behavior, but attributed it to her weakened condition.

That night, when all was still, Dorothy heard the steps outside her window upon the garden path. Her husband was asleep; she distinguished his regular breathing as it rose and fell upon the quiet of the room.  She leaned over him; a gleam reflected from the patch of moonlight upon the floor fell across his face.  She waited an instant, watching him, then rose cautiously, and going to the window looked out through the narrow panes of the casement.  She heard the echoing steps, but saw no one.

Suddenly a tall figure emerged from beneath a drooping willow.  It was Grenville.  He was looking toward her window; the moonbeams fell across his face, bringing his features into clear relief.

"Father in heaven," she murmured, "he has no pity!"  She fell upon her knees by the window. "Have mercy, O Heavenly One, have mercy!" She clasped her hands and bowed her head above them.   Then, as.if impelled by some gigantic force, she trembled as one in mortal terror, rose from her kneeling position, dressed hastily, and noiselessly descended the stairs and went out into the quiet garden.   The watching figure came forward and joined her.

"Away from me!" she said fiercely.   "Away, come not nigh me!   I can live my life no longer; I go to make restitution."

Grenville started back, appalled.   Was she seeking self-destruction, or was she demented?   He did not speak, awed into silence.

She passed him swiftly, her light step making no sound.   She fled through the garden gate, thence down the country road, which was brilliantly illuminated by the white light of the full moon.   Sir Grenville followed warily, keeping her form in sight. She never paused, but straight as the bird flies, made her way to the garden that lay back of the Holden farm, the dear old garden that she had tended so faithfully in the happy days now past— happy, though she had suspected it not.   She hastened to the flowering shrub that grew in the secluded corner, and there she paused.   That she was demented, Sir Grenville did not doubt.

He remained motionless, watching her closely. She seized a stick, and with its assistance and that of her hands commenced to dig rapidly in the earth. Presently she drew forth a small box from the ground, the odor of the damp clay rising upon the atmosphere as she did so. She was speaking to herself, but Grenville stood at too great distance to distinguish the words. She brushed the clinging dirt from the box and turned to retrace her steps.

By slow degrees Sir Grenville reached the conclusion that, after all, there might possibly be a motive in this midnight journey, and that his reasoning had been at fault in considering her mind diseased.

When she reached the road he joined her, and grasped her arm. "What is the meaning of this?" he demanded, drawing her away from the bright highway to the shade of some vines that climbed over a blighted tree near the wayside.

"Hast thou followed me?" she said desperately. "Can I never escape thee?"

"In one way, and one only."

"Then I have found the way," she cried triumphantly. "It is here, in this box; it contains my death-warrant, yet it frees me from thee."

"What does that box contain?" he said.

"My confession, which my husband shall see when the morning dawns. Alas! for me there shall dawn no morning, only a long, long night."

"Hast thou the courage?" he said softly.

"Why ask me that question? Have the poor wretches the courage to give up their lives on the hill yonder? It is their fate; this is mine, and thou canst take this thought to thyself, that thou hast made me what I am."

"No, no, Dorothy, no, no," he said; "say not that."

"I shall say it; it is the truth. Was I not an innocent child when I first met thee? What am I now? A terrified, cowed creature, with no will, no balance, starting at every sound, the prey of mine accusing conscience, living a life of deceit, striving to win my happiness with a lie."

He drew nearer to her. His face was in shadow; she could not distinguish the expression of his features. The clouds were drifting across the moon, and a dull, somber glow had spread itself upon the fields and distant hills. No sound, save the far-off booming of the waves, broke the tense stillness. "There is a way out of all this misery," he said. "Shall I not speak it?"

"There is none," she murmured brokenly. "Oft have I thought, yet ever have I returned to the starting-point."

"There is a way," he said quickly. "Come with me; leave this hated spot, where all is fraught with direst danger. Not alone from the wrath of your husband, not alone from my passing steps at midnight, yet still another source—from the rage of one who hates you, who seeks to harm you—yes, worse than harm—who seeks your life, who holds it even now within her bloodthirsty hand." He had spoken loudly; he paused, his chest heaving with the force of his words.

She recoiled from him. "And thou, thou," she cried, "who once professed a true, deep love for me, now seekst my destruction." She rushed by him to the center of the road, where she stopped irresolute, swaying backward and forward.

He did not follow her; he had expected no different result from his speech. He had given her food for thought, however. That was sufficient for the present.

She started abruptly, not once looking backward, flying swiftly onward. When she reached the little graveyard on the hill near the meeting-house she paused, and gazed over the wooden paling upon the quiet spot. "How calm is their rest!" she said aloud. "Would that I were sleeping with them. Had they ever sorrows such as mine? Do they lie there so still, with secrets hidden in their hearts? I ween not, else they would not sleep so peacefully." She rested for a few minutes longer, her thoughts filled with a vague dreaminess.

The realities of her position departed from her. In truth she saw before her but the last earthly homes of the dead—humble, narrow homes; but in a vision she caught glimpses of the beautiful possibilities of a life eternal, reaching far above and beyond those lowly graves, where all would be made right, and an everlasting peace would fill her immortal soul. She was startled from her reverie by a clear, deep voice at her side, a voice she remembered only too well. She turned quickly, to behold Elizabeth standing near her.

"So thou hast been on thy midnight ride." scoffed Elizabeth, "to the forest. Do thy imps dance gayly on such a moonlight night as this? I ween thou hast been busy, Mistress Dorothy."

"Thou art crazed, Elizabeth. What know I of imps and midnight rides? I might as well accuse thee of such uncanny practices. Wherefore art thou abroad this hour?"

"I am about my business. I saw thee alight from thy charger even at this churchyard, and when thou didst alight the moon hid her face. I heard thee mutter in strange words."

"Go thy way," cried Dorothy angrily. "I am no more a witch than thou art. Thou wilt find it no small matter to accuse the wife of Judge Wentworth. Dorothy Grey would no doubt have fallen an easier victim. I am not afraid of thee, I scorn thee."

At this Elizabeth drew nearer, shaking her finger menacingly, and trembling with anger. "Thou shalt see who has the greatest influence in Salem, I or Judge Wentworth. It were better for thee to bridle thy speech."

"I defy a girl who has no more heart than thou hast. I can see through thy efforts: thou wouldst be in my place. I defy thee, I say."

Elizabeth bent above the defiant girl in the attitude of an eagle about to swoop upon its prey, then, drawing away from her a few paces, she spoke in tones of concentrated passion. "I hate thee, and thou shalt repent thy words. Thou art a witch. Even now the black man is by thy side; thy imps are dancing among the graves—they are near thee to do thy bidding."

Dorothy laughed hysterically. "Cease thy foolish raving! I fear thee not. My husband is all-powerful against thee. So long as I hold his love and trust I am safe." Her last words suddenly recalled her to a realization of the horror of her position. "His love and trust!" Like a bolt from a clear sky these words struck home. She cowered before the wrath of this merciless fiend. "Well," she said helplessly, "if thou dost accuse me, what of it? I shall then be at peace in a land whither thou canst not follow to torment me."

This strange answer nonplused Elizabeth. She did not reply immediately; then, as though struggling to assert again the baleful influence she saw was bewildering Dorothy, she clutched her arm and said, "What hast thou in that box thou claspest in thy hand? I wot it contains love philters and charms—perchance some noisome herbs and drugs that do assist thee in thy evil work."

"No, Elizabeth, no," she answered sadly. "Would that it did contain some spell to dull my conscience, or to blind the eyes of one that believes in me. Alas! it is not so. What it holds is my secret, and one other's."

"I shall not force it from thee, fear not. I wish no acquaintance with the secrets of thy wicked craft."

"It would avail thee little. Yet see," she pointed, as she spoke, toward the east, "it is the dawn; the morning will soon be here. I must away." She turned and glanced timidly into the malicious face regarding her. "Thou wilt not harm me, thou wilt not, for the sake of our girlhood's friendship."

"I am no friend of thine. I shall do the work I have set my hands to do. I have a mission—I shall fulfill it." The tones were cold and calm.

Dorothy turned from her and wrung her hands. "Then I leave thee; I can ask no more." She sped hastily up the street in the direction of her home.

After Elizabeth was left alone, she hesitated some minutes before leaving the lonely spot. She appeared to be thinking deeply. She rested upon the wooden paling and looked gloomily over the graveyard. Then she descended the hill, going toward the north of the village. As she passed the clump of vines beneath which Dorothy and Sir

Grenville had been conversing she thought she heard a rustling of the foliage. She was not mistaken; her sharp eyes soon discovered a stalwart figure coming cautiously forward, though endeavoring to keep as near as possible to the shelter of the hedge. She recognized him, however, as the English lord now domiciled at the inn in the village. She did not address him, but passed on.

When Dorothy, frightened, distracted, hounded, reached the shelter of her room, she found all as she had left it. Her husband was sleeping quietly; her absence had not been discovered. She seated herself on the chair by the bedside, the box upon her lap. She was not terrified, only baffled, at this new link in the chain. Even if she were to be arrested, which in her position as the wife of the popular judge she very much doubted, her suffering could not be greater than that she now endured. The power of her grief did not lie in this reflection; ah, no, but in the knowledge that her life was as a deep pool of deceit, from which there was but one means of extricating herself, and that means she had not the courage to use.

She leaned over her husband, looking tenderly down upon him, then kissed him gently. He stirred in his sleep but did not awake. "If he knew, if he knew!" she murmured. "Ah, that I had told him that day when he found me weeping at my spinning-wheel! He might have forgiven me then; now—now—it is too late."

The faint glow of the early morning stole in through the lattice; the birds began to twitter faintly in the trees near the house; the distant sound of the cattle lowing echoed across the village street; a faint pink tinge crept furtively around the room, chasing the gray light before it. The articles of furniture became more clearly outlined, then the pink glow deepened into red and stole over the sleeping man and the watching woman.

Dorothy knew that the sun had risen, and the task she had set herself must be performed before another hour had passed. She clenched her small hands tightly. "Then I can go home," she murmured. "Perhaps Aunt Martha will take me in. It will only be for a little while; I shall not trouble any one very long."

Suddenly she started; her husband was speaking in his sleep. She listened intently, placing her ear close to his face. A spasm of agony crossed her features as she heard and understood his words.

"Dorothy," he said, "Dorothy, my own!" He was dreaming of her.

Such inexpressible affection was in his voice that she rose to her feet as if struck. "God help me, I cannot tell him, I cannot." A dimness came over her sight; she shook as with a chill, though the summer morning was warm. She advanced to the window and looked over the fields toward the sea. Then going softly up the garret stairs, she placed the confession in an oaken chest that contained some old-time treasures. She leaned her head upon the chest after securely locking it, and burst into passionate tears.

This in her overwrought condition was well, for it relieved the terrible mental strain under which she had been laboring. She then arose, and walked to the small garret window set in the gambrel roof, and gazed out upon the spreading landscape growing gradually from out the mistiness of night to the full glory of a brilliant morning. She was scarce appreciative of the beauties of nature encompassed in the fair rural scene before her.

A dread apprehension had taken possession of her: the fear that some unknown agency outside her will had for its wretched mission the subjugation of her powers. Though she could see and reason aright, nevermore, she believed, would she possess the courage to reveal the misery within her. Perhaps a witch now lying in her cell condemned to die was dealing her this deadly harm, sending her agents forth on this diabolical mission, or else torturing the puppet she had fashioned in the shape of her victim. This was a not unusual conclusion for Dorothy to have reached, considering that witchcraft was deemed responsible for nearly all the ills that afflicted mankind.

# CHAPTER XIV.



THE colony of Salem had reached a pitch of extreme terror and excitement; the people were floundering in a tempestuous sea of doubt and apprehension. That the dreaded circle might possibly be dissembling apparently never occurred to the deluded populace, and the girls were allowed to proceed upon their own wicked way. · They were supposed to be under supernatural guidance and ' fulfilling their ordained mission; consequently they were objects of awe and respect. This attention naturally caused them to become bold and unscrupulous. From accusing individuals in lowly positions and but little considered in the community, they now aimed their deadly shafts at saintly persons of high standing.

Mr. Parris had from the beginning of the trouble been most vehement in his denunciation of the witches. He had helped to fan the devastating

flames that were raging fiercely over the quiet repose of this little New World hamlet.

A secret session was called one afternoon, in the
study at the manse.   Mr. Parris presided, and many
learned men were present.   Mr. Wentworth was
absent; in fact, he had not been apprised of the
meeting.   The stern-visaged men sat in solemn
rows around a long table in the center of the apartment.   Upon the table were heaped many books
and documents.

Elizabeth Hubbard, erect, watchful, her great
eyes, like coals of fire, roving restlessly over the
faces before her, stood at one end of the table, one
hand upon a book, the other resting upon the back
of a chair.   The grave countenances of the men
were turned respectfully upon her as they listened
with the closest attention to the fantastic utterances
that fell from her lips.

" Now sayest thou truly, Elizabeth?  Can it be possible that such dread news must be heralded by thee?"

It was Mr. Parris who spoke, his voice low and
repressed.   He turned to the assemblage.   " Hast
listened well to these awful disclosures? "

All were silent; their faces were troubled; they
shook their heads solemnly.

"Tell us what else thou wast compelled to witness; conceal naught for the sake of any affection or humanity. It is thy duty; proceed."

"When I did look upon her, she did cower as though seized with a great fear. She held in her hand a box; I smelt the damp odor of clay issue from it. Doubtless she had dug it with the aid of her attendants, who accompanied her from the graves in the churchyard. I did accuse her to her face. I was strong with righteousness, I had no fear. She flaunted me, saying she was safe, no harm could reach one in her position."

"What else, what else?" said the frightened company, drawing nearer to each other and listening with bated breath and credulous countenances.

"When she did speak thus I heard laughs come from the hollows in the graves, and strange forms rose into the air and circled about my head. She then did bid me do my worst, and vanished from my sight, whether up into the air or down into the earth I know not, but the place where she was standing became vacant. Then I heard the fluttering of wings, lights danced upon the grass, and a great cry came out of the forest toward the north."

"Horrible, horrible!" said the company. They

looked askance over their shoulders, then shuddered as they placed their heads closer together.

"Surely she has signed a bond with the powers of darkness," said Mr. Parris in a deep voice.

"Yet let us investigate further into this matter," said one. "What wast thou doing at that hour upon the highway?"

"I sleep but little," said Elizabeth, eying her interlocutor malevolently. "I seek ever for proof to cleanse the earth of this dread scourge. Behold, I have been successful: Dorothy Wentworth is of a surety the greatest witch amongst us."

"She is," cried Mr. Parris with decision, "she is. She shall be dealt with as have been all the rest. No youth or beauty or position shall avail her now. Verily Satan hath chosen a fine instrument for his designs."

"Softly, softly," said the voice of the cautious one; "be not rash. Alden Wentworth is a power in the village."

"He possesses no power great enough to shield one who is accused," answered Mr. Parris, "and who is doubtless guilty."

"Let me warn Wentworth. Spring not this appalling revelation upon him."

"Not so; he will aid her to escape.    I shall procure more testimony, then in a few days I shall issue
the warrant for her arrest."    It was the voice of the
presiding judge who spoke.    No one gainsaid the
wisdom of his decision.    So the meeting dispersed
in silence and gloom, the worthy judges remaining
huddled together for some time longer in the study.

They examined carefully the different phases of
this most serious case, and twisted it this way and
that way, always arriving at the same conclusion.
She was a witch; for the good of mankind she must
be immediately dealt with and punished.

"Know you not," cried Mr. Parris, "that ye do
expose your families to a fearful risk in allowing
these fiends to live?    The extent of their power for
evil is limitless."

Elizabeth went her way with triumph depicted
upon her sinister countenance.    After leaving the
manse, she wandered toward the seashore, where
she often sat for hours brooding gloomily.    It had
been her daily habit for months; none questioned
it.    Had she not been set apart for a sacred work?
Her eccentricities were but accounted outward em-
blems of her incomprehensible spiritual powers.

She remained long brooding in the shadow of a

great bowlder that shielded her from the curious gaze of any chance passer-by.   Looking back upon the terrible fatalities committed by these misguided girls, it were no doubt charitable to consider them demented, or as being themselves deluded.   Yet in many of their accusations there appears to have been a perfectly conducted plan, as if they worked from well-defined motives.   At any rate, they succeeded in deceiving the wisest minds of the times.

After some minutes of thoughtfulness, Elizabeth laid her head back against a clump of seaweeds that had collected in a nook near her, and fell asleep. She was awakened by the sound of voices—harsh men's voices.   They were evidently disputing.   She did not speak or move, but remained listening intently.

"You kept back half the gold that rightfully was mine; were it not for the wholesome dread I have of Sir Grenville, I would make him pay well for the silence we keep."

The other voice responded by a coarse laugh. "I ween the pretty little Puritan was a schemer, after all.   To think that she should hoodwink our master, and then catch the worthy young judge! Gad, she is a smart one!"

" Didst see her face well the night she played the
sorry trick upon him?" asked the first speaker.

" Ay, well, in the light of the lantern they carried
on the pommel of the saddle; she had the sweetest
face I ever saw.  When I beheld her yestereve on
the village street, her hand on the arm of the stiffnecked Puritan she married, I was well-nigh shocked,
she looked so pale and wan."

Elizabeth lifted her head, a lurid glow over-
spreading her features, the light of a new thought
creeping into her somber eyes.  A full comprehension of the conversation she was listening to gradually forced itself upon her.  She eagerly gathered
together, link by link, Dorothy's failing health, her
strange words the night they met by the graveyard,
Sir Grenville skulking by the wayside under the
shelter of the vines.

For some moments the voices remained silent,
then one spoke defiantly : " I do not fear Sir Grenville.  I shall go to him and buy my silence.  It is
worth something to him ; if he fails me, I shall seek
the gentle, saintly Mistress Wentworth.  I wot she
never told of her elopement escapade : she would
be hounded from the place.  These saints of the
earth, as they do consider themselves, have no toler-
ance for a foolish deed."

"That would be cruel, mate," said the other, who was evidently made of more gentle fiber than his companion. "Try the master; if he fails, give it up. Say, now, do you presume he caught the pretty bird in the woods that night nigh Boston town, or did she escape him?"

"She escaped him: can you not remember his rage and his curses? I cannot say what the outcome of it all was; I know he lingered near the woods for days. I would I knew why she left him, what he told her, and why he engaged us to wait in hiding, bidding us gag her if need be, should she prove rebellious. What became of her? Did she go to England? And if so, how did she return to Salem?"

"Let us give up the riddle and go, while the fire is hot within us, and demand hush-money from the gay milord."

"Ay, the chance is worth trying."

As the two men arose Elizabeth stepped out from behind the rock which had concealed her presence, and stood before them.

"I have heard whereof ye have spoken," she said calmly; "it is of great moment to me. Seek not Sir Grenville Lawson, rather seek me; I will pay thee well for information on this subject."

"Truly we are poor," replied one of the men, "and would have pay. You must know, however, that to us you are a stranger; we can run no risks."

"I am a stranger: what of that?" She stepped closer to them, her bold glance compelling their attention. "Is my gold not as capable of use as that English lord's ye have served?"

"Yes, truly, but we fear him, and are indebted to him greatly."

"Do not bandy words with me," she said impatiently; "name your price. I construe thou hast no great affection for thy taskmaster; leastways, I judged so by thy words."

"You speak truth there," they said. Then finally the bolder of the two spoke.

"If you can procure for us a right goodly sum, you shall be as wise to-morrow as we are to-day."

"I shall have the money; I shall be here to-morrow at this time. Remember, fail me not."

"You will not use the story to the discredit of sweet Mistress Wentworth? If so, I swear I will not tell it," said the more gentle of the two.

"Hold your prating, fellow," cried the hardened one. "We need the gold; this is no time for silly sentiment."

"A wise and cautious sentence," interrupted Elizabeth with a bitter laugh. "This is no case, I tell thee, for sentiment. Nevertheless, it is a good thing to see heart in one where it is so unexpected."

"She was so fair and young and innocent," said the fellow.

"Thou art a fool!" cried Elizabeth angrily. "When one is young, perchance fair, should that cover sin? I tell thee, when one is old and ill-favored, none show mercy. I show mercy to none."

"She was not sinful," said the fellow stubbornly. "I believe no ill of her."

"Silence! Know ye who I am?" They started at her question. "I am Elizabeth Hubbard of the accusing circle."

The men drew hurriedly apart from her, almost tripping each other in their haste. "Ah, I have alarmed ye! Well, calm yourselves: I shall do ye no harm; the star of witchcraft is not on your foreheads, your wickedness is too apparent." She laughed sarcastically, then turned from them, glancing sidewise upon them as she retreated, regarding them sternly. "Fail me not; I shall be here.

Spare no details of the story; I shall know if there be a falsehood in your speech."

On the following day Elizabeth heard the account of the disastrous journey, and heard it correctly save in one particular—the men not knowing of a certainty whether Dorothy had been recaptured or no.

One might imagine that an evil genius was in waiting upon the will of this demented creature, so aptly and concisely did all the pieces of her puzzle fit. She now had at her command not only the means to drag her rival from her high position, but also to debase her in the eyes of her husband. This latter secret she gloated over with the glee of a miser gloating over his treasures, for truly it was the most formidable weapon in her armory.

The reverend Mr. Parris spared neither time nor pains in procuring witnesses and evidence against Dorothy. This was not a difficult task at a time when the slightest individual peculiarity might be distorted into deeds of witchcraft, and seized upon eagerly by the terrified and credulous people. Mr. Parris was a man of narrow instincts, and evidently considered himself working in the light of godliness. That he was intentionally wicked or cruel, history does not assert; he was only zealous in a mistaken cause. He was not by any means alone in his career of ferreting out the witches; he had helpers among his brother clergymen, and the name of Cotton Mather figures conspicuously in the narratives devoted to those distressing days.

The wretched girls, intoxicated by the attentions conferred upon them by men of such renown, performed daily their ridiculous pranks for their edification, the wise sages in the meanwhile looking solemnly on, wagging their heads and saying, " Of a certainty these poor girls are bewitched; it behooves us to hang the witches."

One of the most heinous crimes Dorothy had committed was her persistency in remaining absent from the meetings on the Lord's Day.

Elizabeth and the rest of her companions asserted that she dared not enter the church, she dared not remain in the presence of good people; that Satan had claimed her for his own, and if she placed her foot upon the threshold of the holy spot she would emit flames of fire from her mouth.

All this was drunk in greedily, with shudderings at the horrible condition of this lost soul amongst them. It was but too true that Dorothy had not attended any of the church services for some weeks. This was partly owing to her enfeebled state of health, but more particularly to a morbid dread of adding to the great weight of deceit which already burdened her conscience. It was absolute torture to sit in her accustomed place, the pew reserved for the wives of the deacons. In those days this was no mean honor. She felt herself humiliated and crushed, that thus she sat raised high in dignity above them all, when had she her just merits she would stand without the meeting-house door, perhaps, excommunicated.

The rigid code of morals of those days would have pronounced a weighty sentence upon even lighter misdeeds than Dorothy's. The almost sacred position held by the clergy of Puritan New England forbade the slightest touch of scandal or gossip smirching the name of the minister's wife, without the most penetrating investigation, and this rigid compliance extended in a great degree to the wives of the deacons. It appalled her when she considered that by her example she was expected to teach others the narrow path of righteousness, when in reality she looked upon herself as a miserable castaway.

In spite of Alden's persuasions, and much to his distress, she obstinately remained at home.  For some time past Wentworth had been uneasy in regard to Dorothy;  he did not understand her strange moods, her perverse broodings, her forced smiles and sudden bursts of tears.  Once indeed the suspicion crossed his mind, engendered by the jeering words of Elizabeth, that Dorothy was bewitched, or—he rejected this latter suggestion with horror—in league with some restless spirit of the air.

One night they were sitting silently in Wentworth's study;  he was writing, and she had been sewing, but had dropped her work.  Her hands were folded over it in her lap, her eyes fixed upon vacancy.  No sound was heard, except the hurried scratching of the quill across the paper.  Now and then the boughs of the trees near the house would brush back and forth across the window-panes with a noise resembling the rustling of the garments of some mysterious visitor.  The hour was late, it was drawing close to midnight.

Wentworth was preparing a paper to read before the magistrates, counseling deeper investigation into the testimony advanced by the reckless and blood-thirsty circle.  Further than advocating such measures he dared not go; living in the age in which he did, it would not have been possible for him to have discredited entirely the supernatural workings of witchcraft. He believed in its existence and was in a measure under its influence, but he did not believe in the power of a chosen few to locate the witches.

Suddenly Dorothy bent her head forward and inclined her ear in the attitude of intent listening. Presently she stood upright; her husband was too busily occupied to notice her movements. She took a few steps, then paused and held up her slender forefinger. Above the sound of the rapid motion of the pen and the swaying of the boughs against the windows came yet another vibration upon the stillness of the night.

Dorothy's face was in shadow; she stood without the circle of light thrown from the candle that rested upon the writing-desk. She turned abruptly, and dropping her extended hand grasped her husband's arm.

"The footsteps," she cried hoarsely, "the footsteps! They are passing, they are taking me from thee, my husband! Save me—save me—thou canst —oh, thou canst!"

Wentworth turned impetuously and caught her in his arms. He held her closely to him, and kissed her passionately. "I do not comprehend thee," he said tenderly; "I hear no footsteps; 'tis but the phantom of thy brain, or perchance the wind."

She tore herself from his grasp, and darting to the window drew aside the curtains, and leaned out into the air. He joined her.

"What dost thou see—a night owl?" He spoke coaxingly, as one does to a frightened child.

"I do not hear them now," she said, "they have gone." Then turning toward her husband, she clasped her hands in the attitude of prayer.

"Alden"—her voice rose shrill and piercingly upon the stillness of the midnight hour—"I am crushed to the earth by a sorrow I have not power to reveal to thee. Wretched and sinful I am; my soul is filled with a great bitterness. Though I cannot tell thee now, a voice within me says thou shalt know ere long. When that time is here, pity me—pity—me—Alden, for the great love I bear thee; it is this love of thee that makes me weak."

Again, like the flash of a lantern in the dark, across Wentworth's brain darted the words of Elizabeth.

"Dorothy, calm thyself," he said sternly. "What means this disclosure? Hast had communication with those instruments of Satan? What is this foolishness? Has the spell been cast upon thee? Art thou in bondage also?"

"No, no," she exclaimed, "'tis not that, 'tis not that. I can say no more, I am weary; let me go; I would rest—the hour is late."

He looked darkly upon her as she walked toward the door. When she reached the threshold she turned and hesitated an instant. She appeared so fragile, so innocent, so childlike as the glow from the candle fell upon her fair face and burnished hair. As he watched her his heart reproached him for his suspicions.

"Perchance thou wilt write much later," she said; "I will bid thee good-night, and God guard thee, Alden, my beloved!" She spoke wistfully. "Forget my words. I have grieved thee; forgive me."

She did not wait for his response, but passed slowly up the narrow staircase to the room above, where, sick and miserable, she found rest at last in a deep, dreamless sleep.

After Dorothy had left the room Wentworth remained for a long time in profound thought. The expression upon his face was stern and severe.   He laid his pen aside and bowed his head in his hands. He was baffled at this bewildering array of emotional tendencies just discovered in Dorothy's composition.   Could it be that in some remote manner she was being influenced by the witches?  That she could be one of them he repelled with horror; not for a moment would he allow such a doubt to find lodgment within him.   He could scarce contain himself from going to her and craving forgiveness that he should have harbored such a thought even for an instant.   He brooded until the morning dawned, and then fell into a troubled sleep in his chair.

# CHAPTER XV.

## THE WARNING IN THE MARKET-PLACE.

THE last month of summer had come, and with
it a great heat. The days were radiant with a
cloudless expanse of sky that throbbed and shim-
mered with a white, intense light, undimmed by
storm-bursts or mists. The foliage drooped discon-
solately in the fields and by the wayside. Along
the well-trodden country road that ran through the
town, thence out toward the edge of the primeval
forest, great clouds of blinding dust rose upon the
air, whirled hither and thither, as the hot wind blew
from the inland. The little brooks rippled faintly in
their shallow beds as they flowed slowly through
the parched meadows. In the gardens the flowers
bloomed scantily. The song of the birds was
stilled, they having sought new homes in the deep
glens and wooded hollows, where the heat scarce
penetrated.

The heat of nature did not exceed in fierceness
the fever of excitement and terror that burned in

the hearts of the people as they clustered in groups in the market-place of the little Puritan town.

It was the 19th of August of the year 1692. On this day five more victims were to pay the penalty of their friends' bigotry and ignorance. The names of these unfortunates were, George Burroughs, John Proctor, George Jacobs, John Willard, and Martha Carrier.

Crowds of men and women, and even children, were standing in knots and scattered groups upon the streets. All were waiting and watching intently for the carts containing the condemned to pass by on their ignominious journey to the place of execution beyond the town. Upon the faces of the crowd, whose cold features seemed hardening into the rigidity of stone, were few signs of compassion or regret. In some cases a few of the unfortunates had friends who, more bold than the rest, dared speak in derision of the magistrates and in pity for the victims.

Such a one was Martha Holden. Her buxom figure and broad shoulders towered above many of the crowd as she elbowed her way through them. Her ruddy cheeks burned to a crimson flush, her gray eyes flashed angrily and defiantly. Dorothy walked close by her side with eyes cast down, except when a harsh, denunciatory sentence would be uttered by some person in the crowd. against the condemned.   At such a time Dorothy would tremble and grow pale, look pitifully about her, and attempt to pass unobserved by keeping in the wake of her portly relative.

" Fear them not, child," said Martha reassuringly. " Put on a bold front; I give not a jot for the opinion of the entire clergy and magistrates," snapping her fingers as she spoke, and pointing contemptuously toward the court-house, from whence would soon issue the worthy retinue of exalted personages to join the procession to Gallows Hill.

It had not been Dorothy's wish to be present at this gathering of the town, but Wentworth had peremptorily bidden her to do so.   His reason she suspected.   Of late he had watched her suspiciously, ever since the night she had lost her self-control and had revealed to him that some secret sorrow was weighing upon her.   Try as he would, a lurking doubt assailed him; he fought against it valiantly, yet all to no purpose.

It was commonly believed that one in league with the witches dared not look upon them as their souls passed to that dread reunion in the realms of their master. If one who understood their baleful workings and dealt in their horrid practices gazed steadfastly upon them, some sign of their brotherhood would become known to the observers. Wentworth watched his wife closely from the windows of the court-house as she stood by her aunt's side on the street below.

The suspicion once fastened upon his imagination that this secret trouble of Dorothy's was connected with the delusion that filled every nook and cranny of the village was gaining slowly but steadily upon him. He could conjecture no other solution of the mystery of her sighs, her tears, her incomprehensible remarks, her desire for solitude, her fear to enter a church. Yet all these things might be explained naturally, he argued; at all events he must first have proof, and strong proof, that she had sealed that fatal covenant. And then—then——He dared think no further; his brain reeled, his thoughts wandered aimlessly, ending in a chaos of doubt and loss.

"The magistrates know their business, Martha," remonstrated a friend who was speaking softly to the excited old woman, who, with shrill speech and harsh epithets, gave voice to her rage at the proceedings.

"Know their business!" repeated Martha. "Is it their business to murder these God-fearing, pious persons? Forsooth, I would I had the right to sit in judgment on these wiseacres. I would place on each empty pate the fool's-cap and bid them march through the streets of Salem."

"Hush, hush, Aunt Martha," said Dorothy; "the people are all looking our way."

"What care I for the people?" She raised her voice until it reached a shout. "I tell them all, and without fear, that they have committed a most grievous wrong—a wrong they can never right. Goodwives, have ye no heart? Will ye look on while these our old friends die in innocence?" With desperate eagerness she rushed forward, and mounting upon a cart that stood in the center of the street, she gazed bravely over the heads of the cold, silent throng. "Will ye hear me?" she cried. "Let these poor prisoners free. Ye cannot know the fearful thing ye do permit. Beseech the judges for their lives; there is yet time."

"Out upon her!" called a harsh voice. "Put the old woman out, drag her from the cart, throttle her!"

"Hush, hush, for mercy's sake!" said Dorothy tearfully, starting forward, and standing by the side of the cart. "They will do thee harm; they are overwrought."

"I will not hush. I have my speech; I shall use it in defense of these my poor friends."

At this a terrible commotion was visible among the people; they swayed back and forth with the intense excitement that possessed them, and Martha was roughly jostled to the ground by the surging mass. On closer examination it was discovered that one of the afflicted children had been taken with a strange and terrible spasm. Her limbs were drawn up, her mouth was twitched to one side, her eyes rolled horribly. From her throat issued piercing shrieks interspersed with denunciatory words against some one who did afflict her, and who, she did assert, was even then standing in the crowd.

"Where is she? Where is she?" cried an emotional individual. "I will strike her," twirling his cane as he spoke, so that it came in rather uncomfortable proximity to the heads of some of the assemblage.

"She is near me! Her eyes are piercing mine,

they burn!   I suffer tortures!   Take her away, take
her away!"

At this juncture a tall, imposing figure made her
way with some difficulty through the closely packed
throng.  The people gazed with awe and respect
upon the new-comer, though not unmixed with a
superstitious fear.  Elizabeth, for it was she, did
not notice their deference.  Going swiftly to the
girl, she stooped over her and spoke some words
close to her ear.  Even as she did so she was also
seized with a like spasm, only, if possible, more
fearful to behold.

"We are bewitched," she shrieked, as she writhed
upon the ground, "we are bewitched!  The woman
who doeth us this harm is standing in the crowd."

"Where, where?" called a chorus of voices.

"There she stands," cried Elizabeth, rising to her
feet and pointing toward Dorothy.  Her face was
pale, her eyes bloodshot, her whole bearing instinct
with a frenzy approaching madness.  "I scarce
dare look upon her—there, with the old woman by
her side.  She is the queen of the witches; they
do her bidding night and day.  I do denounce
thee, Dorothy Wentworth, I, Elizabeth Hubbard,
the inspired."

The people all drew tremblingly away from Dorothy and her aunt. The women hurriedly gathered the little children together and stood in front of them. Dorothy did not flinch; she stood motionless an instant, then looked calmly around upon the clouded faces of her townspeople.

"I have done thee no harm, Elizabeth; wherefore dost thou accuse me?" Her sweet voice rang with dignity and reproach.

"Thou art a witch, thou art a witch! Cast her forth, cast her forth!" The two girls were now calling and shouting like two demons. Dorothy's voice could not be heard above the general uproar.

Wentworth had left the window a few minutes before, having been called to attend to some last requests of the condemned in their cells. Some of the men now rushed toward Dorothy, but Martha stepped in front of her, spreading out her powerful arms.

"Touch her if ye dare," she cried, "and my curse upon ye shall be heavier than any witch's spell!" She was deathly pale; the crimson flush had faded from her cheeks; her old figure was erect, though trembling with agitation. The men drew back a few paces; Dorothy was as one in a dream. The swaying throng, the angry faces, the heated street, the intense blue of the midday sky, all took on phantom shapes, intangible, unreal.

"Away with the witch! She tortures us! Away with her!" again came the cries.

The men started forward once more. "Let us take her e'en now before the judges," they said. "There is still room in the carts for another of these accursed creatures."

"Thou canst not arrest her, thou hast no warrant," cried Martha triumphantly. "Come, Dorothy, come with me; we will leave this place; come to thy home, they cannot harm thee."

The bewildered girl turned mechanically, and Martha grasped her hand. The men stood irresolute; they knew they could not arrest her without the necessary warrant. The two women proceeded a few steps down the street, the people watching them sullenly, then Martha turned. Shaking her finger in the direction of Elizabeth, who stood dark and sinister, watching Dorothy intently, she said, "Thou art a wicked girl. I know thy motive. Thou art a murderess; woe be to thee! The future will bring thee thy punishment."

Dorothy did not speak as they walked slowly

onward. Her throat was dry, her lips parched, but one idea shone clearly before her mind. The beginning of the end had come, the dread expected with all its accompanying horrors had fallen. The hot sunshine fell upon her delicate face, which was growing paler from the effect of the heat, but she scarcely heeded it; no physical discomfort could trouble her now.

"I am tired, Aunt Martha," she said finally; "let us rest here awhile," pausing under the shade of a willow-tree.

Some members of the angry crowd had followed, and a few stones had been thrown by vicious boys; now, however, they had returned to their places, eager not to miss any portion of the procession forming, as they could tell by the heavy rolling of the carts and the distant shouts of the men.

The street on which the two women rested was merely a narrow lane leading from the market-place. It was very quiet, there being few houses in the vicinity, and every one that could attend had been anxious to join the parade of the day, and thus bear witness by their presence to their sympathy with the dictates of justice.

A little child came out of a house at some distance down the lane and advanced singing in glee along the road, all unconscious of the dreadful tragedy which was being enacted close at hand. The little fellow came up to Dorothy and smiled confidingly upon her, laying his chubby hand on her knee. At sight of his sweet face she burst into tears and drew him closely to her side.

"He believes in me," she said sadly. "Happy little boy, thou knowest no trouble as yet. May thy life be brighter than mine has been." She kissed him tenderly upon his forehead, and he nestled close beside her, looking up smilingly into her face.

At this instant a loud cry was heard from a woman, who came rushing down the lane from the direction of the court-house. As she neared the group beneath the willow-tree, they noticed that she was in a state of consternation and fear. "Take thy defiled touch from off my child!" she screamed. "Wouldst thou seek to add his name to thine in the Black Book? Come hither to thy mother." She rushed forward and snatched the child to her breast. "She is a witch, little one; she will harm thee."

At the word "witch" the boy set up a cry of terror; he clung to his mother, then slipped from her clasp and tried to hide amongst her skirts. Martha appeared to be struck dumb by this distressing scene.

"Surely, neighbor," she said finally, "thou canst not believe these lies against the wife of the honored judge, who is also thy friend."

There was indescribable pathos and supplication discernible in Martha's voice; her courage and defiance had deserted her; she was now the supplicant.

"Why, then, does she not attend the meetings on the Lord's Day?" said the woman. "Of a certainty they have found much proof against her." As she spoke she endeavored to still the frenzied screams of the child, who tugged at his mother's skirts and now and then looked forth from their shelter with a glance of fascinated childish terror upon Dorothy.

"They have no proof save that gathered by that wretched circle. I fear not for Dorothy. Alden can protect her. They will not dare issue a warrant against the wife of one so high in favor, and a friend of the governor's."

The woman did not reply immediately; then she said, as she turned from them, "Elizabeth Hubbard hath denounced her; what greater proof need ye?"

She hurried from them along the road, hushing

the child.   She had lifted him in her arms, and she now pressed his head close against her shoulder, so that he could not look back upon the bowed figure resting under the drooping willow branches.

The figure remained motionless.   She might have been dead for all outward signs of animation: her head was bent forward in her lap, her arms hung heavily by her side, stray sunbeams lay upon her brown, waving hair.

" Rouse up, child, show thy spirit."   Martha shook her by the arm.   Poor Martha's courage was well-nigh spent; she fully realized the hopelessness of the case of one denounced by the all-powerful circle; her heart was heavy with a dread foreboding.

" I have no spirit," said Dorothy.   " I have fought so long that now my strength is gone. What matters it?   I am no better than those who have gone before, and who now are at rest."

" Say not so, say not so.   There is still hope, I wot, that Alden hath more influence than those wicked imps of Satan, who desire to drink innocent blood."

" He will not plead for me; he is from henceforth as one apart from me."

"Dorothy, art thou crazed? What is the meaning of such words?"

"Thou wilt know soon, yet not from me; I must tell another first. I can speak no further. Let us hasten home; I hear the fearful din and the rumble of the carts. Let us get within the shelter of the house."

The two women walked silently the short remaining distance. They entered the low gate before the new house—that abode wherein two happy united hearts had thought to live in peace and love. Dorothy looked sadly around upon the familiar scene; her aunt stood by her side, her eyes downcast and filled with blinding tears.

"Alas, alas!" she sobbed, "the child that I tended so faithfully to come to this! 'Tis hard, 'tis hard!"

"Grieve not," said Dorothy solemnly; "thou hast been ever kind and good. I did but ill requite thee. Yet now I love thee dearly. Thou canst not help me in this trouble—none can, save God."

The two women seated themselves in the door of the porch, each engrossed with her own bitter thoughts. The afternoon was drawing near; the sun was already stealing toward the west. The light and heat had become somewhat diminished; a welcome breeze sprang up from the north, rustling the leaves gently with its cool breath, till they looked as though nodding and addressing each other; the drooping flowers appeared less despondent as the shadows of the trees near the house fell across them.

A man came wearily up the narrow garden path. His face was pale, deep lines were indented upon his forehead. He stooped as he walked, and his hands hung by his side. When he reached the porch, the two women arose and waited for him to speak. His words came quickly, thrilled with passion intermingled with anxiety and fear.

"Dorothy, I know all: they have accused thee publicly in the market-place. Thou art under the ban. They will seek to procure a warrant. Yet fear not. God forgive me that I ever doubted thee. Thou art innocent, and I am thy husband and thy protector. I will shield thee, no matter what powers there be against thee. Canst thou forgive me that I ever doubted thee, so pure and good?"

She winced at these words. "Thou wilt aid me

no matter what happens?" she repeated with trembling eagerness. "Art thou certain of thy words—*no matter what powers there be against me?*"

"Ay, I know whereof I speak. I have influence with those high in office."

As if controlled by some recollections, he shuddered when he had finished speaking, and placed his hands before his face.

"Merciful Heaven, spare me the fearful sights I have witnessed this day! I have lost my strength from very horror of the deaths of those creatures, be they guilty or innocent of the charges held against them."

"Speak not of it, I cannot bear it!" wailed Dorothy.

Martha left them as they conversed, turning at the gate to wish them good-night. Wentworth's arm was across Dorothy's shoulder, she was leaning against him. The daylight was waning, the lowing of the cattle sounded distinctly across the meadows. Side by side they watched the setting of the sun behind the low line of hills. The yellow glow stole tenderly across Dorothy's face, and lingered upon her simple gown of blue tiffany. She appeared irradiated by an everlasting glory from another world, so ethereal was her bearing. Wentworth drew her lovingly toward him.

"They shall not harm thee, my own," he said. She did not answer; she was unconscious of his presence. The world was slipping from her grasp. She saw nothing material; she was gazing yearningly into that beautiful new life beyond the sunset.

# CHAPTER XVI.

## THE SCENE AT THE JUDGE'S HOUSE.

No doubt the very tenderness of Dorothy's character increased in no slight degree the enormity of her offense in her own eyes, while an extremely sensitive organization aided in completing her humiliation. She realized to the fullest extent what was expected of one in her position, and also her utter inability to comply with the demands of her calling. The terrible accusations that had been made against her by the witch-accusers had naturally alarmed her. This, however, was dwarfed into insignificance by the dread that daily and hourly tortured her of losing her husband's faith and love. This dread robbed every waking hour of peace, and filled her troubled sleep with wretched nightmares.

There appeared to be no way out of all this misery, and sometimes in the silent hours of night the tempter would warily approach her, and whisper in her ear, "Sir Grenville has pointed out a way; hearken unto him." At such times she would shudder and stretch out her hands in the darkness, as if to thrust aside some reality that loomed up from the shadows that surrounded her.

A week or more had elapsed since the public denunciation in the market-place. An ominous silence had followed the storm, ruffled only by the cold, repelling glances that followed her whenever she left the shelter of her home. The little children scattered wildly at her approach, and doors and shutters were hurriedly closed when she passed down the streets.

The first day of September had come. The weather still remained sultry, though one could notice a perceptible change in the length of the days. A fall haze gathered upon the hills toward evening, rendering them blue and indefinable.

Dorothy was seated one afternoon in the living-room of her home. She was idle, or if she employed herself occasioanlly upon some fine linen work that lay in her lap, it was by fits and starts; she drew the thread in and out in a mechanical fashion, her gaze wandering constantly through the opened window, over the widespreading fields of the farming district. On the broad window-ledge rested her psalm-book. She had been hopelessly seeking its pages for comfort, and had then laid it aside.   A pot of plants bloomed upon the ledge; now and then the breeze rustled the leaves and sent a sweet, penetrating odor into the room.   Her spinning-wheel, with its flax ready at hand, was beside her.   The sun crept around, till its light stole past the window, leaving the room in semi-coldness and darkness.

Dorothy leaned back against her high carved chair, closed her eyes, and sat very still; her work fell to the floor and lay unheeded at her feet.   She was aroused from her apathy by the consciousness of some presence near at hand.   She started, sat upright, and glanced toward the window.   The malevolent countenance of Elizabeth was pressed against the panes.   Dorothy rose from her chair, went to the door, opened it, and standing an instant upon the threshold, she timidly invited her enemy to enter.

Elizabeth came forward, and stood close to her upon the doorstep; then she brushed hastily by her, entered the doorway, and advanced to the center of the room.   She paused an instant, eying Dorothy curiously, then spoke.

" Thou, methinks, art a worthy personage to hold

thine exalted place. It is no doubt a merry prank for thee to sit in thy high seat when thou knowest thou art a hypocrite."

Dorothy recoiled; little gasps came from her white lips.

"What dost thou mean?" she said.

"I know thy secret, thou perverted one. I know of thy escapade with Sir Grenville Lawson. When thou forsooth didst draw the veil well across the eyes of thy friends with stories of sickness and wanderings, it was left to me to expose thee. Thou art indeed a worthy follower of thy master; he has taught thee well the secrets of his art."

"I know not whereof thou hast spoken," said Dorothy faintly. "Where hast thou heard such a story of me?"

"That is mine affair; my knowledge is mine own. Yet know this—that thou art lost, no power can help thee now; for of a certainty thy husband will not be thy friend when he hears of this deception."

At the words "thy husband" Dorothy trembled and grasped the back of a chair to keep herself from falling. Her face appeared to shrivel and grow small and peaked, like the face of the aged.

"Wilt thou tell him?" she gasped.

Elizabeth seized her arm and bent down over her. "Ay, I will tell him, and know well that this is the debt I owe thee. Thou didst take from me the one thing I desired above all others, the one thing that, stolen from me, as thou didst steal it, by false measures, made the world henceforth a wasted place, where I walk without peace or hope."

"I do not comprehend thee," faltered Dorothy, trying to draw her arm from the fierce clutch that held her like a vise.

"No, thou canst not; thy weak, soft nature cannot comprehend my strength; that strength, perverted from its rightful channel, has turned into hatred for thee."

She released her hold upon her victim and thrust her roughly from her.

"Spare me," said Dorothy, clasping her wasted hands, "spare me for the sake of the old days when we were friends."

"I have no pity," cried Elizabeth; "I know not the meaning of the word. Why should I pity thee? Thou hast made me what I am; thou hast woven thy fate—the strands are strengthened by thine own hands."

"Ay, ay, thou sayest truly; yet I have suffered
—thou wilt never know how sorely. Wilt thou not
relent?"

"I tell thee *no*, for all time."

"Then thou shalt not do thy worst. I will tell
Alden of my deception myself; thy cruel lips shall
not reveal to him my error, for error only it was. I
will tell thee the truth: I did fly with Sir Grenville,
to be married in Boston, thence to sail for England.
He deceived me; he was already married. I escaped
him on the confines of the forest. All else that I
did tell is truth, save that I did withhold the name
of the woman who sheltered me."

"I believe thee not; thou hast perjured thyself
once, thou canst perjure thyself again—when thy
life is at stake. On with thy weaving—the strands
will but draw the tighter noose around thy slim
neck."

Dorothy shuddered, and instinctively placed her
hand to her throat. That moment her timidity left
her. Drawing herself up, she raised her head
proudly.

"Thou mayst ruin me if thou wilt; thou canst
take my life; yet it is not in thy power to take from
me the love that has been mine, and which is cov-

eted by thee.   In the clear light of God's throne
the truth is revealed which I repeat to thee.    I
have been foolish and wayward.    I have done that
which I regret in bitterest sorrow and remorse.
Thou wouldst believe worse of me, Elizabeth, for
thine own advancement, but thou art not stronger
than the truth."

"Of a certainty thou hast a cunning manner!   A
few hours hence will tell how much longer thou
canst play thy part.   I go to fetch the wedding gift
I promised thee."   She took a few steps toward
the door.   Dorothy followed her, and grasped her
gown.

"Have mercy, have mercy, as some day, perchance, thou wilt need mercy.   Let me tell my
husband.   This thing that thou wilt tell is false;
yet should he believe it, it would turn his love to
bitterest hatred.   He believes in me—he believes
in me.   There is no proof save in my word, and
that is doubted; but there is still a hope within me
that he will forgive.   Elizabeth, Elizabeth, take that
hope from me and naught remains save despair."

Elizabeth dragged her gown roughly from the
clinging hold and stepped over the threshold.

"Dost thou not know that thou art an accursed

witch?  A witch has no redress; she cannot speak the truth, she is one with the father of lies."

" That is as naught to me;  I did forget it in this greater calamity that has come upon me—this story thou hast heard, where, I cannot conjecture.  I have no desire to live.  No, Elizabeth, all I ask of thee is to let me first acquaint him with the true facts; then do thy worst, cause my arrest.  I care not, if he but believe in me."

Her tormentor brushed rudely past her, saying, " It is too late; thou hast made a puppet of thy fate, tossed it hither and thither in wanton sport; now it recoils on thee for vengeance."

She strode rapidly from the sight of the frenzied girl and disappeared among the trees.

After watching the retreating figure till lost to sight, Dorothy returned to her seat by the window, and to her dreary, hopeless thoughts.  She had at last fully determined upon her course.  When her husband returned, which he would do ere long, she would confess all and abide by the consequences, be they what they may.  This decision arrived at, a great calmness crept over her; she sat with folded hands, a patient smile upon her face.

The weary, useless struggle was over.  The night

came on, and the room filled with shadows.  All was very still without, no sounds of passing in the street.  Nothing broke the silence, save the twittering of the birds, singing sweetly as they flew from branch to branch.

Presently she heard the violent slamming of the garden gate, then hurried steps upon the walk, then a dark figure rushed past the window, and Martha, breathless, panting, dashed into the room.

"Dorothy, Dorothy, child, where art thou?"

"I am here, Aunt Martha."

"Light the candles—hasten, hasten!  I have much to tell thee; I am well-nigh crazed."

As she spoke she lit the candles on the mantel-shelf, Dorothy not moving from her chair.  Then Martha went to her, and taking her hand led her forward to the light.

"How can I tell thee, little one," she sobbed, "how can I?  Be thou brave."

"I know what thou wouldst say, aunt.  Speak; I am strong to-night."

"It is then too true: they have procured a warrant for thy arrest on the testimony of the circle. Alden has been interceding for thee; he is beside himself with grief.  He is e'en now with the judges, and most eloquently has he plead in thy defense; so much so, they do tell me, that the tears did flow down their cheeks, even while they refused to release thee."

"Merciful Heaven!" said Dorothy. "And must I add to grief such as this?"

"What is it thou hast said, child?" queried Martha curiously. "I do not comprehend. Yet how canst thou speak aught of sense, when this fearful fate is before thee?"

"I fear not that—oh no, not that! There are far worse sorrows than death."

"Death!" exclaimed Martha. "I tell thee thou shalt not die by their hands. Dost thou think I shall desert thee? Not so; thou shalt escape. I have brought with me a disguise—see, thou shalt don it—and I have horses waiting on the borders of the forest, and good trusty friends. There is time; the streets are quiet. I will go with thee, and with the help of the Father of the fatherless thou shalt be saved from thine enemies."

"And Alden——"

"He knows of this plan; as a last resource he advises it. He will be here anon, when he considers all effort hopeless with the presiding judges."

Dorothy drew nearer to her aunt, and taking her hand looked into her face. The light from the candle fell upon the girl, upon the bronze brown of her hair, holding its reflection until it shone like a halo around the head of a martyred saint. Martha started as the wonderful courage depicted on those yet almost childlike features betrayed itself to her intent gaze.

"Aunt Martha, I shall not try to escape. I thank thee for thy love and care. I will go with my jailers when they come for me. My heart has been in prison this many a day. What is my body that I should mourn its sufferings?"

"My child, my little child!" She clasped her convulsively and held her tightly against her breast. "I tell thee, thou art beside thyself, and what wonder! Thou must escape! What is this foolish talk of sorrows? Thou art young, thy husband loves thee, thou art honored. Is thy life not worth the saving? I tell thee it is, and I, with the help of God, will save it."

"No, no," said Dorothy, drawing away from her, "I am determined. I shall not make one effort to escape. It is not a sacrifice, as thou deemest, it is retribution."

"I tell thee, thou shalt be saved, even if Alden and I between us carry thee by force and tie thee in the pillion."

"I will even then not go with thee. Be not too sanguine that my husband will aid me. I have something to tell him which I cannot tell thee." She choked and gasped. "Soon, very soon, thou wilt know all."

Martha burst into a torrent of uncontrollable sobs. "Can it be that this is the little babe I brought across the seas from England, that I did love e'en better than all else, that I did take such pride in? And now—now—O Father in heaven, hear me, have pity on me!"

"Hush, hush!" said Dorothy. "Hush, I would be calm this hour. Take not from me my strength."

Martha raised her flushed face, then started to her feet.

"What is that uproar? I hear the tramping of feet," she cried, rushing toward the window.

Dorothy did not speak; she stood quietly within the circle of light thrown from the candle on the shelf. A serene peace rested in the lovely wide-opened eyes. Martha darted back from the window. "Hide, hide!" she shrieked, grasping her arm and endeavoring to drag her from her place. "It is the warrant, it is the warrant!"  She could not move the firm, unflinching girl.  "Fly to the well-house—*I* will face them.   I fear not the whole town of Salem."

"I tell thee no; bide quiet, I wait for them."

"My God, help me!" cried Martha.   "How can I live and see this thing?  'Tis but yesterday, it seems, thou wast a little helpless infant, and now to give thee up to this awful fate—a witch, a witch, hooted, shunned, excommunicated, hung!  Dorothy, Dorothy, I shall not live to see thee suffer!   This hour has broken my heart."

Nearer and nearer came the sound of the advancing crowds, echoing loud and distinctly upon the stillness of the night.  Then arose hoarse shouts and calls, shrill cries of women and children, and soon the people swarmed into the little garden and filled the street beyond.

Dorothy, white and calm, went forth to meet them; she stood in the doorway, looking quietly upon the groups of excited, menacing persons.

"Mistress Wentworth," called the stern voice of the beadle, "in the name of his most worshipful, the governor, we do arrest thee on the charge of witchcraft. Thou hast been guilty of detestable acts and sorceries; thine enemies thou hast tortured, afflicted, pined, consumed, wasted, and tormented."

Dorothy stepped forward. " I will go with thee, and though I am no witch and have wronged but one, for that offense Providence has been most kind, in that I may, by this punishment, ease a troubled conscience."

These words stilled the murmurs of the throng, and though furious glances and gestures were directed toward the fearless girl, they uttered aloud no denunciations.

It was a brilliant night; the gleam of the moon penetrated the surroundings for a considerable distance, serving to illuminate the scene, and defining even objects some distance from the house. On the outskirts of the crowd the tall figure of a man suddenly loomed into view. Dorothy instinctively turned her head in his direction, and bent her gaze upon him. A tremor passed over her, and she uttered aloud a little cry of almost physical pain. The man lifted his head and gazed fixedly upon her, then forced his way through the throng and came close to her side.   She cowered and shrank away from him, as one does in mortal fear.

"Dorothy," he whispered, as he leaned toward her, "be brave, I will save you; be calm."   That was all.   He was gone.

A wailing shriek now arose from among the expectant people: "The devil seeks to aid his own, he hath sent his agents.   One was with her now— the cavalier who did whisper to her, he from the court of the wicked Charles."   At this outburst the crowd began to utter groans and cries.   "Seize her, ere she mount into the air and escape us," cried one.

"See her pale face and eyes of fire!   She doth torment us!   Away with her, away with this fiend!" cried the afflicted children in chorus.   A scene of pandemonium followed these cries.   The girls of the magic circle groveled on the ground in convulsions, horrible groans issuing from their frothing lips.

"I make no resistance," said Dorothy quietly to her jailers; "see, I go willingly with thee."   She held out her hands to them.   "Bind me with thy cords; I am thy prisoner."

"Ay, bind her, bind her!" yelled Elizabeth, like a maniac.   "She will escape.   Already I see a host of demons by her side. To the prison with her! Quick, quick, to the prison, ere we die from the spells she casts upon us!"

"To the prison, to the prison!" came from the hundreds of frenzied persons, now carried away beyond all control.

"Dorothy, Dorothy," wailed Martha, "to come to this, to come to this! She is so young, so innocent. Have ye no pity?" She shook her fists at the crowd and hurled fierce epithets at the girls of the circle.

The jailers now bound Dorothy's wrists together, and stepping one on each side of her, they marched up the village street to the prison. The crowd followed, hooting, shouting, and throwing sticks and stones. "A witch, a witch, a witch! Hang her, burn her, cast her forth!"

When Dorothy reached the prison door she saw her husband standing beside it. He stretched out his arms across the door, thus barring entrance. The look of hopeless misery and utter despair upon his countenance would have caused the most unfeeling heart to move in pity.

"They would not hear me," he gasped. "Till this moment I have labored with them. My God, what have I done that this should come upon me!

Dorothy, my wife, I cannot see thee enter these prison doors, I cannot!"

The jailers drew aside respectfully; the crowd was awed. Such grief as this won at least their silence. The prisoner did not raise her eyes, though she bent toward him, saying, " Let me enter; close not the way to mine atonement; 'tis my desire."

" She is guilty, she confesses! Away with her!" shouted the infuriated populace.

She turned to them. " I confess not to what thou believest of me," she said. Then, turning toward her husband, she knelt down before him, her fair head bowed low in the dust. " I am a grievous sinner, Alden; I have deceived thee, and though I am no witch, I have erred. I go to repent."

The crowd pushed and jostled her roughly. She could scarce regain her feet. " Stop her speech!" they cried. " She casts a spell upon her husband."

She was carried into the prison, and the heavy oaken doors were closed behind her. The angry faces, the moonlight, her husband's frantic endeavors to follow her, faded from her sight, into a mist that deepened and deepened until it became a great blackness and she lay unconscious on the stone floor of her cell.

# CHAPTER XVII.



DOROTHY had been in prison three days. During that time she had seen no one but her jailer, who kept a close and constant watch upon her. He had been warned by the authorities that some of her co-workers might, through the aid of their magic arts, gain admittance to her cell, and thus spirit her away, perhaps through the grated window, perhaps through the keyhole, or possibly down through the stone floor, thence out beneath the earth, to the sunlight and freedom beyond. She had rested upon her bed of coarse straw the greater part of the day and night, sometimes asleep, sometimes watching with wide-strained eyes the rays of light that came at certain hours through the small, high window.

Every time a step was heard upon the corridor without she started and raised her head expectantly, only to let it fall back wearily with a despondent sigh. She knew that by this time Elizabeth had acquainted her husband with the wretched story, exaggerated, no doubt, and painted in colors that would display her in the light of a false, heartless intriguer.

"Yet," she argued, "why does he not come, if only to denounce me? Surely he will hear from mine own lips my vindication."

It was a damp, rainy day; the fall rains were beginning early. The cell lay almost in the gloom of night, so faint was the little glimmer that fell from the grated pane. Dorothy had fallen into a troubled sleep. In her sleep she dreamed Alden was beside her, and so vivid was the dream that it awoke her. She turned her head, and by the side of her cot stood her husband. She recoiled from him in abject terror. Could that stern, cold, pitiless gaze come from the man who had so loved her? She started to her feet, and covering her face with her hands retreated from him, her frame quivering with the misery she endured.

He followed her, and dragged her hands from her face, holding them firmly in his strong grasp. "So thou wouldst hide thy false face," he said.

"Alden, Alden, she has told thee, then. Yet let

me speak ere thou dost wholly condemn; it is but justice."

"Ay, she has told me. I believed her not without proof. I sought it; I have seen those men who did aid in thy scheme. Out upon thee for a fair sorceress! So thou hast duped me well; thy nature is full deep."

"Thou shalt hear me, thou shalt! It is my right! I demand it, and I will have it," she cried. "I have not wholly wronged thee. It was to keep that which I valued above all else, thine affection, that I did deceive thee, for the sake of that love that once was mine. Hear me, hear me, I beseech thee!"

He looked darkly upon her. "Speak," he said. "I hearken."

She then told him all the story, omitting no details. At its close he laughed—a bitter, incredulous laugh. "And so thy voucher is a witch," he said slowly. "Thou hast chosen a valiant witness! Dost thou think I believe thee? No, no, no—a helpless girl like thee to escape Sir Grenville and his tried assistants! And so thine honor hangs on the word of old Goody Trueman."

She crouched at his feet, her head bent low to

the stone floor. "As I stand now in the presence of the Almighty, though unseen by us, I swear I tell thee the truth. Thou *must* believe me, thou must; then mete to me my punishment, I will not repine."

"I believe thee not," he said hoarsely. "I have it within me now to kill thee and send thy perjured soul to its reward." He bent over her as she lay upon the floor. "With my two hands I could strangle thee as thou hast strangled all good within me."

"Kill me, then; I take it from thy hands; it is retribution. Yet, ere I go from thee, look once upon me in forgiveness."

"Away from me!" he said; "thy touch is pollution." He thrust her from him as she tried to draw near upon her knees. "I believe thee not; I will not forgive thee. Thou hast made me what I am; no feeling bides within me, I am turning to stone; thou hast been the sculptor, thy hand hast molded me. How dost thou like thy work?"

"I have no redress further," she moaned; "I am indeed left desolate. My fate draws daily nearer, and I wait for it with joy. My husband, a day will come when thou wilt know me as I am—when thou wilt believe and say, 'Dorothy, I forgive thee;' and I will hear thy voice, though I be in another world, for the love that is between us is sufficiently strong to reach that land toward which my feet are turned." She hesitated and seemed addressing some inner self. "In that day I shall come to thee; thou wilt not see me, yet I shall be near and comfort thee in thy remorse."

"I have no love for thee; thou hast killed it. I shall feel no remorse." He turned away from her. "What once I felt for thee is dead; no medicine can revive the departed. Thou hast gone out of my life and thy memory is no more."

The unimpassioned voice had in its tones no cadence of the past, no echo of the happy days gone by, when he had believed in her and loved her. She clung to him in desperation, her small hands holding like a vise to his garments.

"Thou surely canst not leave me thus. Dost know that in this world we shall never meet again? I beseech thee, Alden, I implore thee—see, I kneel to thee as some poor penitent of the erring flock."

He thrust her from him and she fell heavily to the floor.

"Get thee from me! Can I believe thee when

thou hast stood beside me in yonder meeting-house to become my wife with a lie upon thy lips?—when of a truth I deemed thee as innocent as the angels above."

"Ay," she said, "that is what, perchance, thou didst expect for thy helpmate—an angel—and I was but a woman, a faulty one at that. I would forgive *thee* twice as much for the love I bear thee."

He turned from her quickly at these words. "I go from thee; if thou needst spiritual counsel, Mr. Parris will attend thee. I shall see thee no more."

A spasm of mental agony convulsed her. It was so great that she uttered a low moan, as in bodily pain.

"And thou—thou—wilt leave me thus to die, unloved, forgotten, desolate, hopeless! I tell thee, Alden, when reflection comes to thee thou wilt regret this day. Thou hast made thyself greater than thy God, who forgives all sinners that repent in humble sincerity as I do."

He moved to the door of the cell, her eyes following him like those of some hunted animal when the weary chase is over and life is ebbing fast. She started forward when he appeared to hesitate an instant on the threshold, but he did not turn to encounter her wistful, pleading gaze.

"Farewell," she said softly, "farewell." He heeded her not, did not turn his head.

As he laid his hand upon the door of the cell she rushed across the floor, threw her arms about his neck and kissed him. "Thou shalt give it back to me in Paradise," she murmured, then slipped down upon the floor and bowed her head in her hands.

She listened intently until the sound of his footsteps had died away in the stone corridor, then crouching lower remained motionless, unheeding, her mind filled with confused, meaningless thoughts that crossed and recrossed each other with the rapidity of lightning, conjuring pictures of hopeless despair. How long she remained in this position she did not know. Time passed unheeded, and she noticed no outward things.

Suddenly, though she had heard no steps or the gentle opening of the door, a hand was placed upon her bowed head, and a well-remembered voice said, "Dorothy, look up, look up; a friend is near, one powerful to aid."

Had she slept and died while sleeping? Was this another sphere? And this voice—whence came it? She raised her head. The gray light from the small, grated window revealed Sir Grenville standing by her side. She arose slowly and with evident difficulty from her low position, and stepping to the center of the small cell, she crossed her arms upon her breast and eyed him defiantly.

"So thou hast come to gloat over thy work! Well, what dost thou think? Hast ever beheld wretchedness such as mine? If thou hast desired revenge for the trick I played thee, thou hast it in full measure."

He gazed silently and reproachfully upon her. The utter abandon of her despair was written upon her countenance, and in her frenzied attitude it appalled him and caused the deepest pangs of regret to assail his selfish nature. Her sweet face had lost its childish, innocent expression, but beauty such as hers increases with experience, be it of joy or sorrow.

"I have not come to taunt," he said; "far be it from me to add one pang to sorrows such as yours. I come to save, to help, to protect." He spoke excitedly, drawing nearer and whispering close to her ear, "In Salem harbor there is a merchantman vessel; it lies at anchor beyond the bar. I know the captain well; he is in my debt; he awaits my commands. I have gold—much gold; it is all-powerful. I have bribed the jailers in order to obtain this interview, and if I pay them well these craven cowards will do my bidding.  Do you comprehend my words, Dorothy?"

"No," she said; "what wouldst thou have me do?"

"I would have you go with me; I can save you."

"Whither?" she gasped; "whither?"

"To some sunny isle beyond the seas; to the shores of Spain, perchance, or to that fair city of Venice, or, if your choice be different, we can wander on the shores of the Mediterranean.  But away, away from this land of bleak snows and gales and heartless humanity."

"With thee, with thee?" she murmured, her eyes shining with a radiant glow that appeared almost unearthly.

"Yes, with me.  I love you; I will be to you a slave, a worshiper forever.  I will bring the light of peace and joy again into your life.  I will be all in all to you.  That hated bond in England has been severed by death.  I am free—as you will be free."

"And if I do this thing," she said slowly, as though meditating, "I gain life, freedom, and much that this world can offer."

"Yes, yes," he cried, "all this, and more—you

gain happiness. In time you will forget this hated spot, and all will be as a fearful dream that has passed."

" And if I refuse this gift of thine," she continued in the same low, monotonous tone, " I remain here in this prison for a little while, then I go hence to meet my fate at the hands of man on yonder hill." She pointed as she spoke toward the window, from which they could see the rain falling heavily, and some early autumn leaves, driven by the gale, whirling past.

" That fate is surely yours," he said. " Your husband has deserted you; nothing is left save desolation and an ignominious death."

She hesitated a moment, then replied. " Nevertheless, Sir Grenville, I choose the latter course. Did I go with thee, I should but go to save my miserable life, which is not worth the saving. I have deceived and I have suffered, yet now, thank God! I can make atonement. My life is worthless to me; I offer it as the price of my misdeeds."

" You are crazed," he cried; " this shall not be. A morbid exaggeration of your fault has caused this recklessness. Do you realize your approaching fate? Surely not. And the one that should forgive and protect you is your enemy. Can you still cling to him who scorns you?"

"Speak not of him," she said solemnly. "I wronged him, I wronged him. I lied to him."

"I will not take your decision. Even against your will I will save you. Oh, that some medicine possessed the power to still your conscience! gladly would I procure it."

"There is none; urge me no further, for in this decision I am strong. Go thy way; if thou canst, forget me. In a few short days I shall have gone to my last account. Yet let me warn thee—meet not my husband. In his present state he is as one enraged, and without control. He would murder thee."

"Perchance," he replied scornfully, "or I him. So you have made your choice?"

"Yes, for all time."

"Then I go from you, but, Dorothy, I shall still work to save you." A tear glistened in his eye. "Even though you flaunt my efforts, I cannot see you die, I cannot; the thought unmans me. Though my selfish love has been your dire destruction, yet that love was full deep and strong. Think—think; once again, let me save you, and I ask no price."

"I have made my final decision; have I not told thee?" she said firmly. "Go—go; I desire solitude, I would pray."

He walked toward the door of the cell, then turned and held out his arms, his handsome face pale with agony. "I have brought you to this, I have brought you to this! Forgive—forgive—— " his voice died in his throat.

She looked kindly upon him. "I forgive thee; thou wilt suffer longer than I."

"Ay, truth speaks then; I shall suffer while I live —and remember."

"Thou canst take one grain of comfort to thyself, Sir Grenville, in that by this opportunity thou hast given me to-day thou hast made mine atonement more complete."

At this instant the jailer opened the iron door. "Time is up, my lord," he said.

Sir Grenville looked back once upon the slight figure standing erect in the gloomy cell, and in that look was the reverence one feels for a saint, or for the peace of a dead friend. After his departure the hapless prisoner fell upon her knees below the high window, from which gleamed now but a tiny shaft of light, for the gray day was drawing near its close.

As she looked upward and prayed, she caught glimpses of swift-flying clouds. All the clinging desire of earth departed from her. To her imagination the narrow walls of her cell opened wide, and she stood without them, in the unseen glory of a world where there are no mistakes, no farewells, no tears. Care and conflict were no more, a gentle peace was within her, her soul was alone with her God.

The jailer, passing, glanced into her cell, and the glow from the lantern he carried fell across her features, revealing so unearthly and serene an expression that his heart scarce beat for terror of the supernatural.

" Surely she is not of common clay," he whispered. " If a witch, why that holy peace? To what Deity does she pray that He helps her so greatly in this hour? "

# CHAPTER XVIII.



WHEN Martha became acqainted with the secret
so long guarded by Dorothy she was shocked and
pained, but she did not falter in her allegiance.
Later, when she heard from Wentworth's lips the
second version of the affair which Dorothy had
intrusted to her husband, she believed it, even
when he called it a " parcel of lies."

" Dost thou think," he demanded, " that I can
credit her story?  It is not in the possibilities of
man that she could have escaped that night in the
forest.   No, she fled with this arch-traitor—whither,
I know not.  Can I accept the word of that accursed
creature, the witch Trueman?  Out of this web of
deceit how am I to glean the truth?"

" I know not, I know not," said Martha helplessly.
" Yet this I do know: I have ever loved the child,
and for that love's sake I do forgive her now.
And thou knowest well, Alden Wentworth, that at
the first she told thee she did not love thee; there

was no deceit then.   Then she met this handsome,
wicked fellow, and foolish-like she followed him.
I see it all.   Then for love of thee she kept the
secret of her flight and escape from him.   I believe
her, Alden, I believe her; she thought to make a
grand marriage, poor little Dorothy!"

"I never shall forgive her," he cried fiercely.   "I
leave her to her fate."

Martha looked curiously upon him, then said:
"And this is the fruit of thy religion!   Surely the
teachings of thy creed are cruel.   What says Holy
Writ?   Art thou not a believer in the Word of
God?"

He started as if stung by her words.   "Attack
not my creed; it is the man who has been wronged."

"Alden, Alden, thou hast made a grave mistake.
Take heed; repent and forgive ere it be too late
and thy future life be imbittered by this error."

"The consequences be upon my head," he cried.
"I shall not forgive her."

Some three days after Sir Grenville's visit to
Dorothy in her cell she was brought to trial to
answer the charge of witchcraft.   Eight prisoners
had already been disposed of by the judges, and
had then been taken back to their cells.   Dorothy

was the last culprit brought into court. When taken from the darkness of her prison quarters, the sunshine of the brilliant day caused her to blink in the bright light. Her steps faltered from weakness, her whole frame trembled as she advanced, supported between two powerful keepers.

Owing to the great throng attracted thither by the unusual trial of the wife of a judge for sorcery, the court had adjourned from the "ordinary" to the meeting-house. The place was filled with excited spectators, who jostled and pushed each other roughly. Before the pulpit a raised platform had been built, upon which were seated the judges, with their secretaries. Many distinguished personages occupied chairs upon this raised dais; the poor wretches who were unfortunate enough to be called before this bar for justice had generally been condemned previously by public sentiment. They had no counsel, and in many cases no friends, people being afraid to openly espouse the cause of one against whom public indignation had been turned.

When Dorothy entered the court-room, she raised her eyes wistfully, as if seeking some friend, but quickly dropped them and trembled perceptibly as she encountered the stony glances of her one-time admirers and neighbors. She walked slowly, leaning heavily against the jailers who supported her. She was exhausted from insufficient food and want of sleep. She was placed about eight feet from the judges, and below the platform upon which they were seated.

Between her and the judges, upon the same level with herself, were ranged the accusing girls. She was peremptorily directed to stand erect and keep her eyes fixed upon the magistrates. Moreover, an officer was commanded to hold her hands lest she should afflict some one present. Then the judges held a rigid examination, demanding her reasons for having sold herself to Satan, also her mode of conducting the direful torments she had brought upon these poor, unhappy girls who suffered by her wickedness.

"I am no witch," said Dorothy calmly, not understanding half the confusing questions addressed to her, simply denying her guilt with a grave shake of her head.

"Say the Lord's Prayer," commanded the judge sternly, this being considered one of the important tests of the guilt of the witches. Dorothy had hardly commenced the first words of the prayer before the girls began to fall to the floor in spasms. She ceased, her words became confused, and she stopped abruptly.

"She cannot say it!" they shrieked. "She cannot pray! She is a witch, she has sold herself!"

Presently all the girls became dumb, staring fixedly upon the prisoner, their mouths twitching, their fingers pointed at Dorothy's white, haggard face. Then one spoke in a high, shrill voice: "I see the evil eye upon her! The black man is looking even now over her shoulder! She is one of them, she is one of them! See the yellow-bird perched upon her hair!"

These cries, uttered in a loud, groaning chorus, were certainly sufficient to overcome the nerves of the weakened girl. She endeavored again to repeat the words of the prayer, but her voice fell and broke feebly. "I have done naught, your honors; I have done no harm," she pleaded. But her words were so low they were scarcely heard.

The presiding judge paid no attention to this trembling little protest. Turning to the circle, he said, "Which among you has the courage to approach the prisoner at the bar and touch her?"

They all started forward, but retreated immediately in terror, saying they dared not, she had hosts of demons flying about to destroy them. The judge looked alarmed at this communication, and stared angrily at the prisoner, who gazed gently at him, her blue eyes suffused with tears.

"At what date was thy name signed in the Black Book?" he demanded.

"I have signed no book. I am not guilty of witchcraft; I know none of its practices. I am innocent of the charges brought against me."

"She does know, she does! She is not innocent!" shouted Elizabeth. "She has dug up moldy things from the churchyard—hideous secrets used for our undoing. She deals in all charms and spells; she draws men's souls to destruction. I suffer, I burn, I am tortured in her presence!"

"Hold her hands more firmly, jailer," called the judge, "lest she escape us."

"She has cast a spell even now upon the magistrates," again screamed Elizabeth. "A demon sits upon the platform by Mr. Parris."

Mr. Parris rose hastily, shook his garments, and began cleaving the air with his cane.

"He has fled from thee," said Elizabeth. "Thou art a righteous man—he has no power over thee," and Mr. Parris sat down more at his ease.

The case then proceeded, interrupted presently by the announcement that a great bird was sitting aloft on the beam. At this, all the girls fell to the floor screaming, and apparently in convulsions.

"Take her away, she tortures us, take her away! We cannot live in her presence!"

Dorothy shook as one in violent chills, the horror and confusion of the scene acting upon her overwrought nerves with such violence that it seemed to her she would have fallen dead to the floor.

"Remove the prisoner," commanded the judge in a loud, harsh voice. "Of a surety she is a witch; we need no added proof. Put irons upon her in her cell, let the jailer guard her constantly."

At these words Dorothy raised her head proudly. "I am no witch, honored sir; these girls do dissemble, and ye have committed a grievous error. Nevertheless, I accept what fate has ordained, I rebel not; I accept it as my due for my many sins, and do most earnestly believe that through the mercy of God this punishment will be mine atonement."

"She confesses, she confesses!" shrieked her tormentors.

"I confess nothing; I deny that I am what ye say. I am as guiltless of the acts of witchcraft as ye say ye are."

"Remove her! She hath sent her agents to choke us, to stab us! Away with her!"

Dorothy did not speak again. Amidst the general clamor she was escorted back to her cell, through the densely packed throng of eager, solemn spectators. She was but dimly conscious of her surroundings, until some one among the crowd leaned forward and wiped the falling tears from her face. She glanced up gratefully, to encounter the troubled, sympathetic eyes of Martha. The jailer thrust the ministering hand aside, and the dazed girl was led back to the darkness of her cell.

An hour or so following the trial, a group stood before the meeting-house door, talking eagerly.

"Dost thou think Wentworth believes her guilty?" said a large man, a farmer from the district, who had attended the day's proceedings.

"Of a certainty. He plead not in her defense; he was absent from the meeting-house. They do say he has not entered her cell save once, and that he walks ever restless upon the streets both day and night. He speaks to no one, and if one does address him, he answers him not."

"Truly he is much to be pitied," said a stout woman, a matron from the village. "Ah, that was a foolish marriage. She was ever a wild, idle thing."

"Will they hang her?" inquired a young girl in an awestruck whisper.

"They will, surely; the evidence was most damaging."

"She is so fair and sweet," said the girl sadly. "She was ever kind to me."

"Heaven bless thee for those words," said a voice, and Martha joined the group. "If they do hang her," she exclaimed, looking fiercely around upon the now silenced assemblage, "they commit a murder! I say it without fear, and those fiends that do accuse her will burn in everlasting fire."

"Hush, hush, here comes Elizabeth," spoke some voices in an awed whisper.

"What care I for that bloodthirsty girl?" She raised her voice, and casting her bloodshot eyes upon the sinister but handsome face that now confronted her, she continued: "The day will come when thy power will be gone, and then I wish thee a long life with thy conscience. I trow it will cut deeper than the hangman's rope."

Elizabeth passed by unheeding, the group gazing after her with respectful deference. Elizabeth had not spoken of what she knew in regard to Dorothy's sad story, save to Wentworth and Martha. She had two reasons for this secrecy: first, she wished to establish a tacit bond between herself and Wentworth, that might prove the nucleus of her future plans; secondly, she was astute enough to know that if she brought forward any personal motive for revenge, it would be likely to tell in favor of the suspected one.

By a strange coincidence, the cell in which Goody Trueman had been confined, and in which she now lay, suffering from a fatal disease, was next to that in which Dorothy awaited the last sentence of the court, the day decreed for her execution. The jailer had acquainted Dorothy with the fact of Goody's near abode, she having inquired who moaned and wept continuously so near her. The jailer, who had more compassion than one might expect in a person whose life is passed amidst prison scenes, expressed sympathy, although in guarded terms, for the old woman. When Dorothy begged for admittance to the presence of the sufferer, he consented.

Though Dorothy wore irons upon her wrists and ankles, she had not been shackled to the floor, as was the case in many instances. When admitted to the adjoining cell, which was even smaller, darker, and closer than her own, Dorothy stood a moment irresolute, hoping that Goody would recognize her before she spoke, dreading the possible shock to the already enfeebled heart and body. As Goody did not move or speak, Dorothy went up to the cot, her chains clanking as she advanced. "Goody, Goody," she said, "I have come to speak with thee; dost know me?"

The dim eyes looked up. "Ay, I know thee," she replied feebly. "Whence comest thou? Not condemned, surely not condemned!"

"Only too true are thy words: I am a condemned witch. Yet now I can tell thee all my story, for I have naught to gain in this world, yet much, I trust, in another."

So, leaning her face against the withered hand that lay upon the side of the cot, she told all. At the conclusion she paused an instant, then continued: "I ask but one favor of thee: if my husband comes to thee and speaks of me, that thou wilt plead for me, Goody. Thou wilt?"

"And so my little wild wood-blossom has withered at the first fierce touch of the sun! Ay, my child, and those hot rays which scorched thee were fed by thy deceit. Ah well, the aged cannot always guide the young."

"No, no, Goody, yet reproach me not."

"No, surely I will not, and if thy husband comes to me I will plead, though it were with my dying breath, for thee. But I despair, I hope not. I am an outcast; my word is hooted and despised."

"I know, I know; and yet when one is drowning one clings to even the frailest bark for help. Thou art good; perchance some truth in thy speech might convince him."

"If the chance comes to me, I will, I will, my child."

So Dorothy crept back to her cell, and sat quietly in the dark, repeating over and over again, in low tones, portions of the Psalms which she had sung so often to the droning, dragging tunes beloved by the Puritans, as she stood, in the days now gone forever, within the walls of the meeting-house.

# CHAPTER XIX.



## ON GALLOWS HILL.

ALDEN WENTWORTH was indeed a most
wretched man; the dream of peace and happiness
which had been his was gone forever. In its stead
stalked the specters of buried hopes, dead desires,
and shattered faith. The deadly poison of suspicion
was working within him. All Dorothy's acts and
words tended but to exaggerate his belief in her
guilt. Though he longed to believe her story, yet
viewing them in the light of subsequent events, he
could not. No, she had led him on deliberately,
then duped and fooled him. She had lied to him
once, she would lie again. Much was at stake—her
life—and she was young.

Over and over he said to himself, with clenched
fist and furrowed brow, "I cannot trust her; she is
false. Where she was those four months I know
not, yet this I do know: the truth is not in her,
she has schemed full well, and I am her wretched
dupe."

Though Martha had endeavored by every means in her power to gain admittance to the prison, she had not been successful. This was partly owing to her avowed disapproval of the acts of her superiors, partly for fear that she might achieve some method of escape for Dorothy.

Martha had already come under the eye of the avenging circle, and menacing glances followed her whenever she appeared upon the streets. The bright September days passed rapidly. Nature matured her gifts to man; the fruits of the full orchards were waiting to be garnered into the great barns and outbuildings of the Salem farms. No heed was taken of the rich and profitable harvest, for the decree had gone forth that on the 22d of September the last of the convicted witches should pay the penalty of the law. In the present excitement the people had forgotten their daily tasks, had set aside the natural course of their quiet lives, to take part in the general calamity.

When the jailer brought the final decision of the court to Dorothy she clasped her hands, from which the irons had been removed, saying, " I have waited for some help from my husband; since it comes not, I ask for nothing. I have no requests; I will be ready when thou shalt come for me; I will make no resistance."

The eight unfortunate victims of that day were hanged some hours previous to the time set aside for Dorothy's execution. It was growing late in the afternoon when they entered her cell to conduct her to the cart in attendance, that was stationed on the street without. She did not murmur, but stood calm and silent, her lips moving in prayer. Only once she spoke, when standing beside the cart, the eager throngs pressing near her; she looked up and said sadly:

"I ween I have no friends; yet once I was well beloved in Salem. Has every one forgotten me?"

At these words a woman in the crowd raised her voice and called loudly, "Thou hast one friend, Dorothy—thy Aunt Martha."

"Hush," commanded an official, "be silent. I will place in pillory all offenders against the dignity of this proceeding. Here come the magistrates— step back, step back!"

The procession was then formed. Dorothy, seated upon the rough board placed across the springless cart, was surrounded by officials and dignitaries. Some rode on horseback in advance of her, some on either side. The magic circle walked not far from the side of the vehicle, anxious to witness the last hours of their victim. By their absurd antics they intensified the excitement, which already ran fever high. Elizabeth with a swinging gait strode ahead of her companions, looking backward now and then to gaze upon the bowed figure in the cart, swaying with every motion of the wretched vehicle as it jolted clumsily over the stones and uneven surface of the road. The stern-visaged people walked stolidly forward, speaking but seldom, and then in monosyllables.

At the head of the procession, clad in rich trappings, rode the chief magistrates and high officials with many eminent personages. Prominent among them was Cotton Mather, who sat his horse well, his handsome face set and cold with a fanaticism none possessed to a greater degree than he.

"Truly, my friend," he said, turning toward Judge Stoughton, who rode beside him, "this is a most gracious day for the world; eight lost wretches have we dispatched to their deserts, and now one more"—he turned in his saddle at these words, to glance at the last victim—"who, judging by her countenance, should be as good as the angels. Truly Satan loves to dwell in a fair domicile."

"Well said, well said," replied Judge Stoughton. "We will at this rate soon rid the land of these imps of iniquity. Yet my heart misgives me for the sanity of Wentworth. He neither speaks nor sleeps. This child-wife of his has surely wrecked him."

"He will recover," answered the wise Cotton. "He doeth a good deed; the Lord will reward him." He coughed piously, and crossed his hands, as though in prayer. "He has not rebelled once at the decree of the court; of a certainty he believes her a witch, and drowns his affection for the good of mankind. A most exemplary man is Wentworth."

The soft, warm September sun shone upon the curly locks that fell from beneath Dorothy's cap; it glistened around her sweet face like a nimbus of gold. Her hands were confined behind her back. Her eyes were downcast, the long lashes resting upon her cheeks in a dark circle, causing the whiteness of her face to appear the more startling. She spoke not to those near the cart; she seemed apart from them, already in another sphere.

As the dreadful journey proceeded, she would

raise her eyes at intervals and glance wistfully at the old familiar scenes that came under her gaze. The long, wide, straggling street, with its rows of dormer-windowed, gambrel-roofed houses, their un-shuttered panes to her vivid fancy watching like so many cold, staring eyes this her ignominious, humili-ating ride to death.

The cart rumbled past the meeting-house, where she had worshiped so regularly every Lord's Day through the cold winters and the hot summers, and where—here a tear fell upon her cheek, rested there a moment, thence dropped into her lap —she had been married. Could it be that it was only last spring? That beautiful May-day, seemed years ago, so much had she suffered since then. Then they slowly passed the graveyard with its aspect of quiet repose, and now the houses be-came less frequent, and the farming lands began. A spasm convulsed her as the Holden place came in sight; she noticed with loving tenderness old Rollo tied by the kitchen door, barking and tugging at his chain. "Does he know me?" she wondered vaguely. "He cannot understand. Ah, well for him; he would be but one more unhappy one, for he loved me, kind old dog."

Here the procession halted a moment for rest. Dorothy turned partly around in her seat. For an instant it seemed to her that her heart ceased beating, and that death had mercifully come.

Riding upon a large, dark horse was her husband, slowly following in the rear of the cart. He looked coldly and strangely upon her, as though she were unknown to him, an outcast, a stranger. A peculiar fancy now took possession of her faculties—a fancy that he saw her not, that his eyes had not the power of vision, that another creature looked forth from those windows of his soul, not Alden. The conviction now forced itself upon her that another's will than his own was guiding his actions in his hatred and unforgiveness toward her; in fact, that he himself was bewitched, and unable to do otherwise.

"Hasten, my friends, hasten," called Cotton Mather, "we must not delay; already the day is late, and the road is long; we must waste no precious time."

The weary tramp commenced again toward Gallows Hill, or Witch Hill, as it is sometimes called. The ascent of the hill was slow and irksome. It was a gloomy spot, though commanding an excellent view of the widespreading though not varied landscape. When the large concourse of people had reached the summit of the hill, or rather the spot midway previously designed for the execution, a halt was called, and the prisoner was lifted from the cart.

As Dorothy stood upon the eminence the people halted slightly below her, the circle-girls being in the foreground, while near her stood the officials and clergy, and not far distant the hangman, his face averted. At some little space to the right of the hangman stood Wentworth. Dorothy moved mechanically when they commanded her to do so; her spirit was in another world, she obeyed them silently. She turned toward the west as they directed, and remained passive. Only once her lips moved slightly; it was when she heard a great cry from Martha in the crowd below.

"Let me get to her, let me get to her! Ye are all murderers! O Dorothy, Dorothy, my little one!"

Suddenly a shadow fell across the greensward near her—a long, dark shadow. Her husband faced her. Intense silence reigned; the murmurs of the crowd ceased. It was an awesome moment. Nothing was heard save the rustle of the wind in the forest trees, and over the fields of wheat, moaning as it advanced from the north.

The magistrates remained calm, with bowed heads; they recognized the awful sacredness of the scene—the severing of the strongest bond on earth. Dorothy looked up; her face shone as the face of some unearthly being, the glory of the setting sun casting its reflection tenderly upon her. The purity and sweetness of her beautiful countenance, filled with love and with the resignation of a character made perfect by suffering, appeared to irradiate that lonely hillside with a glimpse of the promised splendors of the infinite. As she gazed upon her husband, no reproach, no coldness was in her look; all was love, tenderness, forgiveness.

"Alden," she said softly, "ere I go hence, say that thou wilt forgive me. When I go from thee thy words cannot follow me. Thou knowest, my beloved, that standing with my feet upon the threshold of that unseen world, I dare not speak a falsehood, when I so soon shall enter the presence of God." He stood like one carved from stone, silent, motionless, unheeding. "Thou hearest?" she repeated. "I ask not for life; only tell me that thou dost believe me; then my body will rest on earth in peace, and my soul will wait for thee. See, I would kneel and clasp my hands to thee, were I not ·bound."

He swayed slightly toward her, held out his hands like one groping in the dark, then, throwing his arms wildly above his head, a cry of agony came from his lips—a cry so loud, so deep, so strong, that it resounded over the heads of the people, and a flock of wild birds soaring above flew affrighted toward the sea. "Dorothy, I believe thee, I believe thee! What am I, that I should usurp the province of the Almighty to withhold forgiveness? God pity me— God pardon me——"

She inclined her head, as though listening attentively, watching him eagerly; then, grasping his meaning, she tried to reach him, but her steps faltered. She crept nearer, her lips moving, though no sound came from them. At length, summoning all her strength, she whispered: "My husband, I have now no regrets; I am happy. Stay thou near me till all is over and I go to my rest."

The sun was sinking behind the hills, the landscape lay in somber tints and shades of the coming night, the delicate after-glow of the pale fall sunset was fading from the sky. Dorothy gazed sadly upon the changing cloud pictures, thence upon the cold, hard faces of her townspeople, thence passed them and looked out over the hills and vales of her home, the distant town, the winding country road, the ships, the harbor, and far away the long line of sea and shores of yellow sand. Then turning, with a smile of unutterable peace, she looked her last upon Wentworth.

"I am ready, Alden, I am ready. Farewell, my own; thou hast forgiven me, I ask no more." She swayed as a reed sways in the gale, her eyes closed, her face relaxed and became still and white as the face of the dead. With a little fluttering cry she fell forward at his feet. Wentworth rushed to her, and lifting her from the ground in his strong arms held her thus an instant, and faced the people.

"She is mine," he cried, "she is mine! Death has given her back to me!"

The powerful personality of the man who could hold them spellbound by his fiery eloquence in the court now asserted itself. The crowd, but an instant before eager to cry, "Hang her, she is a witch!" now became silent in the presence of a sorrow such as this.

He endeavored to force his way through the throng, his helpless burden pressed close against his heart, her head hanging across his shoulder. The people huddled together, the hangman dropped his rope, and the officials began eagerly whispering among themselves. Wentworth had already accomplished a little distance of the descent of the steep hillside, when Elizabeth Hubbard confronted him, holding her arms wide apart to prevent his progress. Her face was black with rage, and like a wild beast deprived of its prey, all reason and humanity had departed from her.

"She is not dead!" she shrieked. "She does dissemble, she is not dead! Even now I see the demons laughing by her side! Release her, she is ours, release her!"

Wentworth turned fiercely upon her. "Out of my way, thou wretched creature, out of my way! Who art thou, that thou canst call the dead to life?"

"If she be dead, then her body belongs to the ditch; no witch can have a Christian burial—she is excommunicated."

"I tell thee depart, ere I curse thee."

She shrank from him in abject terror at these

words; the pallor gleamed through her swarthy cheeks, her face grew pinched and drawn.

"Thou wilt curse me—me," she echoed—"thou, for whom I have imperiled my immortal soul!"

Stepping backward, she threw up her arms, and crouching low to the ground tried to hide within the shelter of the densely packed throng. The populace, almost beside itself at the passionate intensity of the scene just enacted, swayed like the restless waves of the sea when a storm passes over it.

Wentworth hastened to the cart, which had been left below the hill beneath a spreading oak-tree. He laid his burden down upon the floor of the cart, and placing his cloak over it, he stood erect and defiant.

"Who molests her now," he cried, "shall be responsible to me. She is mine; ye have done your worst."

The doctor now drew near, and bending over the quiet form touched the face and hands, listening at the heart. Wentworth watched him intently. The doctor lifted his head and gazed steadfastly into Wentworth's face. Their glances met, they understood each other. Then the doctor turned to the people. "She is at rest—ye need fear her no more. Give her into her husband's charge."

At this announcement murmurs arose among the spectators—murmurs of disapproval and dissent. Some turned impetuously in the direction of the wagon. At this juncture a woman in the crowd called loudly:

"See, a horseman! He rides at great speed along the highway from the town."

All heads were turned in the direction of the advancing figure on horseback, who came onward, rushing headlong through a cloud of whirling dust, urging his steed to the utmost. As he neared the hill he cried breathlessly: "The governor's ships are in the harbor; he has returned from the Indian wars. He is wroth, they say, at these proceedings in Salem. Return in all haste to the town to welcome him."

The people gazed awestruck at each other on receiving these tidings. They darted hither and thither, filled with excitement and indecision, and after much delay proceeded reluctantly to form in straggling disorder, preparatory to returning along the road to the town. The officials also appeared troubled and crestfallen. As for Cotton Mather, he was exceedingly angry. Nevertheless, they all considered it the better policy to welcome the governor properly, and departed slowly in the wake of the procession, Cotton in the meanwhile delivering himself of much pious grumbling.

Martha had closely followed Wentworth when he placed Dorothy in the cart. She now stood near him, her hand upon his arm, and watched the dispersing of the multitude.

"We will not take her to the new house," whispered Wentworth, "she was not happy there; but to the old farm, where I first met her, a little child."

Martha wept softly as she looked upon the silent form. "Ay," she said, "we will take her home."

And so through the misty gloaming of that cool September evening Dorothy was taken back to the scene of that simple life of her childhood. Wentworth and Martha walked slowly by the side of the vehicle with bowed heads.

# CHAPTER XX.

## "IN A FAR COUNTRY."

WHEN Dorothy was lifted from the cart in her
husband's arms and placed upon the bed in her
quaint little dormer-windowed room that faced the
west and the sea, she was apparently dead; and so
the watchers thought, as they leaned above her and
saw no signs of life. The doctor said otherwise.
"It is suspended animation; she may speak again
and know ye. Yet be most cautious; she stands
upon the borderland of that spirit world." He
turned to Wentworth. "Perchance thy voice may
have the power to call her back to life. Watch
carefully, watch."

When the night had advanced and the stars were
shining brightly in the heavens, Dorothy opened her
eyes, to behold her husband. He placed his arms
about her. She looked up with the sweet, gentle
smile he had seen so often. "Have I died?" she
whispered. "Is this another world? Art thou with
me?"

"Thou hast died to sorrow, Dorothy, but thou livest in thy husband's love for evermore, if such a sinner as I deserve such love as thine." .

She did not reply; she closed her eyes and lay very still. He kissed her. The light of the stars shone through the small-paned windows, and a peace unutterable entered into the souls of those present.

That fearful scene on Gallows Hill was the last act of that terrible religious tragedy which disgraced the early days of our ancestors in New England. In October following the entire community became convinced of their fatal error. The light began to dawn, and the power of the magic circle visible in that light of calm reason dwindled and grew pale. "They have perjured themselves," cried many. The dark horror came to an end, the storm settled into a great calm, with the wrecks of homes and hopes and hearts strewing the shore line. The prisons of Ipswich, Boston, Salem, and Cambridge opened their doors, and the poor dazed creatures came forth. The number of those unfortunate ones imprisoned for witchcraft is not definitely known, but it is estimated that some hundreds suffered this ignominy.

Great was the remorse experienced among the

now awakened citizens. They bowed themselves humbly to the earth, beseeching forgiveness for their grievous fault. The governor, Sir William Phipps, commanded that no more cases of witchcraft should be tried, and no more spectral testimony be taken in evidence.

In one of the most remote settlements of the New World, some eight years after the events related in this story, a man and woman might often be seen toward evening, when the day's work was done, leaning upon a low wooden paling surrounding a simple cottage. The man was Wentworth, the sweet-faced woman by his side, his wife Dorothy. He had renounced the brilliant career that lay before him, and hand in hand with her he loved had made a new home in a new country far removed from the sad scene of his great sorrow.

"I am not worthy, I am not worthy," he had maintained, "to point to others the way; no longer can I lead, yet I can follow in all humility. I did transgress upon the province of God."

Though Dorothy had endeavored to persuade him from this course, he was determined. In bitterness of spirit he said, "It was not as though I believed thee guilty of witchcraft; I had not even that to sanction my great sin.  No, I knew that thou wert innocent; it was for mine own wrongs I sought revenge.  In the wickedness of my heart I have been a murderer.  I step down from my high place, a penitent sinner."

"Yet thou art eloquent, Alden; a great future is before thee."

"I renounce it; my great fault has been mine ambition.  I take this as my merited punishment."

So he became a teacher to the Indians, instructing them in reading and writing and in all the practical arts that were known in those days.  Though directed by no law of churchly sanction, his influence for good was sufficiently widespreading to be a beacon-light to those holy men who in later years worked for the advancement of the Indians.

Wentworth was truly a missionary in his kindly, noble life, a father, a helper, and a friend to those degraded savages.

It is the 22d of September.  The afternoon is warm; a soft fall haze is in the atmosphere.  Dorothy is standing in the porch of the tiny cottage, looking dreamily over the little settlement, thence toward the vast unexplored forests of the north. She is presently joined by Wentworth, leading a little girl by the hand. The child is crying bitterly; her apron is held to her eyes, and her hands are covered with fruit stains. Alden looks down reprovingly upon her; she is trying to hide her face with the little chubby hand that grasps the apron, and is endeavoring to hold back and hide behind her father.

"What has Dot been doing?" asks Dorothy anxiously.

Wentworth lifts his little girl in his arms, and she presses her pretty face against his shoulder. "What hast thou done, my child?" he says. "Confess to thy mother."

"I—I—took the fruit—" she pauses and sobs— "that—that—thou didst tell me I could not have." She hesitates and stops abruptly.

"What else, what else?" urges her father.

"I told father I did not take it, and I held my hands behind my back so that he could not see the stains. He took my hands and saw that—I— I——"

Dorothy snatches the child from its father's arms, a look of terror upon her face; she clasps her closely against her breast, and bows her head above the little curly one that rests so near her heart.

"Dot, O Dot," she says, the tears in her eyes, "thou hast told a falsehood, thou hast told a falsehood, my child; that is a great sin."

Alden places his hand tenderly upon Dorothy's hair, saying gently, "She was sorry and did confess."

"And thou, what didst thou say to her?"

He bowed his head humbly. "I forgave her. Could I do otherwise?"

"Poor little Dot," says Dorothy, "poor little Dot! Thine earthly heritage is early apparent."

Together the three remained looking over the lovely rural scene that lay before them, the child asleep upon its mother's lap, the marks of her recent grief upon her face; now and then she sobbed in her sleep, as though into her dreams she had carried her troubles. Wentworth held Dorothy's hand, and they watched the changing clouds above them drifting toward the setting sun.

"We are far away from home," said Dorothy presently. "I ofttimes wonder what Aunt Martha is doing at the farm; yet I long not for Salem, I am happy."

"Yes," said he, "we are happy, and we are not far from home, though on the borders of the great wilderness; we do but bide here awhile, till we hasten to our rest in a 'far country,' where our true home shall be."

The birds began to prepare for the night, the wild wood warblers calling loud and shrill as they flew overhead; the fall insects piped in discordant notes. The dews began to fall, and Dorothy covered the sleeping child with her shawl.

"Dear little penitent!" she whispered, and kissed her.

The sun went down upon the quiet and pleasant scene. If it could have imparted to the watching couple the numerous things it had witnessed in its rounds, it would have told of many interesting events relating to the personages of this story.

In a foreign town it had viewed not long since Sir Grenville Lawson slain in a duel; and when they raised him, so that he might breath more easily, the life-blood had gushed from his mouth; he essayed to speak, and his attendants, bending over him to catch the faltering words, heard him whisper, "Dorothy, forgive!"

"His mind wanders," they said; "we know of no such person."

The day-king had then crossed the seas and looked in at the narrow panes of the Holden farmhouse kitchen, and had shone upon Martha, hale, buxom, as of yore, but alone. Crossing the hill, it rested tenderly upon two graves, not far apart, in the little Puritan "God's-acre." On one simple head-stone is carved *Goody Trueman*, on the other *David Holden*.

The destiny of the girls of the accusing circle, with but few exceptions, was shrouded in mystery; statistics state little of their subsequent career; it is very possible that they retired into their quiet lives and oblivion. I doubt if we could mete to them a greater punishment than that engendered by an awakened conscience, with its pangs of bitter remorse.

It was quite dark now; the night had come. "It is the anniversary, Alden," says Dorothy softly, after some moments of silence, "the anniversary of the day that I was given back to thee—the 22d of September."

"Ay, dearest," he replies, "I remember; the day God opened mine eyes, and I became, by acknowledging myself the greater sinner, in part worthy of thee, my beloved."

"We are happy and united, my husband," she says softly, "the past is forgotten."